NIGHT SHADOWS

STEPHEN L. BRAYTON

Black Rose Writing | Texas

©2024 by Stephen L. Brayton
All rights reserved. No part of this book may be reproduced, stored in a retrieval system or transmitted in any form or by any means without the prior written permission of the publishers, except by a reviewer who may quote brief passages in a review to be printed in a newspaper, magazine or journal.

The author grants the final approval for this literary material.

First printing

This is a work of fiction. Names, characters, businesses, places, events, and incidents are either the products of the author's imagination or used in a fictitious manner. Any resemblance to actual persons, living or dead, or actual events is purely coincidental.

ISBN: 978-1-68513-414-3
LIBRARY OF CONGRESS CONTROL NUMBER: 2023950318
PUBLISHED BY BLACK ROSE WRITING
www.blackrosewriting.com

Printed in the United States of America
Suggested Retail Price (SRP) $20.95

Night Shadows is printed in Minion Pro

*As a planet-friendly publisher, Black Rose Writing does its best to eliminate unnecessary waste to reduce paper usage and energy costs, while never compromising the reading experience. As a result, the final word count vs. page count may not meet common expectations.

ACKNOWLEDGMENTS

In the early years of this century, I worked the overnight shift in the hospitality industry. During those hours, I enjoyed listening to the late-night radio show, Coast to Coast AM. One show featured a guest who spoke of the phenomenon of shadow creatures. That discussion inspired the idea for this book. Right off, I must thank Coast to Coast AM for sparking the creativity to develop *Night Shadows*. In addition, I wish to thank the following:

- To God for giving me writing skills.
- To my family for their love and support.
- To Black Rose Writing for accepting the manuscript.
- To the critique groups of Shades of Ink, the Marion County Writers Workshop, and the Sisyphean Scribes: Writers of the Round Tables. They have helped me improve the craft of writing for over two decades.
- To Kim McKinney for providing ideas on trouble spots within the stories.
- To Principle Insurance for conducting the tour where I discovered the inspiration for the "portal" used in the story. Although I've fictionalized it, the location is an actual art exhibit. I hope I've captured it's flavor in this book.
- And of course, I extend a sincere thank you to the readers. Thank you for your support.

"The most merciful thing in the world, I think, is the inability of the human mind to correlate all its contents. We live on a placid island of ignorance in the midst of black seas of infinity, and it was not meant that we should voyage far. The sciences, each straining in its own direction, have hitherto harmed us little; but some day the piecing together of dissociated knowledge will open up such terrifying vistas of reality, and of our frightful position therein, that we shall either go mad from the revelation or flee from the light into the peace and safety of a new dark age."

— **H. P. Lovecraft, *"The Call of Cthulhu"***

"In this world, everything changes except good deeds and bad deeds; these follow you as the shadow follows the body."

— *Unknown*

"Horatio: O day and night, but this is wondrous strange!

Hamlet: And therefore as a stranger give it welcome. There are more things in heaven and earth, Horatio, than are dreamt of in your philosophy."

— **William Shakespeare, *"Hamlet"***

NIGHT SHADOWS

PROLOGUE

Des Moines, Iowa Midnight, Saturday

It is a special time. The Night. A special place.

Where things are seen but not witnessed. Where promises are made and broken and dreams and wishes fulfilled.

During the day, there is a rushing, frantic pace.

When night falls, movement is quieter and more mysterious. Breezes blow through tree branches, and the soft slap of leaves is heard, but those leaves are not noticed as much as their silhouettes caused by streetlights.

The streetlight's sodium vapor fizzes to life, pale illumination in its own small section of the world, at the same time creating shadows.

Moving shadows.

Elongated shadows, such as the dog and its owner out for a walk along a quiet, residential street. A familiar route for both, but a chance for the canine to track fresh scents and continue the age-old instinctual—if nowadays needless—practice of marking and re-marking its territory. Its owner revels in a chance to breathe the cool air after being cooped up in a stuffy cubicle by day and a stale apartment all evening.

He is cautious, for while he may favor the night, others less innocent also occupy the patches of darkness. So, when his best friend, not a breed to cause hesitation to a potential attacker, stops to sniff a scraggly bush, the man swivels to look in all directions. Ears strain for the lightest footfall or rustle of clothing from someone hidden. Darting eyes pick up any movement. The back-and-forth flow of tree leaves, the silent streak of a darting rabbit not seen by the dog.

There!

Did he notice a curtain edge drop back into place in the darkened house he and his dog now face? Maybe. The dwelling is single story, a small box, with the requisite low-pitched roof, mullioned dollhouse windows. No porch, just irregularly shaped flagstones leading to a gravel driveway. Nothing special, nothing unique. Nothing to fear.

Man and dog continue down the sidewalk, their shadows sometimes guiding, sometimes dissipating as they pass through the patches of street lights.

Inside the house, a figure steps back, letting the curtain fall from his hand when the dog walker turns toward the window.

Did he see me?

Eyes peek around the edge of the curtain and watch as the pair walk out of sight.

No, everything's fine. No one suspects.

A gasp and another step away as car headlights spear the darkness and disappear. Startled, the figure waits until his breathing evens, heartbeat returns to normal. Well, maybe a little faster than normal considering what is about to happen.

Obsessive-compulsive behavior urges another quick check outside. Nothing. No one. A blue flicker of a television from a house across the street, but no worries.

They won't know.

Without as much as the softest whisper of carpet fiber, the figure steps to a door and a flight of descending stairs. Before advancing below, the wraith-like figure double-locks the basement door.

Absolute darkness, but he isn't concerned. He knows the number of stairs and the number of steps to reach the far wall of the basement. A scratch, a brief scent of sulfur, and flame burns one end of a wooden matchstick. The light reveals his scarred and calloused hand, the fingers ends nail-bitten but clean. Those fingers spread the fire to the wicks of more candles resting on makeshift shelves around the room.

The basement is small, as befits the structure above. Not many items are in evidence. The candles, of course—some new and fat, others thin, with castle-like moldings of dripped wax. Others are stubby and ready for replacement. All are colored black or red.

A lectern stands at the far end of the basement. Next to it sits an old wooden chest with an ornate metal lock and hasp.

No windows, no vents. Only the candles, the lectern, the chest...and him.

What was the merest glimpse of a figure behind a curtained window is now a solid man in candlelight, even with a stooped posture. His face and body show the years of a hard life's struggle, ever striving to find that one elusive...something. The creases in his forehead, the scars on his limbs, the gray hairs on his chest and head, the involuntary twitches of leg, arm, and back muscles belie the fact the man is in his late fifties. The robe he wears is inlaid with intricate, complex, and alien designs on a background of rich deep purple.

He lays the spent match in a brass ashtray on a shelf. His heart thuds in anticipation. Quiet pervades the air and the shadows created by the candle flames do a jittery dance against the walls.

The shadows, yes...

A loner by choice for many years, he sometimes wonders why he lives in the city. Rural life would suit him better, away from the people and the noise. Midnight in the metropolis is tolerable, and the traffic on his block is sparse, even during the day.

Unlike Mexico City with its twenty-four-hour-a-day traffic jams, thirty million plus population, and smog turning his snot and lungs black. He had survived the ordeal and obtained his prize. The old chest...and the treasure within.

Years of research and travel led him to the filthy, corrupt capital where he tracked the old Guardian to a forgotten alley in the Zona Roja—the Red Zone—one of the ugliest, dirtiest, crime-ridden, rat and human debris-infested parts of the city. In a sub-cellar of a neglected building, the encounter went as expected. A stubborn, worthless, withered old man lay dead, the chest and its contents he had guarded for decades stolen away in the night.

Now, in another capital city, in an American heartland state, the dreams of the new owner of the treaure can be fulfilled. Power will be the reward for all his tribulations. Power...

From the Book of Sarmangous.

After unlocking the chest, he withdraws the large tome, its cracked bindings, strange textured cover, and brittle pages handled with infinite delicacy. The cover bears strange, timeworn designs, vague human shapes, others more monstrous. Some of them spell out in an ancient language the book's title.

Sarmangous.

He places the book on the wooden felt-lined lectern. Inhaling one sharp breath and holding the air in his lungs, he opens the cover, turns to the correct page deep within the thickness of the ancient writings, and selects the specific text. He squeezes his eyes shut for a moment, still holding his breath. His entire body is a-quiver with heightened nerves, then...then opening his eyes, he utters the correct words, the specific phrases, the weird combination of sounds.

The candles burn brighter.

•   •   •

Another room, elsewhere in the city
One second, darkness, then a flash of swirling purple.

A portal opens.

Whispers like water flowing over rocks fill the air.

In the center of the churning purple maelstrom is a blackness, a malevolence, almost...prescient.

A shape, burnt-gray, slithers from the black into the room...into existence.

It is followed by another and another and...

Pinpricks of red pierce the darkness. The gray shapes expand, grow.

As does their hunger.

•   •   •

The man in the purple robe stands on the dais, gazing at the Book of Sarmangous. He smiles and revels with the energy surging within him. He has unleashed an unstoppable power, one he will control.

The candles flare once and settle back, their flickering erratic, and the created shadows dance.

Some of those shadows move against the dancing silhouettes...move on their own.

And so it begins...

CHAPTER 1

Ewing Park
Four nights later

"Come on, Betty. It'll be fun. Don't you think this is romantic?" The youth coaxed the reluctant girl deeper into the grove of trees and large bushes, the sweet odor of lilacs heavy in the air.

"Joey, we're gonna get caught. Someone's gonna see us."

"No, they won't. It's the middle of the night."

"The car, Joey." Betty pulled back, causing her date to stumble. "A cop is going to find the car and catch us. I don't want to go to jail."

"We're not going to jail unless you don't lower your voice," Joey whispered. "If we get caught, they'll just throw us out of the park. We won't be arrested."

He sensed her hesitation wane.

"Come on, honey. You always complain how I'm not spontaneous enough. Well, here we are."

Betty put her hands on her hips. "Joey, you're carrying a blanket, a flashlight, and a condom. How spontaneous is that? You drove here after we left the club. Don't tell me you didn't plan this."

"Well..." Joey shrugged. "Do I at least get points for originality? Maybe...a kiss?"

Betty pursed her lips in mock consideration. "I have to admit, this is different."

"Uh-huh. What about that kiss?"

"Maybe."

"Maybe...more?"

"At least turn off the flashlight," Betty said. "It won't make any difference how loud our voices are if someone sees a light."

"Mmm..."

"What?"

"I just...well, I wanted..."

"Yes?"

"I want to watch you...undress." Joey leered.

"Joey!"

"It's sexy. The way you look at me and take off your clothes one piece at a time, slow and teasing."

He closed in and nuzzled her neck, whispering more seductive words in her ear. She giggled, then sighed as Joey's insistent body warmed her, overwhelmed her senses, and eased her fears. He touched her skin, brushed her arms with soft fingers, and she reached for him.

"Wait." Joey backed away.

Betty moaned at the broken moment. "Why?"

"Not here. I know a good place. Follow me."

They ran, hand in hand, to a circular clearing within a copse of trees almost in full bloom. The heady lilac scent pushed their pulsing hormones up another notch. He spread the blanket on the grass and removed his shoes. Kneeling, he pointed the flashlight at her.

"All right. Show me," he whispered.

"Don't shine the light in my eyes!"

"Sorry." He aimed the light lower.

She licked her lips with the tip of her tongue while her hands slid across her stomach and up to her breasts. Her fingers played with the first button of her blouse.

"Oh, my!" Joey's eyes widened, excitement building.

Betty moved her hips to a silent rhythm as she popped the first button out of the hole. Then the second button, the third.

A faint sound upon the breeze wafted through the branches. Betty stopped moving.

"What?" Joey narrowed his eyes, upset by the interruption.

Betty cocked her head to one side. "I thought I heard something."

"Ain't nothing out here. Come on, keep going. I'm about to drill a hole in my pants."

Betty giggled again and resumed her routine. When she slipped off the blouse, she crossed her arms in front of her breasts, which all but spilled from her half bra.

"You like?" she asked, voice husky and breathy.

She reached for the zipper on her skirt and soon the garment joined the other.

"Black panties," Joey said with a grin. "My favorite."

"Yes, but it's your turn." Betty pointed. "Time for you to get out of those clothes."

Joey stood, handed her the flashlight, and scrambled out of his shirt.

"Not so fast, lover boy," Betty chided. "I like it slow, too."

He moved his hips in a poor imitation of a Chippendale dancer taking off his pants.

"Yes, very nice," she said.

Joey stepped towards her, hand reaching for her breasts. He hesitated when a slithering sound, like a snake on loose gravel, wormed its way through the trees.

"What was that?" Betty aimed the light around her.

"I don't know. Probably a small animal."

Betty reached for her clothes. "Joey, m–maybe we oughta get out of here."

The sound altered from a slither to the harsh shush of two pieces of satin rubbing together. The volume increased, and the noise became an incensed hiss.

"Joey!" Betty whirled around, flashing the light in every direction. "What is it? What's happening?"

"I don't—"

Another evolution of sound cut off his words. The hiss became a mushy scrunch, like shuffling footsteps in sand or finely broken glass.

Something shifted in the darkness. Too late, Joey realized it wasn't something in the shadows, it *was* a shadow. No, a lot of shadows. Shifting, growing, looming.

Coming closer.

"Betty!" Joey's scream ripped through the night air, but Betty couldn't respond. The shadows enveloped her, and her own screams pierced the darkness.

Although not for long.

Joey tried to run, but other dark shapes cut off his escape...cut short his life.

The flashlight clunked to the ground. Its switch still set to the "on" position. The bulb shone, providing fuel for the attack.

Because with no light, there are no shadows.

CHAPTER 2

Thursday morning

Ring, ring.

Marvin Dirksen, startled by the sudden intrusive noise, dropped the joint onto his bed and fumbled for his cell phone. The lit end darkened a patch on the white sheet.

Ring, ring!

He pinched the joint between thumb and forefinger and transferred it to the small plywood night table, where it smoldered and left a black spot similar to other burn marks on the surface.

Ring! Ring!

The ringtone, a high-pitched, rough-voiced human shouting, *"Ring, ring,"* unless immediately answered, worsened, ever more insistent and nerve-grating. The fourth audible cry for attention cut through Marvin's lethargy.

Marvin answered the phone. "Yeah?"

The voice on the other end was one he expected. His lips formed a lazy smile. His dealer always made him happy.

Marvin had a plan. He wanted to stay high for a week straight with short time-outs for food and sleep. On this, his second day, his mind and soul surged free, flying to the stars. He'd touched his stock of food, purchased for the "trip" when extreme hunger demanded attention.

One snag in the plan, and the phone call soon rectified it. He'd just started smoking his last joint and needed another package. When his supply diminished, a quick message to his dealer's voicemail should have resulted in fresh weed in hours. However, the guy must have run into problems because he hadn't returned Marvin's call. Marvin didn't want to lose what he had worked so hard to attain, although to be honest, only part of his brain bothered to care.

Now, with the phone call dealer confirmed he had come through with the goods.

They'd worked out a great system. The exchange of product and payment occurred via the locked, slotted mailbox in front of Marvin's apartment. Each party owned a key, and Marvin's cash would be replaced with stash.

"Thanks, man," Marvin replied when told he had "mail."

He hauled himself out of bed, slipped his phone and lighter into his pants pockets, made sure to extinguish the joint on the nightstand—no sense taking a chance of burning down the place—and went to inspect the latest offering.

Marvin floated in slow-motion languor out the door to the row of mailboxes. With uncanny precision considering his condition, he eased the key into the lock and turned. The aluminum door squeaked open to reveal a sandwich bag filled with three-inch long joints, enough to carry him through the day and into the night if he rationed them.

He stuffed half a dozen of them into his pants pocket, placed the seventh between his lips, and re-locked the box, leaving the rest for later.

A pleasant walk would do him good. Fresh air to let his mind soar.

He fired up the joint with the lighter as he ambled along the sidewalk. Everything he saw filled him with delight. A budding bush. The street sign with white letters spelling out Indianola Avenue. A gray squirrel scurrying into the trees twenty yards to his left.

He tried to keep a running count of the telephone poles he passed, but lost his train of thought while pondering a fire hydrant. Measured, slow steps, sneakers scuffing the concrete. Take a puff, hold the smoke in for five seconds, then exhale. Inhale, hold, exhale. An easy, unhurried, rhythm.

Before crossing the avenue into Ewing Park, he looked both ways for oncoming traffic like a good boy.

Wow! The marijuana smoke combined with the spicy scent of lilacs sent him to new heights. This early in the morning, Marvin anticipated a day of total bliss.

He wandered among the trees and bushes, weaving from one to another, pushing his nose into each plant, sniffing, followed by a hit off the joint.

He spied a seven-foot tall bush near the entrance to a small patch of open ground. Rounding the corner, he leaned forward for extra momentum…

Thud! A dull ache spread through his body, and his arms and hands were slick with moisture. Why was he looking at blue sky and fuzzy clouds?

"Oh, shit, man!" He tried to maneuver up onto his forearms—his first thought was not the pain in his back from having slipped and landed face up on the hard ground, but the fact he'd lost the joint.

Gore covered his arm. He looked around, eyes widening in shock. What remained of the two human bodies sucked away the marijuana high in an instant. His mind slammed to earth as hard as his body had hit the ground, but stark reality socked him harder.

He uttered a piglet squeal and scrambled away from the carnage. With shaky, red-stained fingers, he plucked the cell phone from his pocket and dialed 9-1-1. Nausea caught up with his addled, weed-affected brain, making his report almost incoherent.

Dry heaves continued to wrack his body even as the sound of sirens filled the lilac park, its beauty now forever ruined by death.

CHAPTER 3

Misty Reznik locked herself in the bathroom and opened the first of two small rectangular packages.

The previous day, she'd debated buying the extra one but decided she needed to be certain. She withdrew the plastic tube with the paper instructions, confirmed the steps she had to take, positioned herself over the toilet, and tried to relax. The test didn't require too much urine to work, but she didn't like the awkwardness of holding the little tube between her legs. A few drops dribbled out while she tried to concentrate on something else...anything else. Footsteps outside the door announced the approach of her husband.

Don't do it, please don't—

She yelped when he slapped the door.

"Hurry up, honey," Harry said. "I haven't brushed my teeth."

Damn it!

His annoying door-slapping habit began long before they married, but it still scared her, taking her by surprise every time. This time, it literally scared the piss out of her. A steady stream shot into the bowl. Flustered, she still managed to open the second box and place the other stick under her before her bladder emptied.

Redressed, she stood before the sink, biting her lower lip, fighting the rising anxiety. The two thermometer-like tubes rested on the porcelain sink processing the information contained in her urine. She closed her eyes, unable to look at the display window. If a minus sign appeared, she wouldn't tell Harry she'd even taken the test.

If the window displays a plus sign, well...

After what seemed an eternity, counting the seconds, she opened one eye in a squint, like a child at Christmas anticipating the one big present still under the tree.

A blurry plus. Blurry because she still hadn't opened her eyes all the way. When she did, the crossed lines cleared. She whimpered in shocked delight and glanced behind her as if Harry might come barging in and discover her secret.

They'd been trying to get pregnant for several months. Frequent discussions had resulted in mutual agreement to try for a baby, and so far, they had enjoyed the effort.

She didn't close her eyes while waiting for the second test but fixed them on the display window, avoiding glancing into the mirror above the sink. She hadn't yet combed her sun-kissed blonde hair, and her sea-blue eyes were itchy and bloodshot. No surprise, after the fitful night she'd experienced.

The positive symbol faded into solidity, and she squealed in delight. She had to tell Harry right now. She burst out of the bathroom and dashed to the kitchen, where her husband stood talking on his cell phone.

"Huh? Not another one! Where? Who? Two kids? Shit. Okay, okay. I'll be out there as soon as I can. Damn, I haven't even had breakfast. Yeah, all right. All right! Get off the phone, so I can go. Bye."

He pressed the *End Call* button.

Misty leaped in front of him. "Harry, you won't believe it. I'm—I mean—"

"No time, baby." Harry reached for his jacket. "Gotta go. Looks like another attack. Two victims this time." He gulped orange juice on the way to the front door.

"But, Harry, I'm—"

Misty followed on his heels but stopped short when he turned, handed her the glass, pecked her on the cheek, said a quick, "See you tonight," and bolted out the door. He disappeared before she could get her lips to move.

"—pregnant," she finished as the door slammed.

The kohl-colored cat stared up at her, mild interest in its pale yellow eyes.

"Aren't you happy for me?" she asked.

The feline cocked its head at her disappointment before padding off to find something more stimulating.

•   •   •

Detective Harry Reznik tried to do two things at the same time: drive and adjust his tie. Rush hour traffic clogged the freeway, interstate, and main arteries of the city. Travel progressed in spurts due to what had to be sentient and evil sets of lights at various intersections. He tried to keep pace with the river of vehicles, steering with his knees while snatching looks at the rear-view mirror aimed so he could see his neck, never satisfied by the placement of the choking knot. He moved it up, down, left, right, returning to the first position like a frustrated husband under the indecisive guidance of his wife deciding on the placement of a heavy planter.

With a sharp screech of brakes, he avoided playing bumper cars. He snarled in disgust, ripped the tie from around his neck, and threw the infernal object in the back seat. A quick finger and thumb motion released the top collar button. He rubbed his chafed neck in relief.

Screw departmental dress code. He hated ties. He wished he could meet the person who decreed the wearing of the torturous pieces of fabric so he could punch him in the mouth. Better yet, choke him to death with his own tie. Besides, he was headed to a murder scene. Corpses couldn't care less whether the detective in charge wore a tie.

Even using shortcuts to avoid the major thoroughfares, twenty-five minutes ticked by before he reached Ewing Park, on Indianola Avenue on the southeast side of Des Moines. Ewing ranked as one of Misty's favorite parks, especially in spring, when the lilacs bloomed. At least once a year during the flowers' brief season, he and his wife drove from their Johnston home and, holding hands like young lovers, strolled the spacious aisles of bushes and trees, enjoying the smells and the serenity.

Today, murder marred the idyllic field. If the facts bore out the initial reports, this would not be a pretty sight. Then again, how many murders were?

Yellow crime scene tape, flapping in the breeze, surrounded the parking area. Harry pulled to a stop half on the road and half in the ditch. Already, more vehicles lined the avenue than necessary. Those not desired were decorated with the myriad letters and numbers of the local media representatives.

The reporters recognized authority and bombarded Harry with questions. If the idiots had any sense, they would realize he wouldn't have any answers yet since he'd just arrived.

Though they kept their somewhat respectful distance, Harry still felt as if he had to wade through the pack like the sole normal human escaping a sea of hungry mutants.

The officer at the barricade directed him to the location of the bodies. Harry advanced as far as he dared and caught the eye of the lead forensics man who bade him come closer.

"Another GD mess, Harry," the man said.

The detective admired Frank Belsom. A ten-year veteran as the county Medical Examiner, the man knew his craft. He retained enough heart to have remorse and regret for the victims, yet could close the shutters on his emotions to do his job. At five-six, he possessed Tom Brokaw handsomeness and carried a pocket watch. He looked at it every three minutes as if he might be late for an important meeting. The quirk Harry liked best was Frank's using initials for swear words.

Harry considered his own features. Thirty-five, athletic, but not a muscular build. Instead of a suave journalist look like Frank, he combined the best attributes of Jack Nicholson crossed with Nick Nolte—at his age, of course.

"How bad this time, Frank?" Harry asked.

"This is a bunch of S." Belsom gestured with spread arms at the surrounding gruesomeness. "When are you going to catch this freak?"

Harry detected a note of desperate haranguing in the man's tone. He decided to return the favor.

"I have a lunch appointment with him at Applebee's to negotiate his surrender. Give me a break, Frank, will you?"

"Yeah, yeah." The other man waved an apology. "I know. I'm just getting tired of being called out morning after morning. Four in a row now. My wife is giving me H about it."

"Stay at your girlfriend's," Harry joked.

"Ha, ha, Harry. You're an F-ing riot."

"Hey, I barely saw my wife this morning."

"Hmph!"

Harry gestured to the scene. "What do you have for me today?"

Frank led him around a corner to a small clearing. "A couple of youngsters out for a bit of late-night nookie. They'd gotten down to their underwear before..." He let his words trail off and pointed.

Although this was the fourth such scene he'd seen this week—and the second one in person and not through photos—Harry still had to control his revulsion. What used to be two kids barely out of their teens now could have been a still shot of a grade-B horror flick with amateurish special effects.

The bodies resembled boiled hams with chunks of flesh removed. Sections of skin bubbled with raw, inflamed blisters or lined with bloody scrapes. Their chests had caved in as if from fallen cement blocks. Each abdomen gaped open after being clawed or ripped apart.

Lots of blood soaked into the ground and more stained the pale purple lilacs. Harry averted his attention away from the slaughter, more to avoid staring than to survey the progress of the crime scene investigation. He suspected, as at the other murder sites, no clues such as fingerprints, footprints, fiber traces, tire tracks, or other forms of identification leading to a suspect would be found.

"Who are they?" Harry asked.

"Car in the parking lot is registered to a Joey McDaniel, Watrous Avenue address. ID in a purse left in the car during the aborted tryst shows the girl one Betty Hogg."

Harry hiked his eyebrows.

"Don't be an A, Harry. H-o-g-g."

"Still. Hell of a name to grow up with."

"No kidding," Frank agreed.

"Place of residence?"

"Ten blocks from McDaniel."

The homicide detective blew air. "Anything else you can tell me?"

"What do you think?"

"Zero, zilch, nada, nothing. Same as at the previous crime scenes."

"Right first try. A big fat F-ing zero." Frank moved to return to the vain search for evidence. "You'll have my report later today with the usual blank space listing all those clues we dug up."

"Thanks," Harry said, with a touch of sarcasm.

Frank gave a slight bow, then straightened up, and pulled out his watch. "We're here only to serve up the very best, even if it turns out to be a bunch of HS."

Harry paused a moment to decipher. He smiled and left Frank to continue looking for his horse shit.

The spring grass crunched under Harry's shoes. He retraced his route back to the parking lot to not disturb any area not cleared by forensics. He stopped to gaze at the broad expanse of the park. From the crest, the long quarter mile of open space ran downhill to a tree-covered valley. Plenty of escape routes for whoever had committed this atrocity. A housing development and the complex design of Easter Park east of Indianola Avenue offered further options.

Before returning to business, Harry walked south along the avenue. Clusters of lilac bushes lined the perimeter of the park in no discernible pattern. He reached a certain point before facing northwest. There before him, the capital city rose from the horizon. Downtown buildings speared the sky—the Principal Building, with its forty-four stories, reigning supreme.

Harry contemplated the vista as he circled the lilacs. Crime scene techs had already cleared the area. This wasn't Chicago, with endless urban sprawl. Rather, it reminded him of Atlanta seen from the air, with patches of city pushing up through the lush trees. A couple of rivers and several creeks lazily wound through the city. They caused problems only when they overflowed their banks, closing off streets and threatening residences.

Des Moines and its suburbs covered the spectrum from wealthy to needy, conservative to liberal, respectable to kooky. Like New York, Harry could always find something of interest. Museums, theater, or a new production at the Civic Center. Even though those were more to Misty's taste, he went along because it made her happy. Every weekend it seemed there was an event along the riverfront or downtown. She dragged him to Art on the Square, the food festival, the farmers' market, or a new-age musician playing at Java Joe's coffee shop.

They both enjoyed Iowa Cubs baseball games and the Buccaneers at the hockey rink. Sticking a finger in the phone book to pick a restaurant. Spending a quiet afternoon picnicking at Union Park, or walking the Greenbelt Trail.

The grassy decline stretched to a single-lane strip of asphalt and a grove of trees. A maintenance truck jerked through gears on its way up the road. At the tree line, the supple, yet powerful, haunches of a young buck froze, wary because it detected a sound or movement. Then, quick as lightning, the animal disappeared with the faintest crunching underfoot.

People should die at home or in the hospital, not amid the peaceful atmosphere of a park. Harry loved being a cop. The job grew on him, and he grew on the job. He'd seen the city in the brightest lights and the darkest blacks, but he still craved the work. All homicides were tragic. Some worse than others. To track down the scumbag who took the life of another brought him satisfaction. Sure, he acted cynical and hard-nosed at times. Sure, he resisted change, but he got the job done.

He didn't want to enlarge his ego but damn it, Des Moines was his city, and someone—some Class A sicko—was running amok.

"I'm coming for you," he whispered. "I'll find you, you bastard, and when I do…"

He left the unspoken vow hanging, certain the city understood.

•   •   •

Harry narrowed his eyes and studied the punk who'd discovered the bodies. He guessed a high school dropout, but Harry wondered what this goofball was doing out so early in the day, sniffing the lilacs with untied sneakers, no socks, ragged shorts, and a T-shirt with a faded imprint of a logo Harry deduced advertised a rock band. While he listened to the kid stutter and stammer through the routine questioning, Harry made a silent inquiry to a nearby officer. Unseen by the youth, the officer smiled and held up a plastic evidence bag containing a handful of joints.

Harry rolled his eyes. He hated punks and in his opinion, any kid between eight and twenty-two with even a hint of a shady countenance rated the title. He didn't mind shorts and T-shirts—Harry owned several of each—but there was a difference between looking casual but respectable even in knock-around clothes and looking like…well, a punk.

Starting five years ago, he deemed that *punk* was the best way to describe the ever-increasing number of dumb-ass bicyclists who ignored every traffic rule, pedestrians who disregarded oncoming traffic while crossing the street, those who giggled and/or spoke into cell phones in a movie theater, or any group of three or more who acted as if they owned a particular corner or doorway and wouldn't respect other pedestrians. How many times had he longed to stick out a foot and send sprawling the disrespectful runts who raced through the Skywalk system?

This particular punk in front of him wasn't his concern. Harry couldn't even remember the doofus's name. He'd let the officer handle the misdemeanor drug charge. Regarding Harry's case, the kid offered nothing substantive other than solid alibis for the dates of the other murders. Intuition told Harry the kid didn't possess the acumen nor the strength to have committed the horrendous crimes.

Before Harry returned to his car, he muttered an aside to the officer out of the punk's earshot. "I'd take him behind those Porta-Pottys over there and put my foot up his ass."

"I could 'accidentally' lock him in one of them for about three hours," the officer offered.

Harry grinned and nodded all the way back to the car.

CHAPTER 4

Many buildings housing the country's police departments were modern and stylish, exuding high class—at least the ones Detective Harry Reznik had visited. The Des Moines police department reminded him of a medieval keep. Built in 1920, the massive chunk of stones at East Court and East First dominated the bank of the Des Moines River. Inside, tiled floors and bland bare corridors echoed the sixties. Small offices became even more cramped when officers created makeshift conference rooms by pushing several tables together with barely enough room for chairs.

Technologically, the force was up to par and still able to claim a patrol officer could respond to a dispatch and arrive at the address in question within three minutes. DMPD also worked well with other metro departments, often coordinating operations.

Robbery/Homicide resided on the third floor with a dozen detectives investigating, on average, that same number of murders per year.

Harry yawned as he entered the room. He'd visited the families of McDaniel and Hogg and, like the punk, they provided nothing worthwhile. He hated leaving them with a hole in their lives. Delivering death notifications was always the worst part of the job.

"Hey, Len," he greeted the detective whose desk sat closest to the door. Len Hillyer had a permanent somber expression and a quiet manner. Sometimes he irritated Harry, but the feeling ran both ways. "Don't look too happy this morning. The fun is just beginning."

Hillyer shrugged and went back to studying his paperwork. Other detectives held phone conversations, typed endless reports, or discussed cases with one another. Because of the recent rash of murders—four in as many nights—several officers worked the baffling cases. After days without results, each was as stymied as the next. No one had discovered any connections between the victims, any pattern in the locations of the killing sites, or any evidence other than the grisly remains left at the scenes.

Talk of an official task force had passed through the office and although the detectives shared everything, an all-out hard-hitting coordinated team would evolve, especially in light of this morning's latest victims. It had to, since some of the killings occurred outside the Des Moines city limits, thus involving suburban departments.

"Forgot your tie, Harry," Gary Wang said from his corner desk. Wang, third-generation American and had no issue voicing his opinions. Many centered on department policy.

Harry brushed a hand through his hair and remembered his tie still crumpled on the back seat of his car. "I don't give a shit." There were more important matters to worry about than whether he wore the fashionable noose.

Truth be told, Harry enjoyed his job—as much as having to look at the myriad forms of dead bodies can be enjoyable. He relished the hunt, the chase, and the untangling of evidence. There wasn't an overwhelming sense of "justice for the victim" syndrome, although every investigator had a touch of it. He came to work five to six days per week because there were puzzles to be solved and mysteries to unravel.

Unlike other brother officers, he read mystery novels, went to whodunit movies, and watched police shows on television. Sure, some scenes weren't accurate regarding procedure, and many of the plots were formulaic and predictable, but the puzzle always existed, a problem to be solved.

"You don't have to be so surly so early in the morning," Wang said.

Harry leaned over Wang's desk. "It's after ten, Gary. I've just seen the guts of two young kids, and the dumb shit who found the bodies couldn't tie his shoes to save his life. Then, I had to tell two sets of parents their babies are dead. Oh, but heaven forbid I forget my tie? You can take my tie and shove it!"

Many people thought him to be a grouchy bear just awakened from hibernation, but much of his attitude came down to simple cynicism. Cynicism, the standard attitude in police work from the mild, straight-faced Joe Friday of Dragnet to Law & Order's veteran Lenny Briscoe. Harry Reznik followed suit, speaking his mind when the occasion called for it and, sometimes when it did not. No one could accuse him of holding back. His co-workers and bosses always knew where he stood.

"Pretty bad?" Veronica Gamba, one of the department's two female detectives, spoke up from the other side of the room. Auburn-haired, with high cheekbones, dark eyes, and elfin ears, she was one of a handful who saw through Harry's facade.

He repeated Belsom's earlier question. "What do you think?"

"This is getting worse, Harry."

"Tell me something I don't know."

"This killer is almost inhuman."

"Listen, Ronnie." Harry rubbed his aching eyes. "This ain't the boogie man or a mutated monster escaped from a secret government laboratory. He'll be crazy, but he'll be as supernatural as Hillyer."

Veronica smiled. "Are you sure?"

"Yeah, but sometimes I'm not sure about Len."

Harry couldn't understand how those kids, the young would-be lovers, hadn't had enough brains between them to find a safer and more sensible spot to boink each other. Maybe they had the "it won't happen to me" attitude.

The metro area was in a near panic. The shock of three vicious murders in three consecutive nights—and now a fourth—proved overwhelming to the public. Many details had not been released to the press, but the horrid nature of the crimes couldn't be shaded.

Numerous companies and organizations postponed or outright canceled evening activities. Restaurant and bar attendance dropped after the second murder. To make matters worse, the bodies weren't relegated to Des Moines proper. Two incidents now in Des Moines, one in Clive, one in West Des Moines. Frantic mayors made endless phone calls, citizens huddled scared in their homes, and every police dispatcher noted an increase in emergency calls registering innocuous reports. Dogs barking, normal house noises, a postal worker delivering mail. These and many other normal activities became suspect as fear increased. In one case, a neighbor's loud video game through open windows caused one woman to cower in her closet. It took most of the departments' patience to maintain calm with everyone wondering when the next murder would occur and what would happen next.

"Next" for Harry Reznik meant a woman who entered the squad room with a tight jaw, straight mouth, and serious expression. She stopped at the first desk and spoke to Hillyer, who in turn pointed at Harry.

What now?

He judged the woman to be in her early thirties, five-eight or nine, with short-cropped but styled black hair. Professional attire, yet he detected a figure shaped by regular visits to the gym. Dark eyes, a fine-boned smooth face, and an intelligent, if bland, expression.

She stopped at his desk and raised an eyebrow in query. "Detective Reznik?"

She might as well have had FED tattooed on her forehead.

"Yes?"

"Agent Lori Campisi, Federal Bureau of Investigation." She stuck out a hand.

Harry shook it while trying to keep his cynicism in check. Failing that, he looked toward the enclosed corner office of his supervisor. Lieutenant Glynis "GG" Gravatte also had noticed the Feeb's entrance. Her expression showed no surprise, rather a look of expectation. Instead of coming out to help smooth the introduction, she placed a phone to her ear.

Isn't that convenient, Harry thought.

She aimed narrowed eyes at Harry and he surmised the unvoiced order. "Cool your jets and work with her."

Right. Thanks, LT for the advanced warning.

Agent Campisi took the initiative. Her voice held little emotion as she said, "I'm here to assist in the series of murders you are investigating." She paused. "Let's not make this the same old story of locals versus feds. It gets tiresome. Shall we make this easy?"

"Easy?" Harry snorted. "'Easy' she says. Show me one time in the past four days when things have been easy. There's been nothing but chaos at every step. Mayors demanding reports every hour, reporters trying to uncover the hidden conspiracy they're convinced exists, grieving families, panicked citizens, no clues, no suspects, no leads. Hell, it's only natural the next scene in our little nightmare would be you people barging in."

Harry closed his eyes and again ran fingers through his hair. Several strands came loose. Was he now starting to lose his hair? He twisted the kinks out of his neck with a few dull cracks. After waiting five seconds and receiving no response to his minor tirade, he opened one eye. Agent Campisi still stood in front of his desk—vain hope she'd been an illusion borne out of a temporary case of insanity or lack of food— impassive expression set on her face, bored eyes.

"Detective Reznik, there are no 'people,'" she replied. "There is only me, and I'm not barging in anywhere. Although I did initiate a phone call with your lieutenant, I'm here by invitation."

"You made the first call?"

"Yes."

Harry narrowed his eyes in suspicion. "Why? Usually you people don't want to intrude."

"Detective Reznik, please stop saying 'you people.' Its derogatory implication is duly noted and ignored. To answer your question, I made the call because I've had experience with these types of cases."

"Serial killings?"

"If you prefer the term, though it's not accurate."

"What?"

"Detective Reznik—"

"Hey," he cut in, "I'll stop saying 'you people' if you'll drop the Detective. Reznik will do, or even better, Harry, since it looks as if I'm stuck with you. No offense."

"None taken...Detective Reznik," she said in a monotone.

"Why wasn't I informed you planned to be here?"

"I spoke with your lieutenant yesterday afternoon and flew out last night. Besides, she mentioned it would be better—not easier, I'll agree—to be introduced to you in this manner. She said said you make a fuss over new partners."

"I don't make a fuss." Harry's volume rose. Gravatte, still on her supposed phone call, continued to ignore him. Hell of a long call.

"At least sit down, will ya?" He gestured to a chair. "You make me nervous standing there like...well, you...aw hell, sit. Please," he added, remembering courtesy at the last moment.

"Thank you." Campisi sat in the chair next to the desk.

Harry sighed. "Where do we start?"

"Tell me about the victims this morning."

"Gravatte fill you in on the other cases?"

"A summary, yes," answered Campisi. "I expect to have a closer look at the reports later today."

Harry described the scene at Ewing Park, including the dork who called in the report. He ended with, "We have nothing to go on. No evidence to lead us down one particular path, no witnesses, and no weapons." He shrugged, expressing the helplessness shared by all the investigating officers. "Any ideas?"

Campisi paused and said, "A few. I have nothing concrete to share at the moment."

"Yes...well..." Harry thought there was something not quite right about this agent. He couldn't pinpoint the source of his suspicion; he'd have to wait and see. "You said you've had experience in these types of cases, yet you don't want to refer to ours as serial in nature. Why?"

Before she could respond, another detective walked in the door, calling Harry's name.

Harry looked up. "What?"

"You responded to the call at Ewing Park this morning?" Harry raised his chin in affirmation. The man referred to his notepad. "Officer Stanfield just reported in. She responded a homeless guy on East Fourteenth just north of the river. Said the guy acted concerned about his buddy who'd been ranting. Something he witnessed in Ewing Park last night."

Harry scrambled from behind the desk. "What's Stanfield's location?"

"Uh, East Fourteenth and Maury."

"Thanks, Bill. Come on, Agent Campisi. This may be our first break."

He poked his head into the lieutenant's office, shook a "We'll talk later" finger at her, and dashed out of the squad room assuming the Feeb would follow. Halfway to the elevator, he stopped short.

Campisi stopped short of colliding with him. "What is it, Detective?"

"Gotta dime?" He dug into his pants pocket. "Never mind."

He fed coins into the vending machine, punched a letter-number combination, and retrieved his selection from the bin.

As he resumed his flight to the elevator, he held up the plastic-wrapped pastry item. "Didn't get breakfast this morning. Besides, nothing's better than blueberry Pop-Tarts."

He smiled at Campisi who furrowed her forehead and cocked an eyebrow.

CHAPTER 5

"You're what? Oh, my God!"

Misty winced at Terry Tucker's outburst when heads popped up over the tops of the neighboring cubicles.

Terry, the perky junior secretary to the advertising agency's manager Phil Sherwood, was always happy-go-lucky even on the worst days when clients called in upset or when designers and sales personnel took a sick day. Nothing ever dampened her bubbly personality. She became even more animated when any positive news came her way, waving her hands and spouting, "Oh, my God," like an eighties Valley girl.

The morning started with Misty spending two hours on a rush job. A client's sudden demands for a series of changes on a project completed just two days ago. While she waited for the salesman to call back with the okay, she tried to adjust her attention to her latest assignment. After the mid-morning break she visited her supervisor to seek time off the next day for the scheduled doctor's appointment.

However, to see Sherwood she had to go through Terry. Even though she had wanted to tell Harry the good news first, there seemed to be no way to avoid the subject.

"When did you find out? I mean, oh, my God! What did Harry think?" Misty started to reply, but Terry babbled on. "A baby! We haven't had a baby at the agency in years. This is just too cool. I hope you won't have morning sickness."

"Terry, is Phil available?" Misty said between the secretary's gushes. "I need to get a couple of hours off tomorrow to see the doctor."

"Of course, he's here." Terry lowered her voice to a conspiratorial whisper. "He's been on the phone all morning with Astrid Rogers. You know, the ritzy ditz from Tiles and More? Don't tell anyone, but I think he's seeing her on the side, and I don't think his wife knows."

Rogers, the president of a home remodeling company, wasn't the only ditz in town. You'd have to be crazy to believe stone-faced Sherwood would even think of stepping out with someone other than eagle-eyed Edith.

Terry, back on the pregnancy topic, let loose with another, "Oh, my God! I can't believe you're really going to have a baby."

At that point, the office door opened and Sherwood's balding head popped out.

"What the hell is with all the racket? Did Bryan land the Denberg Bakery account? It's been two months."

"Mr. Sherwood, great news," Terry squawked. "Guess who's—"

"Phil, do you have a moment?" Misty asked. "I need to discuss something with you."

Terry bounced with such enthusiasm, Misty thought the girl would pee her pants. Sherwood expressed confusion but motioned for Misty to enter.

Misty closed the office door. From outside, Terry cried out again. "Oh, my God!" The sharp tick of high heels across the floor foretold the baby news would spread throughout the entire office within minutes. Oh, well, why shouldn't everyone share in her happiness?

•　　•　　•

The quickest route to Officer Stanfield's location was not to take Court Avenue to East Fourteenth, then south to Maury. Instead, he cut south on East Sixth to Maury, then east, avoiding the capitol complex.

Certain areas of the metro had been renovated, while a few spots could never be improved unless one started at square one, razing everything, plowing up the land, and beginning again. Still, other neighborhoods, though prosperous in their own eccentric way, had never lost their aged appearance. They weren't dead but didn't appear full of vitality.

The Maury Street neighborhood fell into the latter category. Short strips of pitted blacktop led to junk-filled lawns and ramshackle houses. On the western edge, just before downtown, several small industries hunkered behind chain-link fences. As he got closer to Southeast Fourteenth, the neighborhood assumed a veil of dirty brown. Unwashed. Untidy.

Harry drove a department vehicle, a maroon Buick LeSabre. He stole quick glances at Agent Campisi who rode shotgun. She was a strange one. From the moment she entered the car, she stared straight ahead, hands in her lap, her face a blank mask. She remained silent during the brief trip.

Harry struggled to find any opening to strike up a discussion but resigned himself to munching his Pop Tart. He should have grabbed a coffee to go with it. The damn pastry, while delicious, created sticky gobs in the back of his throat.

Officer Stanfield was not at the Maury and East Fourteenth intersection but a couple of blocks south in the parking lot of a closed and boarded-up tavern.

Officer Kelli Stanfield was a short, blonde who exemplified the cute-girl-next-door. She'd adjusted to big-city life after transferring from a hamlet in northeast Iowa. On the force seven months, she exhibited dedication, enthusiasm, and spunk. She was a regular target for most of the bachelor officers, as well as a few married ones. Harry recalled her background that included a no-nonsense father and two older brothers who became All-State wrestlers in college. Hence, she took crap from no one.

Stanfield tried to calm a short man in a dirty overcoat and scuffed black shoes as Harry and Campisi exited the car. A few days' worth of stubbly facial hair matched the color of the tangled gray mess on the man's head.

"Now, Mr. Warton, just calm down," she said. "As you can see, the detective in charge is here and we'll get this matter sorted out."

Warton shifted from one foot to the other as if his soles burned and kept looking behind him at the decrepit bar.

Harry nodded a greeting to the officer. "What's up?"

Stanfield gestured to her nervous ward. "This is Mr. Jeffrey Warton. He said his friend may have been a witness to your murders last night. I can't get the story clarified, but when he mentioned Ewing Park, I called it in."

"Thanks," Harry said, then spoke to the man. "Mr. Warton, I'm Detective Reznik and this is Agent Campisi. Why don't you tell us what's going on? Nice and slow from the beginning."

The beginning kept restarting as Warton stumbled over his words. He was a shaky little guy who readjusted his balance every three seconds, wiped sweat from his forehead, and displayed an inordinate amount of fear for his friend. Harry recognized the pale, clammy skin combined with Warton's near incoherency as two of the signs of alcohol withdrawal. Warton managed to stutter out his story.

He and his pal, Ronald Leahy, eked out a living begging and doing along Fourteenth. With no permanent residence, they stayed in various hidey-holes in empty houses or closed businesses. They often took shelter in the old bar.

That morning, Leahy had staggered in after being out all night. Warton hadn't been worried. He figured Leahy had slept off a drunk somewhere. However, Leahy kept mumbling and rambling to himself when he arrived.

"Rantin' crazy words." Warton's words came quick and sharp. "On and on. I didn't unner...unnerstan' it. It warn't like him."

"What kind of crazy words?"

"I don't know!" Warton hopped in frustration. "Words and h–half sentences. Ewing Park, naked kids, shadows, blood, screaming. I tried to calm him down, but whenever I got near him, he'd scream and push me away. It's like he was possessed."

"Wait a minute, sir." Harry held up his palms. "Back up a minute. Tell me what your friend said about blood and shadows."

Warton swallowed and wiped his open mouth with a couple of fingers. "I don't know, I tell you. No sense, no s–sense at all."

"Mr. Warton—"

"He said he watched two kids take off their clothes."

"Yes, go on," Harry urged.

More hopping. "Then he said sumpun' attacked them."

"Something, not someone."

Warton's voice went raspy. "Shadows. He said the shadows attacked them. Tore 'em up."

Agent Campisi stepped forward and spoke for the first time since the station house. "Are you sure he said shadows?"

"Y–yes."

"Someone came from the shadows and—"

"No! He said the shadows done it. Killed them kids. He's crazy, I tell you. I know he goes off sometimes, but most of the time he ain't so bad."

Harry let his eyes roam over the bar and the gravel-strewn blacktop. He took in the nondescript building to the north. "Where is Mr. Leahy now, sir?"

Warton pointed at the boarded-up tavern. Officer Stanfield explained. "He left Leahy to find help. Waved me down. I figured I'd get his story and then call for backup."

"Right," Harry agreed. "You stay here with Mr. Warton. Come on, Campisi, time to earn your keep."

The dilapidated tavern sat a few hundred yards south of a dive pizza joint, just north of the riverbank, across the street from a park undergoing construction. Piles of dirt dotted the grounds as if from a giant gopher. The tavern itself showed missing pieces of siding near the foundation as if other mutant rodents had chewed through the walls. Plywood, a putrid dark brown created by Mother Nature, covered every door and window. At the rear, there was a sealed door once used for deliveries.

Harry studied the entrance. On the lower half of the door, the two hobos had constructed a three-foot square cutaway rigged to slide back and forth hid the evidence of the secret opening.

Harry squatted near the opening and peered at the darkness beyond with a flashlight retrieved from the car in one hand. He moved his other hand nearer to the nine-millimeter holstered on his hip. A similar weapon had somehow materialized in Campisi's hand.

Strange, he hadn't seen a holster. She didn't even carry a purse.

"Ronald Leahy?" Harry called. "This is the police. Are you in there?"

No answer. Harry glanced up at Campisi. She still exhibited no readable expression.

"Mr. Leahy? We just want to talk."

Still nothing. No sounds except the traffic passing and a few birds.

After a third entreaty, Harry murmured to the FBI agent, "What do you think?"

She shrugged. "Your call. I'm just here to assist."

Harry smirked. "Don't start that shit." He sighed. "Mr. Leahy, we're coming in. We're not going to hurt you."

He hesitated another moment, muttered an expletive under his breath, drew his gun, and advanced through the hole. Just inside, he paused to let his eyes adjust to the lack of light. He shone the flashlight beam in all directions and stepped to one side to let Campisi enter. The flashlight revealed a narrow hall with a couple of doors on one side, then an open entrance to the main barroom. He glanced at Campisi, and they both advanced with caution.

The first doorway opened on a storeroom, empty except for rotten shelves. Even time and the elements hadn't dispelled the faint trace of alcohol still lingering in the musty air.

They halted at the second door. Harry figured it was an office. The previous owner hadn't bothered selling everything. An old wooden desk bound for the landfill rested near one wall. Two of the four slots for drawers gaped empty, another drawer hung broken and askew, half off its rails. A metal file cabinet stood nearby, so rusted the original color remained unknown. Otherwise, the room was bare.

At the opening to the barroom proper, Harry again called out for Leahy, repeated his identification, the purpose of his visit, and received the same silence in return.

The long bar, scarred with countless cigarette burns and stained with endless spills of alcohol, ran almost the entire length of one wall. The one remaining table on the main floor leaned at a forty-five degree angle—the cripple left behind to suffer the indignity of a broken leg.

Debris scattered on the floor evidenced others who'd sought shelter in the abandoned building over the years. Light filtered through small holes in the scattered pattern of shotgun blasts. Pipes or other implements had punched out other holes. The entire scene was nothing but sheer vandalism.

What remained of Ronald Leahy lay bloody in the western far corner.

"Damn!" Harry said.

"What is it?"

He said nothing, just handed her the light. Let her get her first look at what too many others had seen. See what she thinks of the boiled, gouged, bloody remains, the same in the four other scenes.

•   •   •

Campisi stared at the corpse, the flashlight creating shiny patches on the blood-slicked ravages and the darker areas on the far side of the body. She studied the remains of the homeless man with a clinical eye. Her brain registered each wound without emotion, the slightest expression of revulsion on her face.

Opportunistic flies explored the blood and wounds where rats had already feasted.

Another tragedy, another murder victim. She'd seen many forms of death during her career.

What seeped out of her subconscious, to get a tentative finger-hold on her mind, was the location of the corpse.

Inside a darkened room.

A connection clicked to another unknown place even darker.

Where she'd been in the past and didn't want to return.

She closed her eyes. For years, she'd fought a dual mental battle. One part struggled in vain, trying to remember. Where?

No light pierced the constant, impenetrable black.

Another part of her mind, the rational professional part, suggested the current time and place weren't appropriate for the other's exertions.

Jaw tightened, her lips thinned to a stark white line as tension set like cement on her face.

This mental struggle...something new...or rather a familiar one in a new location at a new time. The nightmare, so often experienced and suffered while asleep, now came to her, reaching tendrils into her consciousness, seeking a firm hold.

Why?

Why now? Because of this particular corpse? Because of what she suspected was the cause of death?

Or because of the site of that other dark shadowy place where...

Where...what?

She couldn't remember.

This wasn't the place to fight personal demons. She had a job to do but did not look forward to the near future or the joust with a hard-nosed cop.

Detective Harry Reznik was going to be trouble.

•　　•　　•

"JHC," hollered Frank Belsom when he showed up at the old tavern. "I haven't even finished with the first two from this morning and you call in another? What the F, Harry? You trying to win Des Moines the prize for reporting the most kills? Why don't you let Pleasant Hill or Saylorville have a turn?"

Harry understood the M.E. was releasing a combination of frustration and not a little fear. Fear of the unknown.

It didn't matter if the murders happened in those burbs, because Belsom, the county medical examiner, would still be in attendance. The man stomped off toward the building muttering more bad letters and checking his pocket watch.

While awaiting the arrival of the crime scene unit, Harry had badgered and bullied more answers out of Jeffrey Warton, squeezing out every minute of the homeless man's life for the past twenty-four hours. For most of the time, he couldn't substantiate his whereabouts since his lifestyle didn't allow too much company. He provided alibis for the dates of the other killings but once again, they'd be difficult to confirm.

Harry let Officer Stanfield transport Warton back to the station. He'd be cleaned up, fed, and questioned again at length. The detective also intuited it would all be for naught. Warton wasn't the murderer. He didn't have the faculties to commit one, let alone a series of killings, despite his relationship with the most recent victim. Still, they had to go through the motions.

Agent Campisi, who had exited the tavern a few minutes before, remained silent. She hadn't expressed a reaction to the finding of Leahy's body or its condition. No shocked gasp or small cries of disgust. Rather, she exhibited the straight mouth and focused stare of intrigue.

Her attitude reminded Harry of Spock from the old Star Trek series. Fascinated, yet her countenance displayed no emotions. She had stayed behind, ostensibly to study the corpse, while Harry returned outside to call into the station. Before he did, she crouched next to Leahy, careful not to disturb the scene any more than necessary as she observed everything with a practiced meticulous eye.

She'd remained motionless during Harry's interview with Warton. Even now, with homeless mand gone and the forensic team's operations winding down, she offered no comment or insight.

Harry checked his own watch as he rested his behind on the fender of the LeSabre. "Do you eat, Agent Campisi?"

"Excuse me?"

"I asked if you ate. As in food."

"Yes, Detective," she answered. "Why would you ask such an inane question?"

"It's past lunchtime. Shall we grab something before we head back to the station? I don't suppose the government would foot the bill for a meal, would it?"

Campisi raised an eyebrow just like Mr. Spock and, without a word, walked to the car.

Yes, she was a strange one. He might have to check up on her.

She was going to be trouble.

CHAPTER 6

Misty glanced at the dashboard clock. Twenty minutes to one, but she could be late getting back from lunch. Phil Sherwood wouldn't come down on her too hard as she'd made excellent progress on her current project, completing a couple of preliminary drafts ahead of schedule. Three more designs needed reworking. A couple of hours to tweak the nuances of the ad, including removing the blemishes from the face of the septuagenarian woman model to give the impression the age-defying cream the client's company sold worked miracles.

So, yes, one more store.

After Harry's hasty departure that morning, she'd remained frozen by indecision. Should she dash after him or throw the orange juice glass against the door in frustration? He'd been stressed himself this week, what with the recent murders and the phone call that rushed him out of the house.

Still...

They'd decided to try for a child a few months ago. Although she wasn't hearing her biological clock notching the years, the time felt right. Harry, secure in his career, earned decent annual raises, she had established a solid position at the agency, and their finances wouldn't be in jeopardy if she took maternity leave. She could work on projects at home if necessary—or so she hoped.

Her imagining family life, becoming a mom, and using her body to nurture a child, kept intruding at quiet moments. She and Harry tried to avoid *the* sore topic between them, but a grandchild to present to her parents might help ease the existing enmity sensed and heard over the thousand-mile phone line on each phone call. Even though the problem lay between her parents and Harry, she was caught in the middle. Maybe a baby would change the tense situation.

Now, with the test verifying her pregnancy—to be confirmed tomorrow at the doctor's office—Misty decided if Harry wasn't going to let her tell him, she'd show him.

They would purchase the big items together, of course: crib, stroller, car seat. She would buy the items to be used as a surprise: teddy bears, blankets, bottles, rattles, teething rings—somewhat premature, but what the hell—a mobile, nightlight, stuffed animals to guard the little tyke in his or her crib, and of course, diapers. Three jumbo-sized purple and white boxes of them. Everything filled her car to capacity as if she'd raided a nursery.

She'd laughed to herself choosing items almost willy-nilly, drawing wary stares from other mothers or mothers-to-be. Upon the latter, she gazed wide-eyed, observing the various sizes of bulges and the arched backs, hands on hip postures.

She was destined for this? Did she understand the coming changes to her body?

Another laugh escaped at how much stuff she'd crammed into her car's trunk and interior. A stranger might think she and her baby lived in the car, and that made her laugh again.

She took the Eighth Avenue exit in West Des Moines and drove into the pastureland of parked cars at the Super Walmart. Inside the vast hypermarket, she hustled to infant clothing and examined the variety of jumpers, PJs, shirts, pants, overalls, shoes, socks, frills, soft denim, small caps, and even a tiny white martial arts uniform with a black belt.

Again, she bought gender-neutral—and again, bought too much. With no more room in the back seat, she tucked the sacks into the floor well of the front passenger seat.

She arrived back at work thirty minutes late and, although Sherwood just gave a pointed look at the clock, Terry beamed excitement, still ecstatic over the morning's news.

CHAPTER 7

Mexico City

Wednesday, nine nights earlier

The Delta 747 began its descent. Out his window, the untold millions of lights ended in darkness along the eastern and southern edges of the bowl containing the world's largest city, the surrounding mountains full of sulfur mines. Within 572 square miles, Mexico City contained the combined population of New York City and Los Angeles in its metropolitan area.

He'd never been to the Mexican capital, but he already hated it. For it was no different from the scores of other earthly hellholes he'd visited over the last thirty years. Bangkok, Rio de Janeiro, Tokyo, New Delhi, Tehran, Cairo, Calcutta. Others in China, middle Africa, Russia. Each of them filthy, rampant with crime, and vermin-infested. At least in the parts of those cities into which he ventured.

Neighborhoods unknown to the average tourist and all but forgotten by the majority of locals, including what passed for the local police. Hidden places, unmapped alleys, dark, dank rooms, and basements of buildings long since deleted from any tax records. Areas where humanity and human morality ceased to exist. Pits of degradation where anything–*anything*–or anyone, could be bought or sold. Where unimaginable vile acts were perpetrated without conscience, without remorse, and many times with no consideration for the act itself.

Mexico City was no different. To him, it was just the world's largest human cesspool. Maybe, just maybe, this would be the final shit-hole he'd have to visit. After years of travel, searching and researching, bribing, begging, cajoling, stealing, and yes, torture and murder, in this place, this time, he would find it.

The Book of Sarmangous.

He leaned back in his seat, closed his eyes, and ignored the atmospheric pressure built up in his ears. His mind drifted back over the years. Too many had passed. Too many filled with struggle and frustration. He'd known terror and other things quite beyond terror. He'd visited six of the seven continents, traveled from Canada to the Caucuses and from Austria to Australia. A last-minute revelation of the falsehood of a lead had prevented a trip to Antarctica. He'd climbed mountains, traversed deserts, wandered lost in jungles, and found himself trapped in forgotten caves.

He reached a rough, scarred hand to the briefcase on the seat beside him. To get through customs, he'd have to produce his passport. Not an unfamiliar experience. How many customs officers had searched him, how many stamps in his multiple passports? How many aliases on those passports? So many throughout the years, he couldn't remember his real name. His birth name. It had faded from memory. The current documents listed him as Nathan Burrows, Professor of Archaeology from Princeton University, visiting Mexico City to study the Teotihuacan ruins north of the capital. Although he would go nowhere near the site, he had to present the pretense. Not because he was an international spy, but because authorities in several countries wanted him for questioning. Also, there were others who sought him, and anyone else who searched for the Book of Sarmangous. They would kill him without hesitation, even in front of a score of witnesses, and walk away clean.

Those others, yes...

Keep alert, he reminded himself, but focus on the next hour. For now, the plane's screeching tires heralded the next chapter in his quest.

The Hotel Eldorado was a fifteen-story mold-colored box on the edge of a section of the capital city known as Zona Rosa, the Pink Zone, and very near the Zona Roja, the Red Zone.

The Pink Zone was a tourist haven of restaurants, shops, parks, and markets. Museums or a tour past the fancy homes of government officials were but a short drive away.

The Red Zone's businesses ran to the seedier type, where tourists were discouraged to visit as they ran a greater risk of being scammed, overcharged, outright mugged, or assaulted.

This latter section was his desitnation. For the moment, he wanted to familiarize himself with the neighborhood.

The morning's sulfur-tinged clouds choked the sky. The humidity neared ninety-five percent. After nodding a passing acknowledgment to the preteen bellboy in the lobby, Burrows exited the hotel and stepped onto the sidewalk. Traffic congested the intersection, insistent horns going unheeded. The myriad stifling odors of exhaust, oil, pollution, and rotting trash saturated the air. No hint of a breeze, let alone anything close to a breath of freshness, existed.

A billboard, large and unavoidable, rose above the street half a block west, advertising a popular brand of petrol. To his right, along the fences and walls, hung scores of fliers displaying the colors and slogans of several political parties.

The vehicles crammed four lanes wide on a three-lane street. Over half were Volkswagens. No one exhibited any courtesy. Each driver's attitude was "everyone for himself," as evidenced, in part, by mere inches separating the rear bumper of one car and the front bumper of the next.

He eyed a taxi driver staring in his direction. The greasy-looking man raised his chin and offered a half-friendly smile in a silent inquiry of whether the American would like a ride somewhere. Burrows shook his head. The driver shrugged and buzzed off in search of other fares.

Turning right, Burrows walked past the fliers to the next block.

After checking into the hotel the previous night, he'd taken a short reconnaissance and wound up coming back from this direction.

Elements of the Red Zone were already alive and active. Taxis drivers and their fares lined up so customers could view the choices of street whores.

This morning, the hookers were gone and the more legitimate businesses thrived, including a small bakery. Hot, fresh, yeasty smells wafted from the open doorway. Less than five minutes later and fifty cents American poorer, he exited with a variety of rolls and bread sticks and a couple of pastries. He devoured the treats within a block.

In the next couple of hours, situations he'd seen in many other cities unfolded around him, yet they still amazed him.

Armed guards on the sidewalks outside banks.

Mail spilling out of bags onto the sidewalk outside of postal stations.

No one stopped for auto accidents, let alone reported them. A bribe of a rack of snacks from a delivery driver to an officer avoided a ticket for a wrong turn. The cop secreted the stash behind a row of bushes.

And everywhere, the overwhelming number of poor. Beggars and the homeless dressed in filthy rags. Some of the situations true, others false. Many of the individuals did suffer, unable to find a home or a job in the vast uncaring city. However, many parents put their children out on the street to beg for coinage they in turn would use to buy liquor.

Burrows ignored them. He had more important business.

A wider four-lane thoroughfare separated the red and pink zones. There was a definitive abrupt change in the neighborhood. It was as if he could see into and past the buildings and observe the difference in the people from one zone to the other—the tenants, the business owners, those on the cracked and litter-strewn sidewalks—and experience the devolution from the mediocre neighborhood into the intense and all-pervading corruption.

He waved for a taxi, and it stopped with a sharp yelp of brakes, right in the flow of traffic. Horns beeped and other drivers edged their neighbors aside to move around the stopped cab. The driver looked similar to the one he had seen in the street outside the Hotel Eldorado. Oily hair, long devilish face, raised inviting eyebrows.

Burrows leaned down to the passenger window, unable to avoid the grime on the cab door. His casual clothes of polo shirt and khakis befit his professor persona.

"¿Habla inglés?"

"Si."

"I need to visit a certain building I believe is located in what you call the Zona Roja. Would you be willing to…?"

"Si, señor. Wherever you wanna go."

Burrows had forced himself to sleep the previous night, knowing his skills and mental faculties weren't up to par. His earlier walk had also eased his anxiety and excitement at the notion of possible success in his years long obsessive quest for the Book of Sarmangous.

Now, in his anticipatory state, he made a mistake, one he recognized the instant he was inside the cab. Burrows should have asked for the price of the ride before entering the vehicle. The cabbie agreed too quickly to the stated destination, and Burrows hadn't seen until too late…

The driver pressed on the accelerator and the car jackrabbited with a sharp squeal. Burrows was trapped. Any attempt to exit the vehicle would result in injury. The driver would not take him to the location requested.

A couple of blocks into the Zona Roja, the driver swerved into a narrow alley, shadowed and trash-filled. A couple of garbage cans lay upended.

The driver braked at the extreme right of the alley next to a crumbling brick building allowing just enough room on the left side for the doors to open. The Mexican exited the cab at the same time another door opened in the building opposite, twenty yards back. Two men stepped out and blocked the alley against escape.

Burrows murmured low and fierce, "Shit!"

He surmised the situation as soon as the cab entered the alley. The driver wasn't legitimate. He trolled the streets looking for unsuspecting marks, offered them a ride, and then brought them here to this gloomy alley, or others like it, out of sight of casual passersby. The luckless victim would suffer a mugging, an old-fashioned ass-kicking, or worse.

Yes, worse this time as one of the two thugs waiting behind the taxi flashed a switchblade. A large chain encased the other man's right fist.

The driver tapped the window and said in accented English, "Señor, come on out." He laughed. "Don' make us come in an' get you. I don' wan' my cab messed up."

The other two also laughed.

Burrows nodded in resignation and inched toward the door. The driver, in a mock gesture of courtesy, started to open it.

In a flash, Burrows lifted his legs and kicked the door with both feet. It slammed into the man and he stumbled.

Burrows scrambled outside in an instant. As he cleared the door, he withdrew a switchblade of his own from a leather sheath strapped around his right ankle.

Before the driver could regain his balance, Burrows closed in on him. No hesitation, no second thought. He swung the knife toward the brown-skinned man, flicking the small silver release. A four-inch gleaming blade popped up a second before it pierced the soft flesh of the driver's throat. Blood spurted, the man uttered no sound, and he was dead before Burrows pushed him away.

The others advancing, the one with the knife leading the attack.

Burrows and the knife man resembled a strange, twisted freak show mirror image. Two men, faces in determined grimaces, each holding switchblades, Burrows in his right hand, the other in his left. Besides the men's skin tones, they were of equal height, build, and hair color.

Burrows owned the edge on ruthlessness. He judged the distance and, when the other stepped into range, he turned his body, lifted his left leg, and shot a sidekick to his assailant's midriff. He followed through with an on-target swing of his blade. First, a slice to the wrist and the attacker released his knife. Before the weapon hit the concrete, Burrows' blade cut deep into the man's jugular. Choked screams echoed in the alley and Burrows pushed him on top of his already-fallen comrade.

Chain-Fist was the smartest of the three. He'd kept his distance while the American dispatched his buddies in mere seconds. He wanted to flee but stumbled and fell. As he rose, he stuck his free hand out for leverage on the frame of the taxi, inside the open door. Like Burrows earlier, the Mexican realized his mistake in an instant as Burrows stepped forward and slammed the door.

Bones shattered like stepped-on potato chips.

A swift insertion of the blade between ribs silenced the man's beating heart and his screams of agony.

As Burrows left the alley, rats edged closer to investigate the fresh kills with twitching noses.

Nothing else mattered. Nothing but the Book of Sarmangous.

After the incident with the fake cabbie and his thug friends, Burrows ducked into a dingy tobacco store and, without looking at the owner, headed for the bathroom. He washed as much blood out of his clothes as possible. Back out on the street, he soon hailed a legitimate cab. After hearing the intended location, the driver's face paled. Immediate protests produced a sigh from Burrows. "Take me as far as you are willing."

Fifteen full blocks from his destination, the driver stopped the cab. Promises of extra pesos resulted in an adamant, "¡Absolutamente no más lejos!" Absolutely no farther! The tone implied, "Get out now and leave me alone."

The neighborhood was a pure slum. Condemned, or otherwise vacant buildings, closed businesses with broken signs, a deteriorating street. A rat the size of a raccoon and as ugly as an opossum slunk along the crumbling foundation of an abandoned storefront, hesitating to stare at Burrows. After a moment, it growled and hissed, and continued on its explorations of the filth of the city.

Burrows walked the streets, ever vigilant. At a certain spot, he took a left down a stretch of concrete too narrow to be a proper alley. Shadows and dead air filled the passage in this almost forgotten part of the Zona Roja. After a few moments, he entered a nondescript, unnamed, one-story building, walked to the end of a basement hall, and stopped at a recessed doorway.

The door was wooden, maybe solid oak. Various icons were carved into its surface. Strange and alien to most people, Burrows recognized them as symbols of evil, devilry, and a warning to others the person behind the door was quite familiar, even comfortable, with "dark" practices.

El Minister Negro. The Black Minister.

Catholicism was the major denomination for over ninety percent of Mexico, with a smattering of Islam and Protestantism thrown in. Even smaller in number, yet ever-present—as in all countries—were those anti-God faiths in enough flavors to satisfy all tastes.

He had learned of the Minister Negro from previous contacts. Numerous persons claimed the hideous title, devoted to any number of godless religions, but there was one—this one—in particular...

Burrows entered without knocking to find a room that measure no more than ten paces square. Thick tapestries cover the walls, a myriad of weird sigils both ancient and modern woven into the lush fabrics of red, black, and dark blue.

Five candles provided adequate light, enough to illuminate a man dressed in a black robe, kneeling in front of the far tapestry. Unintelligible words ceased when Burrows closed the door. The man rose and turned to face his visitor.

"I have come for the location of the Book of Sarmangous," Burrows said. "Where may I find it?"

The priest shook his head. "I cannot tell you. I will not tell you."

Burrows again withdrew the switchblade. "Yes, you will."

Sharp and blood-letting persuasion revealed the Black Minister's reputation was a façade. The man was nothing but scared, weak, and old. He did, in time, give up the information.

Burrows left the false priest as he left the false taxi driver and his cohorts. He exited the alley, returned to the place the driver had left him but no taxi. Still wary of his surroundings, he traversed the wider, more populated streets, catching the eyes of the locals who may have wondered why the crazy American stranger risked traveling so deep into the Red Zone. As he neared a cab stand, he caught movement out of the corner of his eye. With instinct honed from experience, he dove into the nearest vehicle, throwing bills at the startled driver.

As the taxi rolled away, Burrows peered out the rear window. Three cloaked figures disappeared around a corner. The same trio seen all those years ago for the first time in Germany. The ones he'd managed to avoid several times since he begun his quest.

The Triune.

A trio of strange—what? Creatures? Men? Demons?—who sought the seekers of the Book of Sarmangous, who killed without hesitation, without mercy. Why they hadn't disposed of him earlier in a more remote area, he couldn't say. His aliases and his fighting skills were no match against these three individuals. He vowed to exert more caution knowing they were here.

He sat nursing a drink in the bar on the top floor of the Hotel Eldorado. Behind him, within the confines of portable walls, men sat at tables or danced with each other to music provided by a DJ who tried too hard to be better than he was.

Burrows recognized the homosexual nature of the bar the moment he stepped through the door. In the last hour, he had rebuffed several advances, including one from a drunk who swore the American resembled a Mexican movie star. He wanted to relax and re-energize for the upcoming excursion deep into the Zona Roja. In many ways, he would trek deeper than when he visited the Black Minister. He needed to have his faculties at one hundred percent after his afternoon trials.

Not that the watered-down piss of a drink would affect him. He sipped from the stained glass as he pretended to study a tourist guidebook to avoid the come-on leers of the other patrons and to ignore the stupid, smiling bartender. If all went well, tonight he would have his prize, the Book of Sarmangous. However, traveling so far into the worst neighborhoods of the city, escape was not assured. Patrols of gangs roamed the streets. Threats of assault or death hid in alleys or shadows.

The danger was nothing new, though, and he was no naïve greenhorn entering forbidden territory.

He frowned when he remembered his earlier escape from the Triune, slapped a few hundred peso notes on the counter to pay for his expensive drink, and left the bar, heading up a flight of stairs to the roof.

The air hadn't lost its clinging heat and wavering haziness, with nary a breeze to distribute the pollution. At the parapet's edge, he gazed at the night lights. Yellows, reds, and blues flashed, winked, and shone. Noise from the millions of cars rushed into his ears.

What he'd seen today, what he'd done today, was no different from his experiences in many other cities, yet he paused to reflect.

Death came in many forms. He had seen scores of corpses, many made by his hand. How many had died to further his quest? He had forgotten their names, if he ever knew them in the first place, as he had forgotten his own. No memory of faces, and blurred recollections of the bodies left behind.

They didn't matter.

She didn't matter.

He inhaled a ragged breath. From where did the memory of the girl spring? Her face hadn't been in his thoughts for...had it been over two decades?

Images flash through his mind of Three Rivers, New Mexico, and the occurrence at the nearby tourist attraction. He recalled his last sight of her—his only child—her physical condition, and the reason behind it.

There had been no other option.

Stop!

He stomped on the memory, driving it deep, back to an empty room. Yes, and lock the door. Think about tonight! His search for the Book of Sarmangous ended tonight... Soon...

Soon, he'd be beyond the memories, he would have the *Power*, and oh, the things he would do...

•   •   •

Another alley.

How many countless alleys over the years? This one was no different from the others...

...and yet the aura that was in itself a presence that emanated around the area gave the alley a distinctiveness never before seen. That aura permeated while at the same time enveloped Burrows' skin...his soul.

Considering his previous experience with taxi drivers, Burrows had been lucky to have found one willing to drive so far into the Zona Roja so many hours after sundown. This neighborhood offered no retail, no squalid apartment dwellings, nothing but abandoned buildings. He'd bet even the gangs didn't frequent this section of the Zone. He hadn't seen one rat or stray dog. This area was preternaturally different. Alien. Again, that *presence* hung in the air, saturated it, a powerful, unseen force boding things unnamed.

He was close.

A dark doorway at the end of the rubble-strewn alley. A recessed entry in the cold, high wall. He hesitated not a second, but opened the door and stepped through. He knew it would be unlocked—unlocked for him and his kind, the seekers of the Book of Sarmangous. Only the bravest—or the most insane—dared traverse that threshold. A flight of stairs descended into the Stygian black...even as the presence beckoned.

Come, come my wandering friend. Nothing to fear, but maybe everything. Your journey has reached its last stretch. You may find what you seek or you may lose everything. Come...see what lies ahead.

He did.

The steps regressed from concrete to stone to hard earth. They descended farther than any normal flight of steps should. Far below the basements, deeper into bowels than any laid sewer system. Hundreds of steps, all uniform, going down, down into the dark. Nothing normal existed now. At the bottom, a tunnel of ancient stone with a rocky dirt floor stretched off into the blackness. His feeble flashlight illuminated but a few feet in any direction, so thick was the darkness. He advanced with caution, not knowing what to expect, but anxious to discover his destiny.

The length of the catacomb stretched out of sight. Hot, heavy air weighed down upon him. Minutes, maybe hours passed. His vision blurred, and every muscle ached with each forward step. The sound of his labored breathing filled his ears. He couldn't estimate how far he traveled but as he knew he must, he reached the end of the passage where he dropped to his knees before yet another door, wooden and solid. He was so tired, tired of finding doors and obstacles. However, this was the last one. One more barrier.

Again, no hesitation. He had come too far to wonder what lay beyond. He rose, opened the door, and stepped into the room.

The size of a monk's cell, it contained a single uncomfortable bed against one wall. Opposite, a rickety table, chair, and an old wooden chest, the latter a yard long and a foot and a half wide with a thick iron hasp and heavy lock. The Book of Sarmangous must be inside. His prize rested a mere two-score inches away.

First, he must overcome one last hurdle.

He closed the door and waited. The challenge had been made. He waited for the other to accept.

The strike of a match and a shadowed hand lit a candle on the table. A flame brightened a darkened alcove at the rear of the room where a figure stepped forth.

The man was age personified. Deep crevasse wrinkles formed an elaborate map of his face. Stiff, scraggly tufts of colorless hair sprouted from his head, chin, and ears. Black sunken eyes and hollow cheeks, flat nose, thin chapped lips. His gnarled body was twisted like an old tree, with threadbare clothes more draped than worn. This was more than age, more akin to living death.

The person known currently as Burrows, though nearing exhaustion, was prepared. Now, seeing this...this thing once a human, victory was already his. The Guardian, protector of the Book of Sarmangous, destined to battle all seekers until bested, had been beaten by one thing even the supernatural had difficulty with—Time. How long had this pathetic figure waited for someone to find the Book of Sarmangous? Could the old man even remember his last true battle?

Though weak, the Guardian spoke, "You have come for the Book of Sarmangous."

A statement, not a question.

"There is no need to say what is obvious," Burrows whispered. "Do not put up any resistance."

A dry convulsive cackle, a high-pitched stuttering burst from the thin mouth. After a moment, Burrows recognized the sound wasn't the old man dying, but sardonic laughter.

"Do not mock me," Burrows threatened. "I have searched—"

"I know," the other replied, a long sigh in his voice, "I know because I, too, once played the role you now have."

"Then you know I have come prepared to take the book. To fight, if necessary, although judging by your condition I do not think any contest of wills and strength shall be required."

The other laughed again, a harsh wheeze. "Now who is the mocking one?"

"Listen, old man."

"No, you listen," the Guardian said. "You know not what you seek. You know not what horrors it will bring."

Burrows' turn to laugh. "You don't know what I've seen."

A low hiss escaped the man's mouth. "Yesss...I do. I, too, once journeyed on a quest for the book."

"This is getting tiresome." Burrows' patience waned. "Give me the book or I shall simply take it."

"I cannot give it to you."

"Then..."

"But you may not possess it."

"Why?"

"You do not understand." The old man took a faltering step forward. "Many have sought the book, have longed for the power it offers. All have failed. As shall you."

"You cannot stop me," Burrows said. "You can barely move. How can you claim me a failure?"

"You are not the one to control the power in the book. No one is."

Burrows reached the limit of his patience. Too many years, too much sacrifice lay behind him. He would not be denied. Not now. Forgoing the switchblade used so often this past day, he withdrew a pistol purchased on an open street corner and aimed it at the elder's chest.

"Give me the Book of Sarmangous," he demanded.

When the other shook his head, and Burrows pulled the trigger. The alien atmosphere of the place somehow muted the sound, but the bullet hit true. The old Guardian staggered back one step, two, until he brushed against the alcove wall. As the figure sank to the dirt floor, the retching laughter continued.

"You...can take it." The dying man uttered his last desperate words. "But you cannot possess it. The...Sarmangous...will possess you."

With a last gurgle, the body crumpled and lay still.

Burrows dismissed the old fool and leaped for the chest. Another shot destroyed the heavy lock. He opened the lid and cried out in ecstasy.

The Book of Sarmangous.

His dream, the prize after so long a journey lay encased in a soft velvety fabric. With tentative, quivering fingers he reached out and touched the cover...and the last of his remaining soul was damned.

He should have waited until he had left the lonely place beneath the earth, until ensconced in his own home before laying his naked hand on the Sarmangous, but he could not deny his hammering heart and soaring emotions.

Now his exit would be so much more difficult, for something—a force—had invaded his mind, replacing the being, the essence once man. The last words of the old Guardian came back to him.

You can take it, but you cannot possess it...it will possess you.

...and so it did.

...and now he faced the hardest, most arduous choice of his life.

Would he be strong enough to claim the Sarmangous's treasures, the ultimate knowledge and power its pages offered, or would he fail, and become the next Guardian?

What had the old man come to understand during his long, years long vigil?

Burrows cared not, for he was strong. His will would not be denied.

He closed the lid and, with a last look at the corpse, he struggled to lift the chest.

The return trip was excruciating, not only for its length, but because of the ordeal Burrows suffered visual, mental, and spiritual torture. Ghastly sights and inhuman, unearthly sounds assaulted both mind and body.

Blood, death, murder, tortuous screams. With each step, visions challenged him, realistic hallucinations of torn bodies, decapitations, crushed skulls. Murdered souls. The screams of the dying knifed into his brain. Bile and bloody entrails bubbled and oozed from the walls, while hurricane-force winds brought Burrows to his knees.

He stumbled and fell but by fierce determination still kept a hold on the chest. His finger—his will—could not let go of it. But he couldn't take only the Sarmangous and leave. He had to protect the ancient tome from others' hands...but the chest was so heavy and awkward.

Crawling and dragging the box, unable to even close his eyes to the horrors because his mind's eye suffered every excruciating second.

The thing, the presence, the invader, and replacement of his soul, howled with devilish laughter. Burrows was being tested by the greatest tribulation so far in his many years of searching. He'd fought mortal men, using coercion, persuasion of any means to gain knowledge, but the current battle raged within, his inner strength and determination given the ultimate challenge.

Yes, the old man had spoken true. He, Burrows, would not use the Book of Sarmangous to gain power. The monstrous essence conquering his mind planned to use the Sarmangous for its own ends.

Burrows, the man, acted as just a shell, a vessel for the entity to inhabit, but was he strong enough—could he summon the will to endure? If not, then he would be no better than the last person to touch the Sarmangous, the poor pathetic creature he'd vanquished. Burrows, upon failing, would assume the mantle of the new Guardian. The force inside him would return to the Book, go dormant, waiting for the next seeker.

If he endured the horror, outlasted it, survived the anguished images, the nausea, the head-splitting pain, he could regain control, or at the very least, be rewarded for his efforts.

Onward he crawled, gagging at the stench, screaming at the blood, crying at the insanity created just for him. At one point, he stopped, collapsed to the ground, and curled up. His stomach revolted, and he puked until he dry heaved, then beyond, gagging on blood.

He groped for the chest, finding the handles on either end.

With a guttural, blood-spitting roar, he heaved the chest to him, rose, and stumbled forward. Now he did not falter, did not fall. He cursed at the hellish images and brayed his voice against the wind and fury.

Until...at last...he rested on the bottom step of the flight of stairs.

He'd made his choice and won. However, he was not his own person, not in total control, but a servant to the power inside.

Weariness pressed upon him, but with newfound strength—strength provided by the supernatural—he climbed.

He inched his head out from the darkened doorway. No one in the area, but he waited five minutes more. No longer, because the gang from which he hid earlier, escaping detection, would return. Also, the night neared its end. He could not afford to be here come dawn. Too many people, many looking for mischief and trouble, would walk the streets.

Forced to walk because no one dared drive these streets, let alone taxi operators, he risked turning a corner and facing death from human hands. With the chest hugged tight to his body, he would not be able to defend himself.

Run. He must run. He took one more quick look and dashed to the next corner. Up one block, down the next, but always veering on a westerly course. The sweat poured from his face. His hands were greasy. Dirty, bloody clothes clung to his body. With the streets and the landscaping all similar, he soon was lost.

He had to rely on luck and instinct to exit the Zona Roja, pack up his belongings at the hotel, and head for the airport for a prearranged special private flight out of the country. Travel by normal means and allowing customs to examine his prize were not feasible.

Distant laughter and echoing footsteps somewhere behind him.

A taunting voice shouted, echoing along the pavement and off building facades. "Run, amigo! Run fast."

The Mexican gang. Was this the end? Wait, another voice, this one different. This one's words drifted like a soft wind, yet clear, on the dead night's air, ominous and dire.

Yes, run, it called. *You have escaped for now. But you will wish you had stayed.*

The voice he recognized as coming from a younger version of the man he had shot hours ago.

The taunts, the laughter, and the footsteps died away upon the last echo of low chuckling from a ghostly guardian.

Another four blocks before Burrows a set of streetlights heralded another neighborhood—and more of those damn Beetles forever cruising.

CHAPTER 8

Thursday afternoon/evening
Present day

Back at Homicide, Harry and Campisi sat at the detective's desk, reviewing notes. The homeless man's death had added a new dimension to the series of murders: a daytime attack.

They had sweated Leahy's buddy, Warton, having him repeat half a dozen times his every movement that morning and his activities for the previous four days and nights. As expected, details proved hard to nail down. Many of those hours he spent seeking the bottom of a bottle. Harry made a series of calls and he and Campisi visited the places where the man had sporadic employment, verifying two instances of his presence. They received similar vague information from the staff at the homeless shelters he frequented. Warton provided reluctant other places he and Leahy often holed up during the nights.

Forensics had zilch on the murders, no tools or machines suggested as the cause of death of six people. For his cooperation, they treated the man to a courtesy overnight stay in the county jail with a meal and a chance to clean up. After an afternoon of fruitless investigation, his material witness stature remained weak, and with no further corroborating evidence, he'd be released in the morning.

Harry and Campisi perused the postmortem reports listing cause of death for each victim as unknown, the corpses in a boiled-like state but with no water residue. Blood still in the body tested thin, soupy. *How* and *why* remained two of the endless questions.

Examinations of the gouges and pieces of flesh missing showed something had torn or ripped the body...but the medical examiner found no evidence of tooth marks. Anything from feline to metal claws or knives could have scraped and gouged the abdomens. No other blood or hair or fibers or skin at the scenes other than the victims'.

Harry sighed and leaned back in his chair. "What do you say, Agent Campisi? Call it a day? Tomorrow will be interesting."

Word had passed through the department. Lieutenant Gravatte, an hour ago, had coordinated a task force to work out of the DMPD—the first meeting scheduled for ten the following morning. Harry and, by invitation, Campisi, were part of the team.

Harry waited for Campisi's response.

She had reviewed the case files whenever an opportunity arose, but Harry thought she'd given them a brief once over, as if she'd memorized every line the first time through. Now, as every other minute of the day, she wore a blank expression. Her eyes didn't blink, and she stared at nothing as if hypnotized.

He smacked a palm on the desk near her. "Hey, Campisi!"

She wasn't startled but raised an eyebrow.

Harry wished she'd stop the Spock act. "Home? Or rather, a hotel for you? What do you say? Come back tomorrow and start fresh?"

She nodded and stood.

"Uh, just where are you staying? In case I need to contact you."

He wondered if her empty look and poignant pause before answering held suspicions he might visit for other purposes.

"The Des Lux," she answered. "It's on—"

"I know where it's located," Harry said. "Pretty fair digs, isn't it? Granted, it's not the Embassy Suites, but not too shabby."

"I couldn't get a reservation at the Embassy," she said. "I'll see you tomorrow."

She walked away, leaving Harry in stunned silence. He couldn't hep but think she was a strange lady. Very strange, indeed.

•　　•　　•

Misty Reznik lit candles and dimmed the dining room lights. She surveyed the table with its linen tablecloth, the special dinnerware, and the crystal glasses. Tender pork chops bathed in mushroom gravy in the crock pot. Fresh salad with honey mustard dressing chilled in the refrigerator.

She almost couldn't contain herself and wished Harry would arrive home soon. Sherwood, despite his reservations concerning the facial cream campaign, had granted her the next day for her appointment. She promised overtime and maybe part of the weekend to catch up. There wouldn't be a problem with the arrangement since she figured Harry would be busy with his murder case.

But until then...

•   •   •

Agent Lori Campisi sat on the bed in her room at the Des Lux Hotel feeling claustrophobic. If she'd known this "suite's" dimensions were so small, she'd have chosen other lodgings. In fact, everything about the hotel was small. Lobby, stairwell, hallways.

She had to admit the staff presented a pleasant atmosphere, designing the hotel with style and unassuming class. However, it wasn't her warehouse back in Washington, D.C.

That's what she called it—the Warehouse—because it used to be one. The single-story building with 35,000 square feet of storage once contained supplies for area schools. When the schools moved their ever-growing amount of stuff to another location, the owner, wanting to quit the warehouse business, put the building on the market, expecting another industry to snatch it up.

Instead, Campisi, desperate to get out of her cramped sanitarium-like apartment building, walked into the owner's office and handed over a check made out for three-quarters of the amount listed. The man went wide-eyed in surprise, but was savvy enough to negotiate for more money. Why did a single woman want the place? What were her plans?

After five minutes of hedging because she just didn't care to have her personal business known, she whipped out her FBI identification and gave the wide-eyed ass some threatening malarkey about federal operations and national security. He clammed up and completed the deal.

She had transformed the warehouse into something she could claim as her own. The usual household furnishings accompanied a training area with free weights, weight machines, and treadmill. She installed a running track encircling the inside perimeter of the building and designated areas for a small library and a music "room." The sound system could be adjusted for localized enjoyment or fill the entire warehouse. Another area held her computer, server, and other electronic equipment. The place and space suited her. She had few friends—none she visited or invited to visit her—no boyfriend, and no family.

Campisi hit the proper switch on the remote control and tuned the television to the local news. With the sound muted, she began her normal wind-down routine of undressing and positioning herself for meditation, as she'd done hundreds of times before, trying to remember...something.

For very few people knew Lori Campisi was not Lori Campisi. At least, she hadn't been before age twelve and no one knew who she had been prior to that. In fact, she wasn't even sure she had been twelve when she had her first memory. She just accepted the age the doctors determined.

In October of that year, she had literally become conscious of the world around her. She "woke up" standing on a sidewalk beside a busy street in El Paso, Texas, all alone, no one holding her hand, no one beside her at all. Every person a total stranger.

A shop owner discovered her crying, scared, and confused and called the authorities. Soon, she became a national sensation. The little girl with no memory. Was she a kidnap victim, an escapee from a human trafficking outfit, or—as some of the wildest theories suggested—an alien abductee just returned from Planet X? Everyone who discussed the story shrugged. No one stepped forward to claim her, no suspects arrested and charged with leaving an innocent young girl in one of Texas' most untamed cities.

The endless doctors and their tests showed her to be in excellent physical health despite her amnesia. Sessions of hypnotherapy proved unsuccessful in revealing her secrets.

Little girl lost. A twelve-year-old Jane Doe. Nowhere to go, no one to turn to for comfort or love.

There were plenty of offers. From the beginning, families across America stepped up and opened their hearts and homes for her. Every offer was subjected to an intense background check in case the girl's original family attempted to get her back to continue whatever abuse had been already perpetrated.

Vern and Fran Campisi won out. They were El Paso residents nearing middle age whose sole child had died in infancy. They wanted to share with this child the love denied to their first.

Other tests showed Lori, as the Campisis named her, to be educationally and intellectually sound despite not remembering anything about her former life. Her intelligence level was above average for her age, and her literacy level years better than a high school senior. She understood mathematics, spoke perfect English and, could speak a few words and phrases of Serbian.

She graduated high school near the top of her class. At the University of Texas, she excelled at computers and became fluent in both German and Russian.

Lori Campisi had always been a somewhat introverted person. In school, she didn't go out for sports, theater, or the party scene. Her few friends didn't stay in contact after graduation. The university's size hampered any lasting bonds with classmates. Dates never went past two, when the guys soon became frustrated at the attractive brunette's apathy to continuing a romantic relationship. Not unfriendly or frigid—as one grade-A jerk once described her to his buddies—Lori just never developed intimate or close feelings for men or women.

She wept for her parents, who died two months after her entrance into the Bureau. She had a fondness for pizza and puppies. Sex, after the few times she experienced it, became something she could take or leave.

After earning a degree in criminology, she had planned to attend law school until the Federal Bureau of Investigation came a-calling. Impressed with her language skills, they were more interested in something else.

At age sixteen, she had developed an interest in all matters paranormal, supernatural, or other-worldly. She read any material she could lay her hands on dealing with ghosts, demons, UFOs, superstitions, legends, sea monsters, other dimensions, remote-viewing, psychics, and much, much more.

She watched movies and documentaries on exorcism and resurrection. When possible, she toured any locale purported to be haunted. An avid listener to the Coast To Coast AM radio program, she had exchanged numerous emails with its host, Art Bell. She was disappointed when he took semi-retirement and although she continued listening to his replacement, the new host never asked the right questions of his guests. At least, not the ones she'd have posed.

She didn't believe those early wild theories about her being taken by aliens up to the Mother Ship for experiments, but, in time, became more open-minded to a many ideas most people thought kooky.

After graduating from the University of Texas—where she had continued to delve into that "weird stuff," as her mother called it—with honors, not too much time passed before a high-level supervisor of the FBI knocked on her door recruit her for the Bureau. After the requisite training and completing her new agent requirements in regard to time and duties, she answered a summons to a sub-basement in the Hoover Building where she met Jacob Pepperdine, who discussed the real reason for the Bureau's wanting her within its ranks.

They didn't call it the X-Files division. In fact, the "department" didn't have a name. She would continue to work out of Washington, D.C. under her current supervisor. Now and then, she'd receive a "special" case. Her supervisor wouldn't question the orders from elsewhere, and she didn't need to explain her cases to him. After the visit with Pepperdine, her supervisor told her in no uncertain terms, "I don't want to know what you do. You do not tell me what you do. Be careful. Get out of my office and do your job."

Her salary increased and her expense account changed to "as needed." Whatever funds she required, she received. When she requested a change in residence, Pepperdine said, "Find something and let us know."

All her furnishings, food, utilities, vehicles, other transportation, and what minor entertainment she enjoyed were paid for, no questions asked or explanations required. Other than the warehouse purchase, she hadn't tested the Bureau's extravagance level. Well, maybe on hotel rooms, but so far Pepperdine hadn't suggested she temper her spending.

During her initial meeting with Pepperdine, she also met the Hound.

•   •   •

The Hoover Building, Washington, D.C.
Ten years earlier
Campisi walked beside Pepperdine while he explained the types of cases on which they worked. She would be required to work solo unless she requested otherwise, gaining assistance from local authorities or anyone else she deemed acceptable.

He informed her that she would not lack for resources. Pepperdine escorted her to a single door at the end of an empty hall. Before they entered, the man pursed his lips and—for a brief and rare moment— dropped his serious attitude. "Mr. Hundt may take some...getting used to. Despite his...idiosyncrasies, he is very skilled at what he does."

The room beyond the door held more electronic equipment than a Microsoft convention. Computers, monitors, servers, keyboards, printers. In one corner, a pile of motherboards leaned next to other electrical detritus. Screwdrivers, tweezers, wires, clips, soldering irons, and other tools lay scattered like debris after an explosion. Four extendable desk lamps provided illumination.

Three eighty-inch video monitors were mounted on the walls. On the center screen, a sleek spaceship executed intricate maneuvers through a backdrop of asteroids. Golden beams of light shot from the ship's nose, aimed at various alien monsters attacking from behind the space rocks. Zips, zings, and slurpy death noises emanated from hidden speakers.

A small man seated on a high stool encircled by the electronics operated the controls of the spacecraft. His crew cut matched the black frames of his thick-lens plastic glasses, and he wore a red T-shirt and blue jean shorts. Campisi estimated the guy's height at a couple of inches over four feet. His legs dangled over the seat of the stool.

Pepperdine sighed. "John."

The man didn't hear him, continuing his battle with a large green blob threatening to engulf his ship.

"John!"

The man glanced once over his shoulder, hit a button on his controller, and a blast froze halfway to the monster. "Hey, boss man." He hopped off the stool. "What's cooking?" When he noticed Campisi, he smoothed his short hair. "Hey, baby. You the new Scully?"

"John, what have I told you about your television references?" Pepperdine chided.

"Yeah."

"And your attitude toward the female staff?"

"Yeah."

"Weren't you supposed to be working on gathering evidence for Agent Lundberg?"

Hundt walked over to a printer and grabbed a short stack of paper. "She called an hour ago," he said. "These have been ready for forty minutes."

"Why don't you give her a call?"

"Right."

"After you meet Agent Lori Campisi. She'll be working our special cases."

"Right." John bounced over to shake hands with Campisi.

Pepperdine continued the introduction. "Lori, this is—"

"John Hundt." Hundt caressed Campisi's hand. "They call me the Hound. Get it? Hundt is German for hound."

Campisi retrieved her hand. "Yes, I know."

"I sniff out whatever evidence you need." Hundt bounded back to his stool. "So, I'm going to be your contact, eh? The Fox and the Hound. I like it."

Pepperdine broke in. "John, her code name is—"

"Too late. Fox it is. You're stuck with it, baby."

Pepperdine's voice lowered in pitch and volume, irritation evident in his undertone. "Why don't you get Agent Campisi the laptop?"

"No problem." Hundt dove under a counter like a rat terrier after his prey, scooted equipment out of his path, and dragged out a soft black vinyl computer case. He presented the package to Campisi. "Here ya go, all set up."

"That laptop is loaded with Internet and email software, plus other basic programs," Pepperdine explained. "There is a special instant messenger program, satellite-linked to John's computer. Absolutely secure. I'll give you the password later."

"Aw," Hundt whined. "I wanted to show her the goodies."

Pepperdine ignored the little man. "Use John for any research you require. He'll be able to...*ahem*, dig it up faster than—"

"Than anyone, baby," Hundt boasted.

Hundt proved true to his word. Campisi used the electronics wizard on all of her special cases and a few times on her normal ones. The man had a unique style but always came through. His humor, sometimes brash, helped her stay out of the depths of her own emotion, or rather her non-emotion. She tolerated his extroverted maleness because she suspected it was all for show.

•   •   •

She never knew how Pepperdine received reports of supernatural cases from throughout the country Whenever she was assigned these special cases, her supervisor made sure other agents handled her other investigations. Regarding this case, Pepperdine didn't explain why the series of murders in Des Moines wasn't some psycho on a rampage or a "normal" serial killer. He'd gathered evidence and some background information and deemed the case compelling enough for her to move on it with expediency.

Hound collected the dossiers on the Des Moines players in the case, Lieutenant Glynis Gravatte, a consummate professional officer, and her detective in charge, Harry Reznik. Presenting herself as a lone agent willing to work with Detective Reznik, offering assistance and advice with no pressure to bring in a horde of aggressive agents bent on control and glory, had appealed to Gravatte.

Detective Reznik already had proven to be a challenge. Experienced and dedicated, yes, but cynical and stubborn. Even though he showed determination to find the answer to these murders, when the time came to show him evidence something other than human hands had committed these heinous acts, his closed mind would be difficult to pry open.

For the moment, she dismissed Reznik and the murders. Instead, she allowed her mind to relax, drift. Wearing shorts and a loose T-shirt, she sat crossed-legged on the bed and concentrated on the shifting light patterns from the muted television in the otherwise dark room.

She often set aside certain times to think of her past, to bring more of it to light. She'd learned a few techniques from the hypnosis sessions undergone after high school when she could be serious about the process and the desired results.

With steady, even breaths, she pushed any extraneous thoughts aside. She took herself back in time, skimming over scenes and images, using them as anchor points from which to further regress.

A drug arrest a week earlier.

Her training exercises for Bureau acceptance. The dormitory at UT.

High school graduation.

As the years fell away, the images became hazy, blurred. She was reaching the point where a blank wall would rise to block access to further memories.

There.

Its surface shimmered like a dark desert mirage.

She was a watcher and also the lone individual standing before an impenetrable barrier.

Her life before age twelve lay on the other side. The years and events before the awful awakening in that Texas border town.

As the watcher, she tried to assist herself, brush away the haze, and see beyond. What images could she make out this time?

Nothing, save for a few stills as if from a jumping film reel. Lots of black spaces, gaps in a memory unable to be filled. The images came through blurred, snapshots from an unfocused camera.

A birthday cake with flickering candles.

A grainy image of two adults. Her birth parents? Then darkness. No more haze, no more shimmering waves, just complete darkness. She hated this moment, but could not avoid the experience. It came unbidden, undeniable...a moment filled with fear.

Wait! A flash of something.

A desert. Rocks.

Childish pictures drawn on the rocks. Darkness but different this time.

Is she alone in the dark? She senses someone near.

Something else waits, seeking, reaching out. Reaching for her. What is it?

It's domineering, looming, and resonating evil.

Her heart rate increased and her breaths became gasps before she shut down the images, breaking away, and returning to the present. She remembered how darkness and shadows related to the current case. She opened her eyes and proceeded to turn on every light in the room, including the one in the bathroom. Then she remembered she needed to check in with her contact in Washington.

The Hound.

She removed her Gateway laptop and its accessories from the protective case. Hooked up, plugged in, booted up, she clicked an icon and a special instant messaging window blinked open. When a username and password window popped up, she input the required information. With the password accepted, two other windows appeared. The bottom one displayed her via the computer's built-in camera. The other showed a darkened room and part of someone's shoulder. She adjusted the volume and a distorted roaring squelched through the speaker.

"Hound, you there?"

Twenty seconds elapsed before the sounds ceased and his face appeared.

"Hey, Fox," he greeted. "You have crappy timing. You caught me right as I was about to complete level fifteen."

"What?"

"*Monsters' Revenge.*" He lifted a colorful box, the container for video game disks. The cover was plastered with a multiple explosion background behind several caricature-type creatures. "I just bought it today. Awesome graphics. You get to trap Sasquatch, then blow him up. On level nine you can wrestle a Chupacabra."

"Hound, I don't care. Did you get the information?"

"Okay, okay. Don't have to get huffy, baby." His face tightened in annoyance. She suspected he felt a bit put out because she didn't appreciate his video games. Her case was more important.

He moved off screen but returned sans game box. The thick lenses of his glasses glinted with streaks and scratches. She wondered how he saw anything through them.

"Yes, I sent it to your email."

"Anything I should know?" she asked.

"No. You've already had a taste of Mr. Fun Guy Detective. Minor smudge on his record. He once told his former lieutenant a retarded monkey could do the LT.'s job better. Otherwise, nothing. The current

Loo is solid and kind of a hot number, you ask me. What about the case? Is it…?"

"Yes, I think so," she replied. "Here's what I need you to send me."

She spent ten minutes briefing Hound on the day's events and what she required from him.

"Right," he said, his standard reply to her every request.

Before she clicked closed the video screen, she hesitated and offered a warning. "I don't know how far-reaching this is. At present, it seems localized to the Des Moines metro. Inform me at once if there are any other occurrences elsewhere. And Hound, keep as much light around you as possible at all times."

•   •   •

"What?"

Misty Reznik's eyes teared, and she flinched from her husband's outburst. She'd been so excited for him to come home. When he opened the door upon all the baby stuff amassed in the living room, he stood stunned, frozen not two steps into the house. She jumped around, resembling Sherwood's secretary at times, picking up a pair of tiny shoes, cooing over a teddy bear. She stopped when he didn't say anything.

"I tried to tell you this morning," she said. "I'd taken the test just before you left."

Harry dropped into an easy chair. "Are you kidding me?"

"No, honey. We're going to have a baby."

She frowned when, instead of showing elation, Harry leaned forward and covered his face with his hand.

"No, no, no."

To Misty, the muffled reply sounded like a whine of complaint. "Harry, what's wrong?"

He stood and walked like a zombie through the forest of baby stuff. At the tower of diaper boxes, he faced her. "This is not the best time for this to happen."

Taken aback, she flashed anger. "What do you mean, this isn't the best time? This is what we've wanted."

"Misty, I'm investigating a bunch of horrible murders. This city has never seen anything like this. I've got dead bodies piling up and the M.E. on my back. GG is forming a task force and today, this goofy android of an FBI agent waltzes through the door, and *boom* I have a new partner. I don't need the extra stress of you being—"

"Whoa!" Misty's command came sharp and unyielding. "Hold it right there, buster." She stepped closer to him, challenging his space. "You spout that kind of shit at the office, not to me. And not about this. You had better take a second and put your head straight. This is me. This is our baby. I just learned I'm pregnant. It's not as if I've collapsed from labor pains expecting immediate help from you. You watch your tongue before you say something you will seriously regret."

She huffed at a couple of errant blonde strands fallen into her face and stared hard into her husband's eyes. She'd learned when to give him time to collect himself. Previous spats and arguments resolved themselves sooner if one or the other said his or her piece, then allowed the other to back down. Few escalated beyond a couple of volleys. In those instances, the one who stepped farther over the line lost. The other walked away, went to a movie, shopping, or just to the backyard. Time, distance, and silence became the reconciling forces with words of apology and a rectification soon after.

Misty sensed a partial truce. Harry inhaled half the room's oxygen and released it through flared nostrils. He nodded twice and even took a surrendering step back, almost knocking over the diapers.

"You're right, baby," he said in a low voice. "I'm sorry. This just came as a shock after all these crazy events. I'm sorry."

Misty measured his apology at about ninety percent sincere, but she decided to meet him there and see if she could coax the extra ten out of him. She reached out and took his hand. "Harry, let's sit. Come on."

She guided him to the couch, flicked off all the lights except for one lamp. The candles created dancing shadows on the walls. Seated beside him, she enfolded his hands in hers. Inside, emotions rose. Tears of uncertainty formed at the corners of her eyes.

"H–Harry?" He swallowed and met her eyes. His also glistened. "Tell me you're happy, that you want this. I know things are tough at work, but..."

His quivering jaw stopped her. "Of course, I want this. Damn it, Misty, why don't you smack me upside the head when I get like this? I forgot whom I was talking to."

She smiled. "Me, too."

"Misty, baby. I love you so much." He breathed again. "The case be damned, we're having a baby!" He sniffed back the coming tears and hugged her. "Look at all this stuff. Did you buy all of this today?"

She nodded and whispered, "Yes."

"Have...you told your parents?"

"I've resisted all day. I wanted to tell you first." Technically, Tucker and Sherwood were the first two, but Harry didn't need to know that.

"We'd better call them or they'll disinherit both of us," he said.

She nodded, but they spent nearly thirty minutes crying, kissing, and holding each other before they called their respective families—longer before they enjoyed dinner.

Lost in their happiness, they didn't notice a flutter, a slight shift in the shadows. The cat growled, hissed, and scampered away. Deep in the corner of the living room, something moved, rose an inch or two until it reached the light, then receded.

CHAPTER 9

Thursday night

The man who wore many names, most recently Nathan Burrows, reveled in what he had unleashed. The power surged within him, the presence that infiltrated, invaded, and replaced his soul in Mexico City grew—hungered. If he wanted to satisfy the internal presence and control the outside forces already feeding, he'd have to offer a sacrifice.

A sacrifice of blood.

He gathered the necessary items and headed out into the night.

Into the shadows...

•   •   •

"Hey, Katy, what's the famous lawyer doing out so late?" Rachel Van Croft called out.

Katy Olson turned to her friend coming up behind her. She rolled her eyes and offered a heavy, mock exhausted sigh. "I had to take a break. This torts paper is killing me. Professor Sheen is such a stickler. She just won't let up. I swear I'll have to retake the entire course."

"Maybe you can sue for workman's comp." Rachel giggled and received a light slap on her shoulder.

"Let's go get a sandwich," Katy suggested. "The diner's still open."

"Okay."

The two girls walked across the Drake University Campus to 25th Street. A quarter mile south of University Avenue the lights of the Drake Diner blazed in the otherwise darkened neighborhood.

"Must be something special going on," Rachel said. "I've never seen it so lit up."

"I don't know," Katy replied. "I haven't read about anything happening."

"You haven't read anything in the last six months that didn't have a case number attached to it."

Kathy sighed. "So true."

They enjoyed the cool spring night. The stream of traffic as they crossed University Avenue trickled by. The two girls passed a row of cars parked along the street, cars resembling some post-modern art exhibit, unmoving from one day to the next. Older two-story houses showed dark, curtained windows. Gnarled oak and maple trees could have come from the forest in *The Wizard of Oz*.

As the two students chatted about unimportant matters, a crackling, wet, slippery sounded behind them. They stopped, turned, but saw nothing, and the noise stopped. It started again as they moved on.

"What is that?" Katy asked

"I'm not sure, but I don't like it."

"Yeah, let's go."

An adrenaline rush of self-defense kicked in. The coeds ran for the diner. They'd taken a couple of steps when Katy screamed. "Rachel!"

Her friend whirled just as the young law student fell face-first to the sidewalk as if she'd caught her foot on an unseen tripwire. Rachel's eyes grew wide when Katy's prone body inched backward. Something invisible pulled her into the shadows.

Katy screamed again and clawed at the sidewalk. "Help me!"

Rachel grabbed Katy's wrist. The crackling-rustling grew louder, more intense. Staccato shushes hissed with each effort of the girls to break free. Katy's foot seemed encased in a dark substance, something transparent yet tangible. It blended in with the shadows. It *was* a shadow. Rachel screamed as the dark shade crept up her friend's leg, gaining a stronger hold.

They both yelled in desperate encouragement. "Pull!"

Rachel wondered why no one helped. It was as if everyone had deserted the neighborhood.

The shadow reached Katy's knee.

Rachel screamed when two red eyes blinked at her while the creature advanced up her friend's body. The lower part of Katy's slacks dangled ragged, her shoe mangled. Rachel didn't want to imagine what her foot must look like.

With a last desperate yank, their combined efforts freed the girl's entrapped leg. Katy tumbled over Rachel, both scraping skin on the sidewalk. Ignoring the pain, they scrambled toward the bright lights of the Drake Diner crying out for anyone to hear them.

Behind them, the shadow's white noise rose to a crescendo and faded. The living shadow retreated.

•   •   •

Beep, beep!

Lynda Kimball opened the microwave and with thumb and forefinger, plucked out the steaming bag of popcorn. After pulling on two opposite corners, releasing more of the buttery steam, she emptied the contents into a stainless steel bowl she sometimes used for mixing batter. Two pinches of salt, a few sprinkles of powdered cheese, a can of Diet Rite cola from the fridge, and she was set for the evening.

She planned to watch her soap operas recorded earlier, catch the news and weather, and go to bed. She wondered about the latest on the recent murders around town and needed to hear the forecast for the weekend. Her sister wanted to drive over to Omaha to visit their mother and do some shopping but not if rain was on the way. Marlene acted like a total ninny when it came to rain. A few drops and her sister refused to step outdoors.

Lynda, dressed in loose sweats, her auburn hair pinned up, settled back into the couch cushions. The first handful of popcorn froze halfway to her mouth when she heard a baby cry. She frowned, cocking an ear. Another short-lived wail rose and fell.

It sounded as if it came from the backyard.

Then she smiled and shivered at the eeriness. She recognized the cries. Once or twice a year in the spring, the feline mating rituals commenced. The uncanny similarity to an infant howling had unnerved her for a second.

Lynda set aside her snack. All she had to do was to step out the back door, make some noise, and the cats scampered away to somewhere more remote to conduct their love dance.

Outside, she waited and when one of the cats cried again, she determined their location in the grayish gloom near the small storage shed at the rear of the lot.

Any other time, she would have tried to sneak up on the cats, observe their unique interaction. Tonight, her desire to be indoors in front of the television overshadowed her curiosity. Besides, her popcorn was cooling. So, with quick steps, she marched across the back lawn.

The cat started its cry, segueing from baby to screech until it sensed the woman and the sound cut off. Both felines stared at her for two seconds before they dashed off into the dark faster than her eyes could track them.

She chuckled to herself and walked back to the house. Inside, she stood by the couch and reached for the remote. While one hand pressed the buttons to operate the cable's recording system, the other reached for the popcorn bowl.

Which crashed to the floor, white fluffs snowing the carpet, when someone else's hand clamped over her mouth.

She froze in fear as her body hugged into a harder body. With no waste of motion, her attacker forced her against a wall. Her eyes widened at the sight of a roughened face with wild, crazy, bloodshot eyes and tangled hair. He wore old, stained clothes.

The man's face loomed next to hers. A heavy breath, acidic and reeking of halitosis, whispered unintelligible words into her ear.

The spell went into effect in seconds. Lynda Kimball succumbed to blackness.

•   •   •

A cave?

Strange symbols on the walls and ceiling. A sharp acrid odor.

Searing pain! No!

Nothing. Darkness again.

Lori sat straight up and shaded her eyes from the bright light in the hotel room. She struggled to hold on to the nightmare, sensing the importance of the familiarity of the images.

Since her foray into the supernatural, she had limited experience with psychics. Most were scam artists looking to steal a quick buck, but she'd met a few whose visions and predictions she couldn't explain. Including what they "saw" regarding her.

An inner void. Shadowed secrets.

A couple of them had told her Lori wasn't her birth name, but neither could reveal her true identity.

The most ominous warning had come from an elderly woman who lived in the hills of eastern Tennessee. Rocking in a porch chair, smoking her corncob pipe, the witchy crone spoke words of divination. "There will come a time when the cause of your affliction is near. You will feel a connection, a link, and the wall will begin to crumble. At this time, you must have the fortitude to endure the pain and suffering you shall experience."

Lori wondered if this city, at this time, could be the fulfillment of the old witch's prediction...and if whatever caused her amnesia lurked just out of sight.

CHAPTER 10

Friday morning

The meeting room designated for the task force's use was filled with an eclectic and, in Harry's opinion, eccentric group of people.

Lieutenant Gravatte, the lead detectives from each of the murders, as well as the county medical examiner, Frank Belsom, pocket watch in hand, all jockeyed for space in the small room. Three other guests also took their seats at five after ten on Friday morning.

Besides Harry and his equitable partner Campisi, Sally Walcott represented the suburb of Clive. A squat chunk of a woman, dark redhead and consummate chain smoker, she hated the policy against lighting up in public buildings. During the meeting, she kept reaching inside her jacket pocket to finger a pack of cigarettes. Harry pitied what smoking had done to her. Years of sucking on cancer sticks had aged her face and given her a sandpaper voice, her skin tight and roughened. If he stared hard enough, he could see some of the former attractiveness, now faded. "Wasted beauty," he termed it.

From the West Des Moines department, Brandon Talbott—with two T's, he'd emphasized—the Second made for an imposing, exasperating character. Harry disliked him in the first moment. Talbott acted suave, his nature too slick and just cocky enough to be annoying, despite an impressive case closure record he also threw out, for reasons unknown.

Harry remained unimpressed.

The detraction from his exquisitely tailored suit, his gelled, styled hair, and his youthful Tom Cruise looks was he couldn't figure out what to do with his hands. They constantly moved. One would run up the back of his neck while the other brushed non-existent lint from his shiny paisley tie. Then he'd adjust his Ralph Lauren glasses, brush his forearm, scratch at an ear.

Harry had the urge to handcuff the guy to the chair.

Gravatte assumed the role of team leader. Professional bearing, standing at just over six feet in height, wearing a khaki-colored suit, her pale green eyes, tired and bloodshot from the late hours preparing for today's meeting, glinted an icy determination. She hadn't taken time to brush the thick stiff ends of her hair, manila folder-colored with streaks of dark pine.

The visitors came in the form of Nicholas Pennock and his assistant, Clarissa Teles. Pennock showed some American Indian in his Dick Tracy chiseled face. Clarissa, with her mocha-latte skin tone, could grace the cover of fashion magazines.

Harry tried to concentrate on what this pair brought to the table. He couldn't wrap his mind around their titles. Doctors of Psycho-whatever and Socio-something. Behind the bureaucratic doublespeak, they were criminal profilers hired out of the University of Minnesota. Earlier, after waving off renewed protests regarding Campisi, Gravatte told Harry she'd begged them to catch an eight o'clock puddle jumper flight to attend the meeting.

Gravatte stood at the head of the table. Cups of coffee, tea, or in Gravatte's case, a can of caffeine-free Diet Pepsi, rested on the table before each of them. Harry wanted to suggest the latter to the jittery Talbott—damn him and his T's. The obligatory box of doughnuts lay half crumpled on a side counter, already pillaged.

"All right, folks," the lieutenant stated. "Let's begin."

•   •   •

Misty Reznik hated doctors. She avoided them at all costs and suffered the flu and other bouts of sickness until desperation and Harry's grousing forced her to schedule an appointment with their general practitioner. Afterward, she refused to purchase prescription remedies to assist in the easing of her symptoms, preferring homemade concoctions, recipes given to her by her grandmother. She claimed the special teas and natural salves were just as effective as brand-name pharmaceuticals.

She ignored Harry's disgusted sneer every time he caught her dipping into the old green tin of Bag Balm. The goop might be older than the Depression and originally intended to treat cow udders, but for skin irritations and rashes, Misty swore by it.

Two recollections came to mind of instances when she needed a doctor's care growing up. Once for a broken arm at age fourteen and again for a required physical before she could play basketball at Iowa State University.

She must have had regular checkups as a child, but for some reason, she'd blocked them from her memory. Maybe the secret of her consternation with doctors lay in one of those appointments. Her mind conjured up an evil man in a white coat with a demonic smile who stuck a plunger-sized needle in her arm over and over.

Before she settled on an OB-GYN, she wrote a list of requirements the person must fulfill. Number one, the doctor had to be a woman. No man other than her husband was going to look, probe, or investigate that area of her anatomy. Number two, the woman had to be experienced and respected. No recent graduate for Misty, no matter how prestigious the doctor's medical school.

With those requirements and a few others in hand, she searched until she came across the listing for Doctor Phyllis Ericsson, twenty years in the practice and still loving the job. Misty continued to dislike doctors, but she'd be able to tolerate and endure Ericsson's annual tests.

While Misty sat in the spacious waiting area skimming through a parenting magazine, she decided most other patients shared another of her doctor disdains. The wait time.

Misty's nine o'clock appointment was over an hour late. She'd perused the variety of magazines, all dated eight months ago. Ironic, considering the posh modern office building with its plush, cushioned chairs and love seats, sound-muting acoustics, complex interlocking diamonds in carpeting, and hidden lighting.

An aquarium in the center of the room featured fish of every shade of the rainbow and in as many sizes. She'd gone to the restroom and walked the perimeter of the waiting room twice. She wanted to berate the syrupy-spoken receptionist—"Fill out this form in its entirety, please."—but it wasn't the woman's fault.

Misty's jumbled nerves exacerbated her impatience. She considered herself lucky to even get an appointment the day after the home pregnancy test, let alone in the morning. But she paid the price with a lengthy wait.

Damn, she hated doctors.

"Misty Reznik?" A butterball nurse called out to the waiting area from her I'm-not-moving-any-further-into-the-room spot beyond a half divider. When Misty acknowledged the nurse by walking toward her, the woman stated the obvious. "The doctor will see you now."

•   •   •

Harry approached a large display board someone had crammed into the room. Several pictures tacked to the board showed an array of corpses, similar in condition save for body features and hair color.

"Stacy Owens, forty-eight." He pointed to the person in the first photo. "Lived on Northwest Second near Broadway. Mother of one, separated, husband employed at an engineering firm up in Mason City. She worked as an accountant for Lenz Business Services. Killed Sunday night. Found Monday morning at the end of her driveway. No reason she would have been out there. Best guess, she'd taken a walk, enjoying the night air." He gazed around the room before shrugging. "You all can say ditto to this next part for your cases. No clues, no evidence, no solid explanation how or why she died or by who."

"Whom," Brandon Talbott corrected.

Harry smirked at the arrogant pup. "Well, *whomever* did it, didn't attract attention. No one heard a thing."

Harry pointed to the next two photographs and described the scene with the two lovebirds in Ewing Park. He then spoke about the homeless Leahy and his buddy Warton. When the other detectives unconsciously leaned in, Harry guessed they thought maybe with the most recent victim, there might be something to grab onto, some hook heretofore unseen. Disappointment registered when Harry described Leahy's demise.

Sally Walcott stood to speak next. Harry noted she had gone so far in her craving for a smoke she'd pulled one from the pack and sat playing with it while he'd given his litany of the Des Moines murders. She left the cigarette on the table and shuffled up to the board. Her report was short and succinct.

"Timothy Hancock, eighty-nine." Her rough voice grated on Harry's nerves, as if expending a great effort with every word. "Lived alone at the end of Greenbelt Drive just north of Greenbelt Park. Friends and neighbors say he stayed in exceptional health and loved morning walks. Which he took Tuesday morning. A couple of bicyclists came upon him along the trail. Just as you said, Harry, ditto to cause of death and lack of evidence."

•   •   •

Misty danced on air as she left the doctor's office. She floated so high she almost forgot to schedule the next appointment with Dr. Ericsson.

The doctor had made it official: Misty was five weeks pregnant.

She had known before the doctor told her, even before she took the tests the previous morning. Other than her missed period, she'd started having early food cravings. Never a fan of seafood, she was hungry for shrimp. Lots of shrimp. And lasagna. And peanut butter. Together.

At six in the morning.

Before work today, she'd driven by Red Lobster and Fazoli's to find neither opened until later in the day. After her appointment, she blew by a cop to get to the nearest Olive Garden. She was lucky the officer was busy with another speeder.

Misty tuned the car radio to her favorite country station. She decided to head downtown to do some shopping since she'd taken the entire day off. She checked her watch.

Harry's meeting had started at ten. As excited as she was about the baby, she wouldn't interrupt him. Instead, she'd try to catch him during his lunch hour. On the freeway, she turned up the volume and sang along to the lyrics, appropriate to her current condition: Little Texas's "Kick a Little."

•   •   •

Nathan Burrows hunched over his bowl, scooping generic macaroni and cheese into his mouth at a regular pace. He barely took time to chew and swallow one mouthful of the congealed glob of pasta and cheese before his hand shoved in another helping.

For days, he had eaten when his stomach growled. Mac and cheese was easy to prepare and had been a dietary staple for a long time. Red and yellow boxes lined his kitchen cabinets. Sometimes he'd buy brand names if they offered a special at the grocery store, but generic was just as good.

At the moment, he wasn't concerned about food. He put all his focus on the woman gagged and bound in the basement. Miss Kimball lived alone. The sacrifice already planned, he had kept track of her schedule, learned her habits, and waited for the night to use her to complete the ritual. A simple break-in, and a quick spell rendered the woman unconscious. He had returned unseen to his house, the woman slung over his shoulder.

He finished his food and left the unwashed bowl in the sink atop other food-encrusted dishes, wiped his hand on his pants, and returned to the basement. In the corner, the woman shivered with wide-eyed fear. He gazed at her for a time, knowing she feared rape and torture, but her body would serve a higher, more worthwhile purpose.

Turning away, he studied the sacrificial knife and other accouterments for the upcoming night's witchery. He ran his hands over the cover of his most precious possession, the Book of Sarmangous. The pressure and the power rose and throbbed within him.

And reveled in it.

•   •   •

Brandon Talbott stood as if to receive the Investigator of the Year award, brushed his pants legs, scratched his shoulder, and shifted his glasses up and down. He walked to the display board and stood a moment. Serious and grave expression like he was going to deliver a eulogy. With reverence, he touched the photo of the West Des Moines victim. He offered his most serious expression and allowed a dramatic pause to settle upon the room.

Get on with it, you little prick! Harry glanced at Campisi. Behind her stony expression did he detect a similar urge to take out her weapon and pistol whip the cocky bastard?

Talbott coughed once and spoke. He sounded like a high-class lawyer presenting his most famous court case.

"My friends," he began, and Harry stifled a groan. "I give you the tragic case of Carol Eden, a beautiful woman of twenty-nine years. She had been preparing to depart for the Big Apple—New York City—to begin what no doubt would have been a successful acting career beginning with a continuing role on a popular soap opera. Tuesday night, she arrived home after a lovely evening with her boyfriend. He dropped her off and from what I can determine, she let her little dog, Princess, out for her nightly toilet. A neighbor, annoyed at Princess's incessant barking, investigated the little animal's distress and discovered Miss Eden dead on her front porch."

Talbott acknowledged Frank Belsom. "Our esteemed county examiner, while being a consummate professional, could not offer a cause of death. To date, we have no evidence leading to the person or persons responsible."

Harry swore if Talbott took a bow, he'd throw him out the nearest window. Instead, the West Des Moines detective offered a what-tragedies-we-must-endure smile and shrug, sat, and brushed the already clean table in front of him.

Lieutenant Gravatte stood. "Thank you, Detective Talbott. Speaking of dog walkers, we received a report from the Crocker Street area about another attack last night. It's in the attached reports. I won't go into detail, but the man did escape. As did two university students. They caused quite a scene stumbling into the Drake Diner last night. The responding officer reported the girl's left pant leg and her shoe were both shredded and her foot is going to require extensive surgery. The injuries to both the pet owner and the student resembled the ones on each murder victim." She gestured to the collection of photos.

Harry and the others read the incident reports. Neither victim described the attacker other than a shadowy figure or dark object.

Rachel Van Croft stated a shadow crawled up her friend's leg.

Shadows. Harry recalled Warton claiming his buddy, the deceased Leahy, ranted about shadows. What did it mean? Was there a connection?

Ned Pennock and Clarissa Teles took the floor next. They made an odd pairing, delivering the profile piecemeal, each following on the heels of their partner, finishing each other's sentences. He wondered if he'd fallen into a black humor situation comedy with every character in the meeting two steps away from the norm.

Also, he wondered about Misty's appointment. Did the doctor confirm her pregnancy? Maybe he'd ask Gravatte for a break, give him a chance to call his wife.

The psychobabble team brought his mind back to the present.

Pennock started. "We have made copies of our profile and you can take time to read them at your leisure."

"We believe the person responsible for these heinous murders to be a white male," Teles said.

"Twenty-five to thirty-five years of age," Pennock added. "Professional businessman."

"A loner."

"Single, but that's not always true."

"Based on the area of killing, he is local and familiar with the metro area."

"He's organized."

"Meticulous."

"Mentally disturbed."

"His cycle of violence is short. The period between his 'need for satisfaction' may be shortening even more, as evidenced by the case of the homeless man and the attacks last night."

And so on, and so on. As much as Harry wanted to stay interested, he ended up tuning out these clowns. Their typical claptrap B.S. added nothing to the investigations. *A young white male, employed, maybe married, and mentally disturbed.* Throwing a dart at the phone book would produce a better result. These two might be professionals, but their profile was so vague as to be useless.

The meeting dragged on for two hours. When the clock read near noon, Harry's stomach churned with hunger. He beamed a telepathic message to Gravatte. To his surprise, she seemed to receive it. Politely interrupting the Minneapolis duo, she suggested a break to digest some food as well as the amount of shared information. They would take an hour for lunch, then return to discuss the next stage of the investigation.

Harry made it to the hallway first, but Agent Campisi had not followed him. She still sat at the table, her folder closed and set aside.

"Hey, Campisi." He snapped his fingers. Her attention had strayed again. "Let's eat. I'll even buy."

She rotated her head to look at him. "Detective Reznik, please wait," she said, voice low.

"Huh?"

She motioned to a chair, and like a student in detention, he sat. When the room emptied, save for the two of them, she arched one eyebrow. "Detective Reznik, I need to speak with you about these murders."

"That's all we've been doing all morning. Whatever you have to discuss, bring it up after lunch."

She pursed her lips. "You, of all the investigators, appear to exhibit the most common sense and proper attitude. Not discounting your lieutenant, I believe you are best able to handle the information I need to give you, though I suspect you won't accept it."

"Agent Campisi, what are you talking about? My stomach's growling. If I don't get a burger or a piece of chicken within the next ten minutes, I'm going to start gnawing on this table."

She pursed her lips before nodding. "Yes, let's get something to eat. However, I think you'll want to hear what I have to say."

Harry narrowed his eyes. "If you have something to add to this investigation, why didn't you tell me last night or share with the group this morning?"

"I received some information this morning, right before the meeting." She hesitated a moment, something Harry found surprising. A chink in the solid armor?

She continued. "Detective Reznik, I've worked some strange cases, and this one is unique. For each of them, I've confided in one or two people because if I presented my reports to large groups, such as this task force, I would be met with skepticism, ridicule, and be invited to go back to Washington."

Harry sighed. "Agent Campisi, I have no idea where you're coming from, but I suppose I'm willing to listen. Let's please get something to eat, okay?"

•   •   •

Misty drove the ascending spiral into the downtown parking garage at Seventh and Locust. She favored this garage because of its central location. The elevators to the skywalk opened to a walkway and a balcony above an expansive food court located on the ground level. A couple of hallways brought her to the major shopping skywalk area known as the Hub. When she tired of the glitz, she could browse the no-nonsense shops along the street.

She plucked her time-stamped ticket from the dispenser and the admittance bar rose. Everyone preferred the lower tiers, and she had to drive to the fifth level for an open slot. She grimaced at the audacity of some people. Slots reserved for compact cars had SUVs jammed in the narrow spaces. Several jokers had parked on top of the yellow dividing lines, hogging two spaces.

She parked her Ford Taurus between a cookie-cutter minivan and an old Dodge Dart. Exiting the car, she needed to walk a half level up to get to the elevators on the other side of the garage. Her senses went on alert.

As the wife of a homicide detective, she recognized her situation: a lone female in a darkened parking garage. Four months ago, she had taken a self-defense course offered by the taekwondo school on Army Post Road. The woman instructor presented several techniques to practice, as well as common sense tips. As Misty walked toward the elevator cubicle, she kept her keys in her fist, two of the jagged points sticking out between her fingers.

The faded yellow glare from the security lights added a layer of shadows to the aisles of cars. Sunlight from the outside didn't shine very far into the levels, brightening only the front ends of the vehicles. The odors of concrete and exhaust permeated the air.

Thirty yards from the elevators, a sound closer than the muted rush of traffic far below caught her attention. She halted mid-step, scanned the parking lot, and even squatted to get a glimpse under some nearby cars. The noise reminded her of a soft brush sliding across a snare drum. It echoed from the concrete walls and ceiling.

She wasn't scared, but the suddenness of the noise made for an uneasy ache in her stomach as she prepared herself for an attack. She tightened her grip on the keys, ready to slash or strike for an assailant's eyes.

The shushing became a paper-crumpling white noise. In the concrete garage, the echoes soon became overwhelming.

Survival instinct commanded her to run.

Preparing to make a run to the elevators, she caught a movement in her peripheral vision. A shadowy figure rose from between two cars. It flowed up the wall to a height of eight feet, part of it distorted on the ceiling. It detached itself and advanced. Two blood-red orbs full of evil stared at Misty.

Her uncontrolled screams filled the garage as gray tendrils slipped around her body.

CHAPTER 11

"I knew there was something wacko about you, Campisi," Harry said. "At first, I couldn't figure you out. Maybe your Bureau training sucked all the emotion out of you so you'd be the female version of the stereotypical, stiff-backed, don't-give-away-answers Fed. For a while, I wondered where you kept the black sunglasses. Now, I come to find out you've lost your mind. Shadow creatures are killing my citizens? What kind of bullshit is Quantico feeding you people these days? What are you trying to pull over on this Iowa hick? Shadows! Damn, that's a good one."

Lori Campisi erected a mental blank brick wall in the face of the detective's ranting. She hated this part of her special cases. The initial blow-up of unbelievers. Harry's reaction was typical if loud for the setting.

He had driven them to a cozy, respectable restaurant with floor-to-ceiling windows on two sides, so everyone on the sidewalk could see inside. Located on the corner of East Locust and Fourth, it catered to an average crowd. She guessed the customers' tastes lay in the gray area between chic specialty coffee shops and Chinese fast food. Harry admitted he hadn't cared for the place until he tried a cheeseburger fit for a trucker.

They occupied a semi-private high-backed booth in a front corner. The warm sun shone bright and glaring through the eight-foot windows. The place displayed a kaleidoscope of brown tones, from the faux oak paneling to the glossy pine round tables and the hardwood floor.

She'd waited until after the waitress took their lunch orders. He'd chosen the nauseating, artery-busting burger while she'd opted for tofu stir fry. When the waitress departed, Lori slid a manila folder across the table.

Harry hadn't gotten more than a paragraph into the material Hound had sent before he blew up. She hoped they weren't asked to leave. His volume must have attracted undue attention, though she didn't care to look.

"Wait a sec." Harry said. "Shadows. That homeless bum we talked to, Warton. His dead buddy, what's his name, Leahy? Warton said Leahy talked about shadows killing those kids. I remember you spoke up and questioned him. One of the girls from Drake also mentioned a shadow on her friend's leg." He pointed to the small stack of papers. "Is this what you meant yesterday when you said these weren't part and parcel of a serial killer?"

She nodded.

Harry belched but had the courtesy to excuse himself. Then he continued his haranguing. "Who the hell are you, Campisi? Did the Bureau send you, or did you win your badge at some carnival as a prize for throwing darts at balloons? I hoped you had something substantive to offer, not Rod Serling on a stick. Cripes, GG's going to love this."

"Detective Reznik." Lori dreaded the continuation of this half-conversation, half-rant, but knowing she had to try. "I'm not your mother, but please lower your voice. Now, I understand this may be difficult for you to accept, but—"

"Difficult?" He took a deep breath to launch into another complaint, but she spoke first.

"Please allow me to offer some corroborating evidence, some sense of credibility. Hear me out. If you still think I'm crazy, then I'll leave and pursue this from another angle." She waited a heartbeat before softening her voice. "If what I say is true—and I know how much skepticism you have—then more people are going to die. I don't know who may be safe."

Reznik's glare lasered through her before his lips twisted in capitulation. She breathed a sigh of relief. Maybe he'd at least pretend to listen.

"You've already made my burger less enjoyable." He picked up a French fry and pointed it at her. "But maybe I'll get a laugh or two out of this. You, uh, don't mind if I continue eating?"

"By all means, Detective. I'd hate to deprive you of moving closer to the date of your first heart attack."

"Hey, the lady agent has some spark behind the ice."

She reset her jaw and began. "Despite your sarcasm, I am a real agent. You may confirm my credentials with Washington. I can give you the name and number of my supervisor. You'll discover I've been instrumental in solving many cases, including the rash of bank robberies along the East Coast last year."

"I read about those," Harry said. "Sneaky bastards, having a different inside man employed at each of the banks."

"Yes," she agreed. "Anyway, what my supervisor will not confirm, will emphatically deny, is from time to time, I'm called to investigate certain...special cases."

"Strike up the X-Files theme music," Harry quipped.

"Damn, how I hated that show," she murmured.

"Why? Because of the goofy plots?"

"No, because many of those stories, unbeknownst to the writers as far as we can tell, were based on fact."

"What?" Harry leaned in and waggled his fingers at her. He adopted a mock conspiratorial tone. "You mean Bigfoot *does* exits, as well as vampires and aliens beaming people to the Mother Ship? Hey, why do those Grays do the anal probes?"

She let her impatience seep through. "We're wasting time, Detective."

"Sorry. Go on."

"I don't expect you to believe all of it, but I've seen some things…difficult to comprehend. You won't hear the media report those cases because my department provided, well…alternative explanations."

"Cover-ups."

She paused before nodding.

Harry dipped a fry into a glob of ketchup. "Are you allowed to mention any of those cases?"

"I could but as I've said, you would have difficulty obtaining corroborating information from anyone."

"Yet, I'm supposed to go along with your theories about shadow creatures on blind faith."

"I'm asking you to at least consider the possibility, to open your mind, especially in the face of the lack of evidence otherwise obtained from your crime scenes. Read the information I've presented, ask your questions, then decide."

"You said if I tell you to shove off, you would find other ways to deal with these murders. How?"

"There are avenues I can explore," she stated. "It would be easier to do so with…a partner, of sorts."

She waited while Reznik digested the information and ingested the rest of his lunch, her meal all but forgotten. He opened the file and skimmed the first page as he munched the last half dozen fries. After a couple of minutes, he set the paper aside.

"There is much speculation and most of the alleged incidents are reported by average Joes. Where did these come from, websites on the Internet?"

"There are many sites that deal with the paranormal and the supernatural," she answered. "Many of them have a section listing individual incidents."

"And we all know if it's on the Internet, we can believe it," Harry said, full of sarcasm. Before she could respond, he backed off. "All right, sorry about the potshot. Listen, instead of me reading all of this line-by-line, why don't you give me a summary, hit some of the high points, and maybe tell me where we should go from here."

She cocked an eyebrow.

Harry held up the incorrect number of fingers for Scout's Honor. "I promise to listen and try not to discount anything right out of the chute, okay?"

Campisi shifted her gaze to scan the room. Most of the other patrons had departed back to their daily grind. The remaining few ate meals in their own little worlds. A young couple chatted in a far corner. A lost-looking guy pored over a city map. An elderly woman read a book. She still kept her words from going beyond the immediate table.

"First, the history of shadow beings is extensive," she began. "People have claimed to see them for centuries. They've been called different things, but the similarities of the reports are amazing. Documents and reports from almost every culture exist. Stories passed down through the generations, some of which evolved into fairy tales or so-called urban legends. In the last decade or twos, there have been scores of sightings. Anything from a brief peripheral glimpse to impressions of recognizable figures, and not just human. Many people say they've seen shadow animals. Cats, dogs."

"What do these creatures look like?"

"Various shapes and sizes. Blobs, cloaked figures, spheres. Even the form of a human body. Many reports share common elements. A person wakes to see a dark figure standing at the foot of the bed. A shadow leaning over the bed. Something gray staring through a window. Some of the more frightening experiences include people seeing and feeling a shadow being on top of them, pressing on their chests. In at least one case, a young boy suffered severe burns where a shadow touched him."

"Anyone come up with an explanation of what they are?"

"Many theories. Ghosts, demons, people experiencing out-of-body experiences. Of course, many say it's all imagination."

"I can see why," Harry jumped in. "Those at night can be written off. Who's to say these instances aren't a holdover from a dream or nightmare? Doctors can explain the pressure on the chest."

"True." Campisi offered a weak smile. "Who knows? There have been many daylight sightings. Anyway, a very popular explanation—and one I am drawn to—is that they are something from another dimension."

"Cue the Twilight Zone theme."

She ignored him. "If you do any research at all, you'll find many scientists agreeing on the existence of parallel dimensions. So, maybe, whatever might occupy this other place finds a door or other ways of touching ours."

"Okay," Harry said. "This is all fine, and it sounds like hours without end of fun discussion of these theories and sightings. How do what you say and these reports relate to right now to the cases we've been investigating? Don't tell me this has happened elsewhere."

Her momentary hesitation lasted just long enough to set him off again.

"Damn it, now you're shitting me. Come on, Campisi. If there had been people slaughtered like this in any other state, there's no way you Feds would be able to cover it up."

"No, I'm not saying this exact thing has happened elsewhere on quite the scale as here in Des Moines, although we've had rumors of similar deaths in Australia. Many of the reports are injuries and attacks similar to these two Drake University students."

"What are you saying, Agent Campisi? Give me the benefit of your experience. Best guess on what we're facing here."

She inhaled and told him what she'd been contemplating for the last day. "Reports say many shadow beings are friendly. They appear, stand around for a while, and disappear. Most physical interaction, however, is threatening or injurious, and now, I believe, fatal. I conjecture that these more malevolent creatures have entered our world through an opening, one created for them."

"Why here? In this city?"

"Who knows? Maybe the portal is somewhere in the metro area. I do know one thing: if we don't find a way to close it, a lot more people are going to die. Think, Detective. There are shadows everywhere, all day and all night. Who knows when one of those gray gloomy patches will come to life?"

Harry, immersed in the moment, jumped and swore when his cell phone ringer cut the tension.

He said hello, and his face went through an agonizing transformation from cynicism to rage and fear. Not even saying goodbye, he punched the button to end the call, threw some bills on the table, and grabbing her arm, pulled her out of the booth.

"Come on," he growled and they bolted out of the restaurant.

•   •   •

Pain!

She couldn't move, couldn't cry out, but her mind screamed. Her body was as if hundreds of fire ants covered her body, all biting at the same time.

What happened? Where was she?

Despite the torment, she remembered...concrete. A garage. Yes! A parking garage. She had parked downtown. Walked toward the elevators. Then darkness...and pain.

Whispers haunted the shadows of her mind. Something, maybe many things, still lurked out there. Still hungry. They craved blood. They had a good taste of hers, and they wanted more.

•   •   •

The Buick's tires squealed up the Locust Street parking garage's circular ramp. The admittance bar had been locked in the up position. Good thing, or else Harry would have crashed through it. Before he reached the fifth level, an officer waved him to a stop. He didn't recognize the kid, so figured he wasn't the senior officer on the scene. The patrolman pointed to Officer Todd Colfax, speaking with a couple of other uniforms near a car parked blocking the aisle. Colfax's lean figure complimented a square clean-shaven jaw and gray-streaked hair.

He broke away from the group and approached them. "Damn it, Harry, I'm sorry. It happened minutes ago. The ambulance just left. Didn't you pass it?"

Harry shook his head. "No, I didn't see it. What the hell happened?"

Colfax gave him a pained look. "Another attack. Harry, Misty man, she ain't doin' so well. They took her to Unity Point."

Harry fought the urge to hit something. He ground his teeth. "What happened? Who found her?"

Colfax beckoned to a woman standing with another officer a few steps from the driver's door of the parked car. She walked over and Colfax made the introductions.

"This is Theresa Harrison. She came upon the attack in progress. Ms. Harrison, this is Detective Reznik, husband of the victim. Tell him what you witnessed."

Harrison had dull curly brown hair, an egg oval, blanched face. She wore jeans and a loose T-shirt. Mid-forties, Harry guessed.

Her voice quavered with each word. "I was looking for a parking space. I hate these garages. They're so dark, and I have to use my headlights. I had just rounded the corner and saw a woman near one of the support posts jerking and screaming like she was having a fit or a seizure. When my headlights shone on her, she stiffened and just collapsed. I didn't know what to do. I went to check on her and—" Harrison paused and shivered. "Her face, her arms, they looked...horrible." Sobs drowned her words.

"It's okay, Ms. Harrison," Colfax said, consoling her. "Tell us what you said before, just before Mrs. Reznik collapsed."

The woman sniffed and wiped tears from her cheeks. "I don't know. Just as my headlights shone full on her, she stopped moving—froze. But there was something...a gray shadow, I guess...it disappeared. That's when she collapsed."

"What do you mean when you say the shadow disappeared?" Campisi asked.

"This shadow—I don't know what it was—covered her. Then it just faded away. But before it did..."

Harry was close to snapping. "What?"

"I swear two red eyes stared at me."

Colfax broke in. "We're searching the whole garage, Harry, but the guy could've taken several exits into the elevators, onto the skywalk, or out to the street. Hell, he could be hiding in any of these cars."

Harry had stopped listening. He lost focus as his mind tried to get a handle on the woman's words. A shadow? A shadow attack?

He caught Campisi's eyes and took one step toward the agent, intending to shake some answers out of her. Instead, he checked his actions. He had to go to Misty and raced to the car. Just before he stomped on the pedal to send the Buick into reverse, he remembered Campisi still stood with Officer Colfax and the woman.

For a second, he contemplated the release of built-up tension if he shifted back into drive and plowed right over the federal agent. Serve her right for bringing this madness to his city.

She hadn't, though. She'd brought a moronic idea about shadows. What a crazy notion, despite the witness's description.

Harry settled for leaving Campisi in the parking garage.

He roared off to find his wife.

●   ●   ●

"Everything will be all right," Nathan Burrows whispered to the bound woman as he caressed her quivering face. Her eyes were like oil-stained white dinner plates filled with fear. Fright had dehydrated her, but Burrows didn't care. He hadn't fed her, but no matter. Her demise would not result from thirst or hunger, but he hoped she wouldn't die from sheer terror. She needed to be alive until the sacrifice that night, when *he* would have the power he desired, not the force within.

He aimed the flashlight at the pile of items gathered near the dais. The Book of Sarmangous rested upon its stand, above everything. It was the source, it begged reverence, even worship.

Forgetting the woman, he began to arrange the items in their proper order, to set them in their assigned places. In his concentration, he didn't respond to the woman's whimpering and sobbing, but took notice of the moving shadows around him and the pairs of red eyes, watching…waiting.

"Soon," he whispered to them. "Very soon."

CHAPTER 12

Iowa State University campus

Fourteen years earlier

Pages turning. Pens scratching across notebooks. Soft tapping on a keyboard of one of those clunky laptop computers growing in popularity.

For a space designed for quiet study, the campus library was full of sound. Endless rows of book-filled shelves dotted with oases of work and study tables occupied by students ignoring each other unless a whispering pair labored over a joint assignment.

The spring semester the library had yet to experience the rush of exam-maddened bodies desperate to infuse months' worth of information into a single night's brain-numbing study session.

Harry Reznik, dressed in jeans and a polo shirt, brow creased in frustration and confusion, pored over a god-awful thick book on religious history in the United States. He'd already flunked a pop quiz in the class and he'd vowed not to get blindsided again.

Reading about the people bored him to no end, though. The Quakers, the Protestants, the Lutherans, even the first-century Catholics. Who cared, and why did they matter?

It wasn't as if he planned to become a minister or immerse himself in archaeological studies—although this choice had sounded fascinating at first—or even become a teacher. The education field seemed to be one of the few in which he was remotely interested...and one he hadn't dismissed.

As a freshman, along with all the required core classes, he'd chosen to major in business...until he became confused by a simple ledger book. Then he considered communications, but the field was so broad he couldn't choose a specific venue. Art? Not a consideration, since he couldn't even draw a decent stick figure, let alone paint anything worth the effort.

For two years he'd hopped around from subject to subject, enjoying none of them. He'd even tried botany but dropped out after the third week when the professor said part of the test required him to memorize all of those Latin names for each species.

By the start of his junior year, the increased pressure from his parents and the college counselor forced him to choose a major and stick with the decision.

With reluctance, he'd settled on education. Maybe a history teacher, but damn, he'd had no way of knowing how mind-numbing a lot of his studies would be. Sure, the wars and the political scandals held his interest. He enjoyed learning how various societies dealt with criminals and how laws were implemented—how morals changed from one century to the next.

These religious people, however…

He wasn't an atheist; in fact, he grew up in a Methodist family and attended Sunday school and church. Anything more, however, as in researching the history of some of the more goofy sects and denominations...

He leaned back in his chair and rubbed his tired eyes. Another hour of this and he'd go stir crazy.

"They made beautiful furniture," a soft voice said. "My parents own a table and chairs made in the style."

When he opened his eyes, the person next to him took his breath away. Sun-fired honey blonde hair, sea-blue eyes, delicate angelic face, and a centerfold body. A guy could spin out of control on those curves.

He sat speechless. Did this girl, this modern-day Venus, actually speak to him? He resisted the urge to glance around, but no one sat nearby. He was alone. Well, alone except for her.

His expression must have registered as inquiry of her comment, for she added, "The Shakers. They made wonderful furniture."

"Oh," he said, and before he could stop himself, blurted, "Yeah, but they didn't believe in sex. Don't understand why they didn't have many converts."

Instant embarrassment warmed his cheeks. Nice going, dumb shit. See if you can force your foot any deeper down your throat.

To his surprise and relief, the girl laughed. Wow, what music. Her joyful reaction to his sarcasm sounded genuine, not forced.

"Yes," she agreed. "Ironic. I wonder how they thought they came into the world?"

He couldn't believe it. Instead of changing the subject, she'd added her own humorous comment.

"My name is Misty." She offered her hand. "Misty Stokes."

Harry swallowed and, at the last second, remembered courtesy and tried to stand, but forgot to push the chair back first. It took two attempts as if he had the word FOOL stamped on his forehead.

"Hu—Har..." he stuttered, then unscrambled his tongue. "I mean, Harry Reznik."

Misty, also a junior, played second-string on the women's basketball team while studying for a Bachelor's in Communications. She said she'd always loved art, so she'd opted for a degree in graphic design. "Didn't I see you a year or so ago in an art class?"

"Probably." He explained his difficulty in choosing a major. Way to impress her, he thought, show her how clueless you are about your future. In an attempt at recovery, he said, "I'm interested in Criminology."

Quicker than a blink, he made both career and life decisions. He wanted to be a cop, and he wanted to share how ever many decades afforded him with Misty Stokes. Clarity came in the form of a blue-eyed blonde goddess who didn't walk away after the first ten minutes.

They ditched the books for the night and found a coffeeshop. Later, when he dropped her off at her dorm, he delayed too long on the follow-up, and she ended up asking him to dinner that Saturday night.

•   •   •

Friday afternoon
Present day

Harry sniffed back tears at the memory. After their first evening together, Misty Stokes became an integral and vital part of his life, of his very being.

His heart pounded and ached as he paced the waiting room. He hated feeling so helpless, and the stifling, stuffy room with its neutral-brown carpet, subdued hidden lighting, olive-green sleeper couches, and navy-blue cushioned chairs, all designed to induce serenity and calm did nothing for him.

A muted television mounted on the wall in the corner showed Fox News. A pleasant-faced, sympathetic nurse sat behind a rounded desk near the door. Graceful stairs led up to a second level. A chapel in the upper hall waited for anyone who needed spiritual succor.

Harry was immune to the serene influences. Misty had been in surgery for over two hours with no word on her condition. Every minute with no report fueled his anxiety. He'd already driven two people up to the second level with his back-and-forth, nerve-wracking movements.

If he didn't settle down, he'd punch a hole in the wall. To distract himself, he scowled at the television. While figures from the New York Stock Exchange scrolled across the bottom of the screen, the banner headline announced a plane crash in Thailand. A small square to the right of the perky reporter's head showed a live feed of the smoking ruins.

Harry punched the television's power button, and the picture winked out. He did not need to view tragedy in another part of the world with plenty of suffering in his city.

On a table, lay a thick, heavy book on the history of the hospital. He opened it and started skimming the pages. Unity Point Hospital opened its doors as Iowa Methodist in 1901...trained personnel needed to combat the flu epidemic...an additional twenty-four beds added four years later...major advances in medicine...

Advances in medicine. Were they enough? He closed the book, and as he had that night so many years ago in the Iowa State University library, he leaned back and closed his eyes.

Could the surgeons save Misty and the baby?

"I'm sorry, Harry," a voice said.

Instead of an angel, when he opened his eyes, a devil—in the guise of Agent Campisi—stood before him.

"So, now it's Harry, huh?" His voice came out strained and tired. "Why so informal all of a sudden?"

Campisi didn't respond. They both knew the answer: because matters had become personal.

He waved off the question and asked another. "What did GG say?" Campisi would have reported Misty's attack to his superior. "I suppose I'm off the task force."

"I have not spoken with her and cannot predict what your lieutenant will decide."

Harry stood when a doctor entered the waiting room. The man, tall with black, thinning hair, dressed in white, stopped to whisper to the receptionist. She glanced at Harry and the doctor approached. A name tag pinned to his lapel read Dr. Michael Elstor.

"Mr. Reznik?"

"How—"

The doctor held up a hand. "Let's sit down."

"Tell me, Doc," Harry said. "No bullshit, just give it to me."

Elstor inhaled, pursing his lips. "Mr. Reznik, your wife is in critical condition. At the moment, she is in a coma. We've repaired the injuries as best we can, but she lost a lot of blood. She suffered a great deal of internal damage."

"And the baby?"

Elstor nodded. "I understand she was several weeks pregnant." Another pause. "The internal injuries included the womb. I'm sorry to report the embryo didn't survive. Mr. Reznik, your wife needs time to heal, what with the multiple injuries..."

Elstor's words trailed off. Harry had stopped listening. A boulder-sized lump lodged in his throat, and he couldn't inhale. Campisi hadn't moved. As usual, she remained as emotionless as a stone with her impassive expression and set jaw.

Rage poured into his veins as he recalled their discussion at lunch. He lashed out, grabbed Campisi's lapels, and drove her back until she smacked hard against the wall.

"What the hell is going on around here, Campisi?" His breaths were audible, and he spoke through gritted teeth. "If you know something, you'd better damn well spill it, and I mean right now or so help me, I'll—"

"Mr. Reznik," Doctor Elstor implored. "Please!"

Harry snarled in the man's direction. "Back off!" Then he returned his attention to Campisi. He leaned in, his face inches from hers. "I don't give a damn whether you're some weirdo federal agent, and I'm coming real close to forgetting you're a woman." He shook her. "Talk, damn you. This wasn't a couple of hormone hot lovers in the park. This was my wife." He shook her again.

"Harry, please." She stared into his eyes. "This is not the time or the place." Her voice dropped to a whisper. "Go see your wife. She needs you."

He shook her a third time for emphasis before releasing her.

"Get out of here, Campisi. Go do what you need to do, but get out of my sight." He stepped toward Elstor. "Where is she? Where is Misty?"

Elstor nodded once and led Harry out of the waiting room to an elevator. They rode up one floor to the intensive care unit. Six rooms formed a C around a central nursing station. Monitors beeped and computers hummed. Elstor directed Harry to the third room but grabbed his arm at the door.

"Mr. Reznik," he said in a low voice. "I understand your emotions, but you must control yourself. I can allow you a short visit. We'll be changing her dressings often and watching for infection."

Harry's cold stare bore into the doctor. "You don't understand shit," he rumbled. "Now, remove your hand, and let me see my wife."

.   .   .

Harry sat on a step in the stairwell, head in his hands. The stark white chamber connecting the hospital's floors echoed every sound.

After visiting Misty, he stumbled down the hall, forgoing the elevator. Even though he'd seen the ravages of the heinous attacks—the gouged, boiled skin, and slashed abdomens—before, those same conditions on his wife's body shocked him speechless. Her breathing, labored and sporadic, was aided by a machine's plastic hose taped over her mouth and nose. She lay in the bed like an abused and forgotten rag doll.

What could perpetrate such violence on a human being? Shadows? How? Shadows were intangible, not real. Not alive.

He jerked his head up when a scream penetrated the stairwell from the second floor. Another ripped down the hall as he crashed through the door. A couple of people crowded the chapel entrance.

"What happened?" he asked.

A path opened, and when he entered the sanctuary...

Shit! Not another attack. Not here in a hospital.

The elderly couple who'd ascended to the second floor of the waiting room must have sought further comfort in the chapel. Instead, death waited inside. Their bodies lay ragged and bloody on the floor in front of the altar. From the wall above, Christ on the cross peered with haunted eyes upon the grisly tableau.

A nurse approached, took one look, and rushed to sound the alarm, calling for emergency medics. Harry stood motionless. Two more victims. Two more lives literally torn asunder.

The chapel, full of shadows because of the low ambient light, boded evil. Harry's eyes darted to one corner. Did something move? Had he seen the slightest shifting of an indefinable form? Something in his peripheral vision? When he looked straight into the gloomy corner...nothing.

Attendants brushed him aside and out of the chapel as white and green-clad doctors took over. Outside in the hall, he almost collided with Campisi.

"Damn it, Campisi. What are you doing here?" He didn't allow her time to speak. "Do you see what's happened?" He pointed to the activity in the chapel. "This is a hospital. I've had people attacked in a hospital!" He grabbed her arm and pulled her into a side hall. "What the hell is this?"

"The shadows—"

"Don't give me some bullshit about shadows. Shadows don't rip people apart. They're not alive."

Campisi freed herself from his grip. "How else do you explain it? Listen to me, Detective Reznik. First, you will cease putting your hands on me. Second, you've read the research and listened to my explanations. This is what we're dealing with. Living shadow creatures. They're the best explanation and the only one that explains the reports. I know it sounds ludicrous, like supernatural nonsense, but look at the attack scenes. Parks, a darkened porch, a low-lit chapel, a parking garage."

Harry's sharp look silenced her for a moment.

"They're full of shadows, Harry. That's the connection. Look around us. We're safe. This hall is brighter than outside, but the chapel is dark. Parks are nothing but trees and shadows, and worse at night."

Harry wiped a hand over his face and breathed in frustration. Campisi changed tack. "How is Misty?"

"She looks like that." He gestured toward the carnage being rolled out of the sanctuary. "Except, by some miracle, she's still breathing." He snapped his fingers. "Shit, I've got to call her parents."

"May I offer a suggestion?"

"Does it involve me punching your lights out? Because I'm about five seconds away from doing so."

Campisi ignored him. "Call this in, give your contact information to the doctor, and then drive me back to the station. We need to discuss the situation with your lieutenant. Wait." She held up a hand to stall his protest. "I know you want to be with your wife. However, at the moment, you're unable to do anything for her. Your best action at this time is to be a detective, to investigate this matter, and find a solution."

Her monotone words cut through his emotions. In a strange way, they made sense. He stared at this enigmatic woman, so unruffled, never expressing worry.

"Frank Belsom is going to hate me," he murmured after a moment.

"I'll help smooth things with the hospital staff."

Harry nodded and reached for his cell phone. "I'll meet you at the car."

"I know where it's parked," Campisi said.

Without another word, Harry walked away.

The medical examiner arrived twenty minutes later, disheveled and weary. After he'd sorted through the chaos, he approached Harry. "What the F is going on in this city?"

"Frank—"

"You can't let me have a break. As soon as I finish up with one corpse, you call in another."

"Frank, this is not the time."

"JC, Harry." Belsom sighed. "I heard about Misty and I'm sorry. I haven't gotten a decent night's sleep since this all started. Nothing like this is supposed to happen in Des Moines. You'd think we were living in F-ing New York City."

"I know," Harry said. "We're all feeling it."

For a few moments, they commiserated, each with his hand on the other's shoulder, heads bowed.

"How's she doing?"

Harry shook his head. "Not good, man. Not good."

"Listen," Belsom said in a low voice. "I, uh, I gotta go do...this."

"Yeah."

Belsom shuffled away. Harry hoped the medical examiner would be all right. After a while, he finished up and went to find his car.

Harry drove, not looking at Campisi in the passenger seat. "I suppose you want to be in charge, bring in more of your people to handle this case. You won't need us locals anymore."

Campisi paused before speaking. "No, Harry. I still need to work with the local department. I need you. These are still the task force's cases. As strange as this situation is, I cannot step in, and at this time, I don't want to assume control. Not with as little credibility and evidence as I have. As I told you at lunch, imagine the reaction. I wouldn't get very far."

"So, what do we do now?"

"After you speak with your lieutenant, I suggest you find something to eat and get some sleep. I understand, though, your need to go back to the hospital."

"Yes, but what do we do...I mean, I'm not saying I accept this shadow beings business. I'm trying to get a handle on this." He blew out a breath. "Let me ask you something. You mentioned these—whatever they are, shadow people or creatures—have been around for a long time. You claim the best theory out there is they come from some other dimension. They've been pushing the boundaries or walls of this dimension and making themselves known to us."

"Correct."

"So, if these things found a way into our world, why hasn't there been a mass slaughter? Why a relative few in the Metro area?"

"At the moment, I have no answer. Maybe the portal or gate isn't very big. Or maybe only a few came through."

"Shadows," Harry reflected. "Cripes, Campisi, there are shadows everywhere. Under desks, in corners, alleys, houses."

"Yes."

"Nowhere is safe, especially at night."

"True."

He eyed her with a grave expression. "More people are going to die, aren't they?"

She chose not to answer the rhetorical question. Instead, she said, "I'm in touch with a co-worker who sent me the information I gave you today. I'll contact him tonight to see if he has anything further to help us. I do agree we're likely up against a time factor. It will get worse."

"In the meantime?"

She paused and stared at him, flat eyes unwavering. "Stay in the light."

•   •   •

Yesterday, a ten-acre building sitting just north of the Interstate, sold hundreds of items—both antique and not so much. Everything from used recent best sellers, their dust covers stained and torn, to books with hard faded covers from the early twentieth century. Furniture, lamps, cribs, toys, dishes, tools, records, magazines, advertising, postcards, matchbooks, videos, knickknacks and gewgaws, and so much more. Signs reading *Country Lane, Sawmill Road, Bishop Road,* and other quaint names hung above the aisles. Near the front, three aisles of glass-fronted display cases stretched half the length of the store. The wares in these ranged the collectors' spectrum: watches, pewter, miniature cars, figurines of soldiers, dolls, political buttons, and countless other items on six shelves per case.

Colleen Farrington loved *Yesterday.* A regular patron, she almost never left without at least one item to add to her antique display at home.

Her project, never-ending and always changing, featured a different decade in each room of her house. Six main rooms, six ten-year stretches beginning in the 1900s through the 1950s. Anything newer than 1960 she regarded as too modern.

Colleen herself had been born the year before, in 1959. Four years later, her family's reaction to John Kennedy's assassination tarnished her birthday. Her mom cried for two days and mourned for months afterward.

Colleen wanted her home to reflect the "happier" years before the sixties' tragedies and radicalism.

That morning, she'd decided her thirties collection deserved more books.

Randal, one of eight cashiers, waved to her while he rang up a customer's selection of glassware. She strolled by the looping video hawking expensive furniture polish, past the concession stand and seating area. Here, reference and history books lined the walls.

She took a right at *Willow Tree Lane*. This aisle, like many others, was divided into several units, each a unique collection. Some of them had created a theme for the individual area: furniture, bottles, a young girl's toy chest. All aged and paint-flecked, dusty, and browned and yellowed by time.

Colleen enjoyed the bookcases overflowing with no organization as to genre, title, author, or publication date. A set of faded hymnals leaned against an Abraham Lincoln biography standing next to *Basic Mathematics*. Time had faded the covers to a worn dark brown or blue, gold lettering tarnished, pages torn, yellowed, and dog-eared.

Colleen loved books. She also liked the arrangement of the cases, some of them forming narrow L- or C-shaped alcoves where she could kneel or sit, unseen by other shoppers, and peruse the dusty, musty books in peace.

She crept into the first shadowy alcove and sat cross-legged, three sides of books within easy reach. At random, she selected the most promising-looking volumes, those surviving the abuse through the years.

A pioneer drama, à la *Little House on the Prairie*. Too bad the first thirty-four pages had been torn out.

First Aid. Printed in 1953.

A small, bound dictionary of shorthand symbols.

Her eyes widened as she pulled from the stock a first edition Mary Roberts Rinehart novel, *The Red Lamp*. Published in 1925, but still…

Sometimes, one found treasures tucked away in the gloomiest corners.

A soft crackling sounded behind her as if someone was crumpling newspapers or book pages. Heaven forbid she caught someone abusing a book.

A slight shift in the shadows between her and the corner leading out of the alcove caught her attention. When her hand touched the floor to push herself upright, the shadow latched onto her wrist, pinning her fingers to the floor. She opened her mouth to scream as the shadow moved up her arm, shredding skin with each inch. A second shadow covered her head like an executioner's hood.

The Red Lamp streamed with red blood as the shadows became Colleen's executioner.

•   •   •

More death.

She experienced the latest victim's terror, how the shadows gouged and ripped and absorbed the blood.

Their strength and power increased with each death. They grew bolder, stronger.

Why did she continue to suffer? What was the connection between her and these amorphous phantoms? She wished she could speak to Harry, to warn him. She remained trapped in her mind, unable to move, unable to tell anyone of her plight.

CHAPTER 13

Back at the police station, Harry met with Lieutenant Gravatte in her office. After offering sympathy for Misty, she launched into a long speech detailing why she should remove Harry from the task force and given leave.

"Agent Campisi, despite your brief acquaintance, had some decent insight about you." Gravatte waited until Harry met her eyes. "She said you need to stay focused on the case and if removed from it, you'd strike out on your own to catch the asshole who's been killing our people. I believe she's right on both counts."

Gravatte gave him a few moments to comment, then added, "I'd like to run your ass back to the hospital where you belong but from what you report, there's nothing to be done there except wait. Meanwhile, we've got to keep going. I'm not one to rebuff a federal agent out of hand. If she says you're needed, then..."

Harry didn't respond, just faced his superior with a concrete frown.

"I also suspect you two have discussed these murders at length. Have you anything to share?"

He was on the verge of sharing the conversation he and Campisi had in the restaurant and on the drive back from the hospital when a detective stuck his head into the office.

"Lieutenant, we got trouble."

"Damn it," Gravatte muttered. "What is it now?"

"Reverend T. A. is across the street. We've been asked to help with crowd control."

Gravatte uttered a throaty growl. "Take the Fed with you. Introduce her to one of our fine upstanding troublemakers."

Harry and Campisi exited the station by the main doors and maneuvered around people milling around on the front steps. Officers hurried toward the mass of people on the far side of Court Street. Across the street, on the bank of the Des Moines River, close to a hundred people listened and responded to a man speaking from a makeshift platform. Portable speakers amplified his deep, resonant voice.

"I say then..." The rich baritone resounded across the street. "...I say the devil has come to town!"

A hail of "amens" rose from half the supporters. The man held up his arms for emphasis. A burly figure—skin the color of an aged walnut, with large meaty hands, sweaty face, shining bald skull—wore a too-tight, too-expensive suit.

"The Devil! Killing our citizens."

More "amens." The speaker held up a thick, well-used Bible for all to see. "This, dear ones, is where we must turn. God's Holy Word! It is all we have to combat the evil on our doorstep."

His voice rose, the two amplifiers warbling with the distortion. With each statement, the crowd shouted the appropriate response.

"The police can't help us!"

"No!"

"The governor can't help us!"

"No!"

"Only our merciful God can answer our prayers!"

"Amen!"

"Only the Glorious Redeemer can!"

Campisi stared without expression. "Who is he?"

"The good Reverend Titus A. Samuels of the New Hope Christ Redeemer Church, the fastest growing church in town, services twice on Sunday morning and others throughout the week. He's been in the area for a year or so. Hardly a month goes by when he doesn't gather his flock for a public forum on whatever current evil he has on his mind. It's no surprise these murders would have put a spark under his ass. I thought ole Tits and Ass would have shown his face before now."

"Tits and Ass?"

"Oh, yeah. Samuels loves the ladies. See the entourage off to the side?"

Harry pointed to four women grouped ten yards from the podium All wore dresses that emphasized their curves. "Ushers and greeters. Ain't just Samuels' charm keeping attendance numbers high."

Samuels continued his harangue. "The Lord requires more than prayer! The Lord requires us to act!"

"Oh, shit," Harry moved toward the bottom of the steps. "He's going to say the magic words."

"Harry?"

Harry chose not to respond as he observed several young punks standing on the fringe of the crowd. Their enthusiasm pushed toward frenzy, eager attitudes ready to stir up trouble.

He leaped down the resmaining steps, calling back over his shoulder, "Come on, Campisi. Whip out your Federal badge. It might help dispel a riot."

A squeal of brakes and Harry jumped out of the way of a passing car. He smacked the trunk in anger as the vehicle rolled on.

By now, the crowd in front of Samuels murmured, some shouting, all bodies moving in reaction to the Samuels' words and the energy of the massed people. They were ready to hear and obey his directive.

"Listen, dear people," the preacher said in a confiding voice still audible to everyone. "Now is the time for action! Now is the time we need to demand action! Say 'Amen.'"

"Amen!"

"I say, we march across the street, up those steps into the office of the police chief himself, and demand resolution. If he does not respond, then we should take action ourselves."

The crowd shouted their approval. The cordon of officers closed in to prevent the crowd from spilling out onto Court. Harry ran along the perimeter of the mass. He had to get to Samuels, to try to quell the growing fervor.

He shouted to the nearest officer. "You call for backup?"

"On its way," the cop yelled.

In Harry's haste, he collided a man not of Samuels' flock. The punk wore black jeans and a ripped T-shirt, similar in style to the rest of his buddies. Each youth exhibited lanky strength, with skin the color of a chalkboard—a pasty black. As Harry disentangled himself, the punk pushed him.

"Hey, Five-Oh," the youth said. "What the shit? We ain't doin' nothin'."

"Get out of here, asshole," Harry growled.

Samuels' followers pressed in on Harry and the gang. One tripped and fell. Another blamed the man next to him. Someone else pushed against Harry. More shoving devolved into flying punches. Harry couldn't distinguish between the gang members and the un-Christian mob out for justice. People shouted and cops brandished nightsticks. More tires screeched as drivers tried to stop when the fight spilled out onto Court Avenue. Harry moved his head aside in time to avoid a punch. He grabbed the guy's wrist and followed through, throwing the man over his hip. Not stopping, he plowed his way through the crowd, knocking aside those who had yet to enter the fracas. A quick movement caught his eye. Campisi also struggled to reach the podium.

A member of the gang stepped in front of her. "Say, bitch!" He waved his knife in her face.

Campisi's foot lashed out and the toe of her shoe caught the guy square in the crotch. He went rigid, the knife falling away. She followed up with a palm heel to the punk's nose and blood sprayed. "Harry, we've got to stop this."

"What do you think I'm trying to do?"

Samuels displayed a shocked expression at the chaos, but his subtle smile indicated the preacher enjoyed the scene.

"Samuels!" Harry shouted when he reached the podium

The preacher's face lit up. No longer concerned about his people getting injured, he fell back into his antagonist preacher role. "We asked of the Lord and He has delivered." He leaned in toward the microphone. "My dear people, we have before us an example of the ineptitude and the inefficiency of the police department in our fair city."

While most of the crowd ignored him, some turned to see the unfamiliar face on the stage.

"What have you to say for yourself?" Samuels's oily voice overflowed with sarcasm. "Why is this city cowering in fear instead of enjoying the Lord's gifts? Why must we lock ourselves behind our doors at night instead of being able to gaze upon—"

Harry twisted one of the preacher's arms behind his back. Keeping a firm grip, he growled into the man's ear. "Stop this, Titus. This is not what you want."

If he hauled the reverend off the podium, the crowd would become even more agitated, and he'd have a full-scale riot on his hands. Only the outer edges of the crowd were battling each other and the police.

Samuels offered a broad, knowing smile. "Detective, I want what everyone in this city wants. A killer brought to justice. If you and your fellow officers cannot do the job, then my brothers and sisters will find someone who can."

"You're going to be arrested for inciting a riot," Harry said. "Put an end to this or more people are going to get hurt. We don't have time to deal with your shit right now."

Samuels' smile, if possible, widened. "Detective, we have a moral right to demand the police in this city live up to their responsibility. To protect us from the invaders of homes, from those who wantonly destroy our lives."

The crowd grew even more restless, demanding to be let in on the exchange between the two men upon the podium. Harry knew he had to dispel the tension. He leaned even closer to Samuels' ear. "Reverend, cut the shit and get everyone out of here. Tell them to go home. You go home to your wife and kids."

"But—"

Harry moved to stare the preacher dead in the eye. He lowered his voice to a whisper. "Unless you want me to tell them where you spent last Saturday night. Which commandment did you ignore? The seventh or the tenth?"

Samuels's eyes narrowed and his lip twitched. Harry could tell the man wanted to deny everything but changed his mind. Instead, he gave a tiny nod. "All right, Detective. You've made your point, but I hope you understand mine. These killings have to stop. I'm not the lone voice crying in the wilderness. There will be others. You won't be able to threaten us all."

"Who's threatening, preacher? Now, I'm going to step off this podium and you're going to send these people home. If not, I'll slap you in handcuffs and lock you in a cell so fast you won't have time to play the martyr for the cameras. Sure, your lawyers will get you released. In the meantime think of what can happen. You know how rumors get started…"

While Harry spoke to Samuels, the authorities gained the advantage, quelling the riot, and handcuffing gang members as well as a few of the preacher's flock. Others withdrew, not wanting to be arrested.

Harry backed away and stepped off the podium. He walked back across the street with Campisi. Samuels stuttered and stammered through a weak recovery and urged the remaining masses to stay vigilant and pray.

"You handled yourself well out there," Harry said. Campisi's face creased in concern. "What's up? Listen, I wouldn't worry too much about Samuels. He's a blowhard. I just threatened him with, um, exposure on some minor, uh, infidelities."

"You have proof?"

"He doesn't know I didn't, but I must have hit the mark. The truth in his slimy eyes gave him away. They don't call him Tits and Ass for nothing."

Campisi nodded. "My concern is not for his lack of morals."

"Well?"

"The sun is setting. I hope his congregation breaks up soon or he may have fewer followers in his pews come Sunday. Even so, going home may not be safe either."

"I don't understand."

Campisi stopped short. "While most of the attacks have been outside, Mr. Leahy was killed inside an abandoned building. The elderly couple was murdered inside the hospital." She paused. "As you said, Harry, shadows are everywhere."

They gazed at the sun, now hidden behind a growing bank of clouds.

•   •   •

Misty still lay in a coma. The doctors had patched her deepest wounds and salved and wrapped her other injuries. Her IVs fed her a slow but steady drip of antibiotics and nutrients.

Harry paced the floor, munching on his lean-fixings sandwich purchased out of the hospital vending machine, and questioned the nurse in charge of the intensive care unit.

After three hours his feet ached, the sandwich lay half-eaten in the trash, and the nurse assured him more than once the staff was doing everything possible.

Several friends and fellow officers had stopped by to visit and extend sympathy and support, but their words offered only a temporary distraction.

He sat next to Misty's bed and skimmed through a magazine, every five seconds looking over at her blank face, her closed eyes. Every third breath coincided with the next drop of amber-colored fluid in the IV tube.

He'd called his parents, who were enjoying a three-week cruise in the Caribbean. They hadn't yet returned to the ship after a day's excursion on Antigua, and he ended up leaving a message.

The second call proved much more difficult.

His happiness with Misty was marred by one—well, two—people: her parents. Roger and Barbara Stokes raised sheep in the rugged wilderness of Wyoming. Ranchers to the core, they understood their daughter's desire to attend the wonderful agricultural university of Iowa State, but not her choice of major. What did design and advertising have to do with herding sheep?

They weren't in favor of her choice of boyfriends either, including the local hayseed who'd decided on criminology and law enforcement in his junior year. Marriage to a cop caused more than minor disgruntlement. Cops meant guns and lonely women waiting to become widows.

Holidays at the Stokes' ranch were strained affairs with Misty playing peacekeeper. The Stokes' rare visits to the big bad city lasted, at most, a weekend, and they didn't care to see the local attractions. The time they came for the State Fair was filled with tension. No corn dogs, no edible something on a stick, no concerts, no sky glider, just uninteresting visits to the livestock barns. All in all, a wasted day in Harry's opinion.

The previous evening, Harry and Misty had held each other, laughed and cried, and talked late into the night. They'd almost forgotten to call their parents to announce the good news about her pregnancy. Not twenty-four hours later, Harry related a tragedy.

Both Stokes had seen news reports about the rash of murders in Des Moines. Even Harry's strained, hoarse voice and choked-back tears couldn't dispel the anger from Roger Stokes. Misty's father put the attack on his daughter squarely on Harry's shoulders. When he told Roger about the loss of the baby, the silence on the line portended menace. Stokes' voice came back, at last, low and full of hate.

"You damn son-of-a-bitch," he said. A thunk indicated he'd dropped the phone. Barbara retrieved it, and although she could be as objectionable to Harry as her husband, she was the lesser of two evils.

Now, mid-evening, Harry remembered the gist of the phone call. The Stokes planned to be on the next flight out of Wyoming, didn't want Harry to pay for airfare, or even pick them up at the airport. He told them the hospital and room number. The attitude was the shouldn't be around when they arrived.

Aw, to hell with them. Misty was their daughter, but also his wife. He had as much right to be with her as they did.

Except he had to get away for a while. The hospital made him cramped and restless. Misty's condition hadn't changed in the time he'd been there. In the doctor's opinion, it wouldn't improve for the foreseeable future. Harry loved his wife, but he needed to clear his mind, take a break.

At Grand, he turned west, admiring the office buildings and other businesses along the avenue. Downtown still fascinated him, even after all these years. He loved taking Grand to Seventeenth, then looping around to take Locust east toward the capitol building. After, he would take the shorter streets of Walnut and Cherry. Sometimes, he'd take the numbered streets north, then south, and back again just to look at the old buildings, the new shops, and the people. He loved Des Moines. Big enough to have a few traffic jams, small enough it didn't take forever to cross downtown end to end.

His thoughts drifted to Campisi and shadows. They'd both said it: shadows were everywhere. He couldn't think of a safe place. The sidewalks, offices—hell, even the gloominess inside his car—anywhere could come alive with a shadowy creature, couldn't it?

Damn! It made his heart beat faster and brought a nervous tingle to the back of his neck.

Harry's head jerked right when figures disappeared behind a corner nightclub on Fifteenth Street. The Gaslight bar hosted both local and national blues bands. The place was a decent venue for those who enjoyed that style of music.

Harry wasn't interested in a slow saxophone, though. This shadow business would have him jumping at every dark patch soon enough. What with Campisi guessing these creatures crossed over from some other dimension, well...did he just see one, maybe two?

He pulled over and parked at the curb near the main entrance to the nightclub and flicked on his flashers. He grabbed his weapon and a flashlight from the glove compartment and exited the car.

The Gaslight occupied the ground floor, with apartments above. A flight of steel steps attached to the rear of the building ascended four stories. Nightclub patrons parked along the street, but the tenants used a gravel lot at the rear.

He eased around the eastern side of the building and, with the weapon pointed at the ground, inched his way to the rear corner where the shadows disappeared. What would he do if they returned? Shoot? Would bullets kill a shadow? He stopped when voices drifted around the corner of the building.

"Come on, already! You got the cash or not?"

"Yeah, yeah, give me a sec. Let's see the rock, man."

"Cash first, asshole."

Damn it. This wasn't a shadow creature ready to jump out at an unsuspecting passerby, but just two punks dealing crack.

Harry wasn't foolish enough to take on two human unknowns in the dusky light. He ran back to the car and radioed for backup, then retrieved an extra set of handcuffs. He'd wait until the pair behind the club waltzed out into the open where he'd have more room to keep them covered.

He had just replaced the radio unit when an all too horrified and pain-filled shriek filled the air, followed by an expletive cut off mid-swear. Harry sprinted for the rear of the building, flashlight and gun at the ready. At the corner, he tripped on an eroded portion of concrete. He hit the ground hard, uttering a few choice words himself.

He rose to a crouch, gun pointed at the darkness. No sounds came from behind the blues club. The screaming had stopped.

"Police!" He eased his head around the corner for a quick look. Oh shit! Nothing but shadows, and he couldn't be sure, but had some been moving. "This is the police. Lie on the ground, arms spread. Do it now!"

No reply.

Someone might be injured, but Harry had to think of his safety first. He didn't know who, or what might be waiting. He aimed the flashlight and gun and eased around the corner.

Half a second before he came upon the two dead drug dealers, there was a quick movement of...what? Had those been red eyes winking out as his flashlight illuminated the grisly tableau?

•   •   •

No more! Please, no more!

More death. More pain. More blood.

Something laughed deep in her soul. The shadows? Or her mind going insane?

•   •   •

Lights blazed in Lori Campisi's hotel room. Not just the lamp next to the bed, the standing lamp by the recliner, the two over the desk, and the series of round bulbs in the bathroom—but also several lanterns Lori had purchased before returning to the hotel. These she'd positioned around the room to negate any shadowy corners, obliterating the gray in the desk's knee hole and near the door. The one place not completely lit was beneath the bed, but enough light shone she didn't think there would be any danger.

Lori had changed into sweats. She sat cross-legged on the bed, picking at the last of a tuna fish sandwich.

After dealing with Reverend Samuels and the mob and finishing some paperwork at headquarters, Harry headed back to the hospital while Lori sought the nearest hardware store. She hoped to spend most of the night conducting more shadow research. She and Harry hadn't had a serious discussion about the situation other than at lunch.

His reaction to her broaching the subject had been what she'd expected. With the attack on Misty coming on the heels of their initial discussion, followed by the incident at the hospital, and then the egotistical reverend, there hadn't been time to pursue the matter.

Besides, if Harry decided the shadows were an outrageous idea, she couldn't imagine what his reaction would be regarding the Sarmangous.

The Book of Sarmangous.

Did the fabled grimoire exist somewhere in this vast world, under the care and protection of a Guardian? If so, where? How close might it be? Within the Des Moines city limits?

More likely buried in some forgotten, foul-smelling dungeon or hidden in the deepest darkest jungles of Africa or South America.

However, if the book still remained undiscovered by seekers, what explanation for the shadows in the Iowa capital? As far as she knew, the Sarmangous and the spells contained within were the only ways to call forth shadow killers.

The exception, as she had mentioned to Harry, had been in Australia. In that case, the form the shadows took differed from the current situation, even if the casualties and fatalities were no less tragic.

A tribal chief, driven insane through isolation, heat, and narcotics, had used all but forgotten magic to call forth vengeful creatures of shadowy substance. The native chief wanted the dark spirits to avenge the wrongs the white man had inflicted on the Aboriginal inhabitants since the Botany Bay settlement.

Lori, dispatched to deal with the problem, hadn't taken time to examine the bodies or discuss matters with the local authorities. Instead, she'd used Hound and his computer expertise and hired a local tracker to hunt down the chief. With cold, unemotional prowess, she ended the horror with one bullet. The shadows' essence, linked to the man's life force, had dissipated with his death.

She didn't think the solution to this case would be so easy if the Sarmangous was involved.

She opened her laptop and, after a few clicks, connected to her database. The information was both plentiful and sparse. Many references, but few with substantive value.

Rumored had it caused Caligula's madness.

A soldier reported one of the Knights Templar cached it away during the Second Crusade.

A fellow conquistador of Pizarro wrote in his journal about a strange book mentioned by an Incan priest.

These, and many other references, read like fabrications, enhanced tales of daring, plunder, and discovery. Despite their number, despite the apparent lack of knowledge of previous tales, each took on an air of legend.

Other longer and descriptive accounts were more plausible. They were written by associates of the individuals who had searched for the Sarmangous. Personal journals and reports stopped without an ending to their journey. Either they died along the way or possessed the book and the consequences were too horrible to document.

Power was the great aphrodisiac and using magic to gain it were always the causes of downfall and death, a selling of the soul that in the end backfired.

However, if she believed the reports, a few death spells appeared to have worked.

Entire villages in Africa wiped out overnight and a power monger in control of nothing but the dead.

An instant accumulation of gold to buy a Chinese township.

Lori was not so green as to accept every account as fact. She, like Harry, stayed skeptical about certain paranormal or extraterrestrial subjects. A doubting mind came with the territory. Unidentified Flying Objects, for example. She just couldn't grasp the concept.

Although many her cases involved supernatural beings such as ghosts, goblins, and the like, she'd spent some time researching and discussing alien encounters with Hound. How many hundreds of reported sightings had she read, how many scores of photos had she studied?

She'd come to a general conclusion that, although she couldn't explain all of them, there was a definite lack of worthwhile detail—similar to the Sarmangous accounts.

"It had these flashing lights. It hovered for a moment and then flew away."

Triangular, cylindrical, and time-honored saucer shapes were the common details reported. In fact, as far as she could determine, the observers' accounts related more to extraneous matters than the actual "craft."

At least the shadow creature stories offered variety. She and Harry had discussed the topic of shadow creatures before his wife's attack, but so much more information existed. She'd mentioned most "shadows" seen or glimpsed exhibited a non-threatening attitude, sometimes even comfort. A wife saw the form of her husband who had died in previous days—not a ghost, but just a vague shape before it faded away. Most shadows just watched the subject for a brief time before disappearing.

The difference with the Des Moines area shadows was their disposition. The instances she'd mentioned to Harry regarding the burning sensation or injury when a shadow touched someone numbered in the single digits. Certainly nothing on the scale of the merciless slaughter of the past week.

Thoughts of the Sarmangous brought to mind such a high level of violence...and evil.

Since joining the FBI, she'd encountered a multitude of evils. Merciless mob bosses, sleazy drug runners, serial killers, and worse. When she accepted the assignments under Jacob Pepperdine, she came up against other forms of evil. The results of those cases, save for a few outstanding moments that included her first case when she investigated a haunted house, were resolutions that satisfied everyone.

Although she wasn't comfortable with the paranormal, she have a familiarity with it. Said familiarity also scared her. Because of the amnesia, how close to it was she before the age of twelve.

When she read the report of the attacks in Des Moines, she'd wondered about a possible Sarmangous connection almost as soon as Hound had. The damned book popping up, even in passing, brought a tingle to her senses.

Had she heard someone mention the book in her past? Had she seen the Sarmangous or a drawing of it?

White chalk drawings or pictograms on rocks flashed in her mind.

She fell back onto the bed, eyes shut tight.

Mountains.

A voice mentioning some people called the Mogollon. More darkness. A shocking pain.

Then, the inevitable wall.

This time not quite so solid, so unyielding.

The words of the wizened psychic returned. *"There will come a time when the cause of your affliction is near. You will feel a connection, a link, and the wall will begin to crumble. At this time, you must also have the fortitude to endure the pain and suffering you shall experience."*

The pain receded. She sat up and rubbed her eyes.

Her struggle to break through the memory wall had intensified as of late, occurring more often. How close was she to the source of her amnesia? Or worse, the Sarmangous?

She had to deal with a cynical skeptic ready to lash out at her suggestions and the possibility of encountering the ancient grimoire.

An icon on her screen blinked, announcing a request for conversation from Hundt. A click of the mouse and a window with Hound's image opened.

"Hey, you sweet Fox." The little man perched on the raised swivel chair.

"Yes, Hound," she said without inflection. She'd learned not to react to his overt flirtation even though she had acquiesced to calling him by his amusing nickname.

He leaned toward the monitor screen. Wide-eyed, he said, "It's so bright there I gotta wear shades."

"What do you have for me?"

"I'm still sniffing out the clues." Hound's face loomed too close to the camera. "Sure happy to hear from you."

A certain ominous tone laced her contact's words.

"Why?"

"You are in some serious shit out there, baby. I would hightail your pretty butt outta there ASAP if I were you."

"Cut the flowery language and tell me what you have."

"Very little, but big."

"Just make your report," Campisi ordered, exasperated after the long day.

"As you know, some of the documents, journals, and papers I'm looking for are extremely rare."

"Please, just tell me what you have."

"You're not going to like it."

"Stop stalling," she ordered.

"Well, we've discussed it before." He hesitated a moment. "The Book of Sarmangous."

"Hound..."

"I know you're on the fence about its existence, despite various references throughout history to the contrary. You may change your mind after reading what I sent to your email."

Why couldn't he tell me this first?

"Give me a minute," she said.

She tapped several keys and clicked on a few links to access her private email. Hound referenced various sources, most relating to the Book of Sarmangous, sometimes known just as the Sarmangous. She'd viewed some of these before. The one he'd highlighted originated from a twelfth-century Turkish scribe. The writing, she deduced, was part of an entry from a personal journal, told of his master's acquaintance with a wizard who—

"—*With strange utterances loosed the shadows, and they wreaked havoc,*" the translation read. "*And with more words from the ancient tome he sought control over them, but they would not obey. There is death in the shadows and nowhere to flee...*"

Most of the page had deteriorated, the rest of the entry obliterated.

Campisi stared past the computer screen, not seeing the walls of the hotel room as she considered the words she'd just read.

More vague references, obscure words. A scribe and his master and the master's friend? A few score of those ran around eight hundred years ago. The same number of spell books then as now, most stupid and more a novelty, but others...

The scribe's journal entry contained a connection with her current assignment.

Death in the shadows.

She remembered the still-open window with Hound and clicked back to it. "Did you find anything further? Did the scribe describe if anyone stopped the shadows and how?"

"That would be too easy, baby. They'd write it down in the supernatural solutions manual, wouldn't it?"

"Okay, thanks for your efforts."

"What do you think, Fox?" Hound stared through the camera at her. "Does it exist? Has someone tapped into its secrets?"

She hesitated before answering. "I don't know, but I won't rule it out."

CHAPTER 14

Friday night
8:53 p.m.

Burrows hated hunger, hated scurrying through his kitchen liked a starved rat. He wanted to be in the basement with the woman and the book. The time approached when everything he wanted would be his. No longer would the power residing within him dictate his every decision. He would use the power for his every want and desire.

The pangs protesting the lack of food gnawed at his stomach. Annoying intrusions affecting his concentration and focus. Out of macaroni and cheese, and with no time to prepare it anyway, he scrounged through cabinets. He shoved handfuls of stale crackers and dry cereal from mouse-chewed boxes into his mouth. He scraped the sugar-encrusted bottom of a honey jar. From the refrigerator, he grabbed a couple of eggs—purchased when?—and swallowed them raw, followed by the sharp alcohol sting of the last cup of fermented orange juice.

He opened another cabinet, where he remembered a package of cookies, and instead…

His hasty movements ceased and with shaky hands, he removed the faded four-by-six-inch notebook. He hadn't seen it for years and didn't remember when or why he placed it in the cabinet on the top shelf. Fingers trembled as he opened the cover and perused the pages, remembering each entry, replaying each scene in his mind. So many years, so many miles. A long-forgotten name—his own—popped back into his mind. He returned to the first entry and remembered another journal and the beginning of his descent into madness.

•   •   •

The Gutach River, near Freiburg, Germany
33 years earlier

Peter Monaco had never seen anything so beautiful. He stood at the guardrail over the Gutach River cascading down seven rocky steps, over 160 meters, to the mist-enshrouded bottom. The majestic awe, the rush of noise. Only Niagara Falls outclassed it.

Behind him were a parking area and a quaint little gift shop where his wife, Kris, shopped for trinkets or another unique clock. Heaven knew they'd seen enough clocks during this trip. A collector of clocks and watches, Kris had insisted they visit every shop during their vacation. Meanwhile, Peter enjoyed the scenery, the people, the jagged saw-tooth mountains, and the thick old trees in this area of the Black Forest.

They planned this trip months ago. Peter, a financial investor at a regional bank in St. Louis, and Kris, assistant manager for a local branch of a large grocery chain, had dreamed of a European vacation since their first week of marriage. Years of hard work, saving, and avoiding credit cards and other debt, paid off with promotions, raises, and accrued vacation time.

The vacation had been extra special because a week before their departure date Kris broke the news of an addition to the family due in just under nine months. They almost canceled the trip, but after some budgeting, decided they could afford the vacation and still be financially stable when the baby arrived.

Germany and France. The Rhine and the Seine. Baden-Baden, Paris, and many points in between. They planned for three weeks, and after receiving the doctor's approval, boarded the plane.

Only a week into the trip, Peter could not get enough.

He loved the culture, the museums, the mountain trails, the magic of it all. They arrived near the end of the carnival season and the awe-inspiring parades and celebrations. Peter enjoyed the costumes representing the German myths of witches and gnomes of the woods. He felt the oldness of the people and places trying to hold on to centuries past.

He leaned back against the rail separating the viewing platform from the rushing waters. February in the Black Forest was cool, with lots of sunshine. Where should they go next? Maybe Furstenberg Castle, east of Feldberg, maybe another hike...unless the walking would tire Kris. Despite being a few weeks along, her hormones and metabolism had changed. She'd been eager to see as much as possible, yet careful not to over-stress herself.

Late afternoon arrived and Peter stood alone on the platform. Other tourists made a last visit to the gift shop while Peter contemplated on what he and Kris would have for dinner tonight. Maybe something wild, like bear or fresh trout, with warm pumpernickel, and always, always, couldn't eat too much Black Forest cake with all the cream and chocolate.

Peter always had a yen for travel. He'd always felt as if something was missing in his life. A great job, a beautiful wife, a house, a car, friends. What else could a man ask for in life? *Something* else, but he couldn't be more precise.

For years an emptiness, a hole in his life he couldn't explain, affected his daily behavior. He once tried discussing the matter with Kris, but couldn't find the correct words and the conversation ended with her confused and worrying about his mental faculties. No, he didn't want a divorce, and he wasn't seeing a younger woman.

Early midlife crisis, she'd called it. She was wrong. He called it wanderlust, a calling to a place or a state of existence as yet unknown. Something more had to be gotten out of life beyond money and love and material gains.

He hoped to discover a clue to filling the void on this trip.

A sudden movement caught Peter's eye. A figure stumbled from the trees line across the road. Peter reeled when he recognized the lurching and bedraggled creature was a man. Torn, dirty clothes impeded his progress. He tripped, fell, rolled over the blacktop, and righting himself in the small ditch on the near side.

Who is this person? Monaco thought. What is he doing? Why is he heading for me?

The pathetic figure spit out of the thick vegetation reached out to Peter, imploring, desperate, yet kept looking behind him at the trees as if afraid.

Something chasing him? A wild animal?

Peter froze in indecision. As the man staggered closer, Peter spied something square and brown under the other's left arm. Over the white noise of the river, the man's cough and strangled cry reeked of desperation and terror.

The man tried to utter words, but nothing escaped except a gurgle, a choked whimper.

The ragged stranger fell into Peter's arms. For such a small, hunched stature, he had surprising bulk and weight. Peter almost fell himself, but at the last second heaved the man upright.

"What's happened? Who are you?"

A talon-like hand clawed Peter's jacket. The other hand removed the object, not lost throughout the entire ordeal, and slammed it against Peter's chest.

"T–take it," came the strained whisper. "Hide it."

"What?"

"Don't let them have it." The strangled voice faded to a whisper but became more frantic. "Don't let them see you with it."

"I don't understand," Peter cried. "What's happened? Who are you talking about? Is someone after you?"

Again, the man pushed the object, a small notebook or journal, into Peter's hands. "Hide it! Please."

Keeping the poor creature from collapsing, Peter took the man's offering and tucked it into an inside jacket pocket.

"Now, let's get you some help." Peter tried to lead the stranger toward the gift shop.

Instead, the man lurched away and stepped toward the railing. Peter's eyes widened at the man's intentions.

"No! Wait!"

He moved too late. The stranger took one last look at the woods, stared at Peter, and in a flat voice, stated, "I'm already dead."

Before Peter could reach him, he toppled over the railing, rolled off the small bluff, smashed into the first rocky step, splashed into the water, and disappeared as the Gutach River claimed the body for its own.

Peter stifled his lingering cry stifled when he turned away, sickened, and his gaze landed on three cloaked figures emerging from the woods. They stopped before they came into full light, choosing to remain in the shadows. Although hoods hid their face, a deep chill ran through him. Their attention focused on him. He glanced over the railing, then back at the woods. As if realizing the demise of their quarry, the trio disappeared into the dark without a sound, dissolving to nothing in the camouflage.

One week later, Peter Monaco sat at the kitchen table of his St. Louis home, alone. His wife, Kris, lay up in their bed, asleep...again.

They had cut short their European trip not because of the death of the strange man and the brief appearance of his mysterious pursuers, although the incident dampened the overall enjoyment. The authorities detained Peter, for an unnecessary length of time in his opinion. The man's body could not be recovered and, after an intensive search of the nearby forest, the case went cold since no identification existed. For some reason—fear, curiosity, maybe a twisted sense of obligation because of the man's fate—Peter had chosen not to reveal the existence of the object, a journal of sorts, to the police or anyone else. He kept it hidden, not daring to examine it unless alone, indoors, with little chance of interruption.

Kris' pregnancy, combined with the adventure of travel, had drained her of energy and stamina. Nausea, dizzy spells, and her inability to keep food in her stomach forced the abrupt return to the States. The doctor said she needed rest and quiet, to stabilize her health.

The little notebook wasn't a journal in the strictest sense. The first time Peter skimmed through the dogeared pages, he couldn't comprehend anything. Strange words, unknown dates and locations, alien phrases, vague references, weird drawings, and unrecognizable symbols filled many pages.

Others related quotes and passages from unnamed people and a multitude of sources of research material.

After further, more intense, examinations, Peter estimated the man wrote his first entry between fifteen and twenty years before his tragic plunge into the Gutach River cascades. Peter counted over a dozen countries to which the man had traveled. Remote locations, abandoned castles, unmapped caverns, ancient ruins.

All in a quest for an ancient mystical book that promised riches, treasure, and power to whoever read certain passages. Many of the entries questioned the existence of the book since many references were second and third hand. After many years of searching, the writer wondered about his sanity and inability to cease his journey.

One of the concerns he had was the ever-present fear of capture by an unknown trio of beings, or supernatural creatures, referred to as the Triune. This roving group either also wanted the book, or sought to kill any others who did.

Peter read an entry describing how the Triune disposed of someone considered an enemy.

"And I overheard the man inquire to the market seller about a certain necklace shaped unlike any jeweler's product—fashioned with weird, alien symbols, maybe originating from a race of men long ago deceased. The necklace may be a talisman used as part of the morbid and forbidden spells listed in the Book of Sarmangous."

And further on:

"I followed the man, who dressed in shabby clothes to appear inconspicuous to the other poorly dressed residents of this filthy city. From years of instinct, I maintained a fair distance. I consider myself

fortunate, for as he passed the mouth of a narrow alley, shadowy hands grabbed him and pulled him into the gloomy passage. I crept along on the other side of the street and hid in the darkness of the opposite alley. Not twenty yards from me, two hooded figures held the man against the side of the building, their grip so solid the poor man could offer only scant resistance. A third individual withdrew a wicked blade and, without hesitation, gutted the man from groin to gullet. Screams issued forth, echoing for blocks, but the few passersby acted as though deaf.

"These merciless beings, be they men or demons, possessed a supernatural aura. They could strike without warning and without fear of reprisal from any authority, for one of the persons who passed by the alley's entrance wore the uniform of the local police. He neither attempted to rescue the tortured soul nor even acknowledged anything out of the ordinary. I had been warned of this group, the Triune, and I scurried away before their murderous, soulless eyes fell upon me."

Within days of reading the final entry in the notebook, Peter understood the quest of the doomed man was what he, Peter, had been looking for. This Sarmangous could fill the void in his life, give his existence completeness. Using the notebook as a guide, he started his own journal. His quest for the Book of Sarmangous was underway.

Despite the vow never to fall into the insanity of his predecessor, his life soon underwent drastic, irreversible changes. Within mere months his morality, ethics, and adherence to man's laws, all disappeared.

He embezzled money from the bank, stole from his friends, and even pulled off a few successful armed robberies, all to fund his travels. He neglected and ignored his home, his wife, and the forthcoming baby. On the day his daughter entered the world, he was lost in some cold, isolated, and foreign land.

When not traveling, he scoured libraries and museums to borrow or steal rare books and manuscripts. He risked prison or worse by raiding private collections.

The obsessive quest became the sole purpose of his life.

He granted Kris the easiest divorce in history and wasn't around to demand or deny anything. She and the girl moved out of state.

Peter's pursuit of the elusive grimoire paralleled, then exceeded, anything the other man accomplished. What sights, and sites, he encountered; the dangers he faced. In time, he lost all sense of right and wrong, obtaining information by whatever means feasible, covering his tracks, and moving on. He eluded the authorities, sometimes resorting to murdering government officials. He sank to the lowest depravity, changing identities countless times, even losing his sanity for periods of time, yet knowing he would one day rise above it all, above everything.

The Book of Sarmangous.

After hearing about the sudden death of his ex-wife in an automobile accident, the tiniest bit of humanity cried out from beneath the filth of his existence. He assumed custody of his daughter, and—for two years—tried to hold on to something from his past, to maintain the semblance of a family.

However, rather than settling down and caring for her education and development—instead of trying to create a solid, loving relationship—Peter hauled the girl along on his ventures. He didn't know why he wouldn't leave her in the care of the state or at a foster home. His and Kris' families were all dead, so maybe he just couldn't quite let go. He hired paid sitters, some not noted for their trustworthiness, when he visited places not fit for most adults, let alone a child. Other times, he had no choice but to leave her by herself. She received her schooling piecemeal from various sources, including nuns, nurses, tutors, and even some deluded sense of education from Peter himself.

His obsession was always present and so controlling, so pervasive, he stepped over the line once too often. After the horror in New Mexico, Peter's familial responsibility and his journal-writing both come to an abrupt end.

•   •   •

Present day

He finished the last entry and the memory of the attack in the cave by an unknown creature haunted him, choked off his air. The harm to his daughter. He agonized for hours before making a final, fateful decision to separate father and daughter forever.

The same question came to mind that did over a week ago in Mexico City.

Whatever happened to her?

His eyes darted to the clock.

No time. Out of time.

He dropped the journal on the counter, memories of his daughter swept away. Wiping sweat from his face, he descended to the basement. The woman lay bound on the floor, prepared according to precise directions. The correct number of candles flickered at her head and feet. After cutting a gash into each of her calf muscles, he used the flowing blood to paint a pattern of weird alien symbols on her forehead, stomach, and on each wall in the basement. Flames danced as if responding to the silent crash of instruments in an unseen symphony— as if they, too, anticipated the next step in the ritual.

As it had five nights ago, the Book of Sarmangous rested upon the stand, opened to the relevant page. Next to the book, point glinting sharp, a ceremonial knife. Everything was as it should be.

Peter Monaco, his heart beating hard enough to cause a slight ache in his chest, stepped up to the dais. This was the moment—his time. The force within him drove him, guided him, but he relished the certainty that once he offered the sacrifice, he would be in control, having the power to rule over the shadow creatures he had unleashed upon an unsuspecting world. No one would oppose him. He would be a king. No, even greater—a god.

The shadows gathered and red eyes stared unblinking at him and the woman. The shadows flowed and ebbed as if vying for space. They awaited the next phase.

He checked the woman one last time. She was beyond terror. Her eyes had gone dead, the stare vacant, her fragile mind unable to accept the reality around her. No matter, her mental acuity need not be intact. A sacrifice was a sacrifice.

Back at the Sarmangous, he lifted the knife and held it aloft, presenting it to the shadows. With a hoarse, yet reverent and commanding voice, he spoke the first few lines of the ritual. The words originated from a time all but forgotten by mankind, their syntax a jumble of undecipherable sounds and strange phrases. As his voice rose and fell with the litany, the shadows thickened, darkened, and flowed toward the woman. Monaco also moved in a prescribed pattern across the floor tracing strange angled patterns in the air with the knife.

A discordant accretion of noise filled the basement. His voice, the swish of the knife, the scuttle and crackle of the caliginous shadows, the woman's cry of confused horror.

Shadows. Knife.

Sarmangous. *Power!*

A cold rush of energy surged through him. Starting at his feet, up through his legs, and to his midsection. As it flowed up into his chest, it transformed into warmth, then heat, then burning. Too late Monaco realized something was wrong. The inner fire consumed him, sizzling nerves, seizing musculature control. With a scorching throat, he cried out. "No, this cannot be!"

The truth slammed into him, all too abominable. The invader of his soul showed itself to be a trickster, never intending to relinquish power to the human. Monaco could not reverse the spell. Words uttered, the spell was complete.

His body stiffened. The knife fell unused to the floor.

While his inner being raged with an unquenchable fire, his mind raced, seeking an alternative to the spell. There must be a way! He'd striven too hard, too long to be denied.

Denied he was, for as the shadows advanced upon the woman, they also reached for him, surrounded him, engulfed him. The ritual was not a way to gain power. Instead, those ancient words and almost unpronounceable alien phrases released more power to the shadow beings. When Monaco died, his being, his essence, his spirit would transfer to another dimension to be stripped, tortured, mutilated, and devoured over and over for all eternity.

Screams filled the basement, now a chamber of horrors, and the shadows feasted.

•   •   •

Deep within the coma, the pain impacted her with pure white-hot agony. Her mind disintegrated, shredded, and fell to pieces. Incoherent thoughts coalesced, intermingled, floated off into the ether.

Nothing remained. Even the continued fiery torture was dulled. The laughter was her own. It reveled in the shattering of her soul as it waited for new victims.

Waited for more death.

CHAPTER 15

"Well, Cheryl, I like the direction of your story," Audrey Daston commented. "The action is riveting, and you keep us involved. This chapter you read tonight slowed in one place, but not so much we're bored."

"Just a minor pause to let the reader breathe before getting right back into things," Cheryl Kubert responded.

"I think you need to keep it," Alice added.

Audrey listened to the others critique Cheryl's novel in progress. A glance at her watch reminded her to wrap up the meeting for the night.

She smiled and congratulated herself on the success of the writing group, with the endearing name Shades of Ink. This group sure beat some others she'd been involved with over the years.

Once upon a time, she'd attended weekly meetings of writers, writer wannabes, and writer never-should-bes. Open to the public, attendance varied with people drifting in and out. Soon the group developed a core of regulars and a few newbies every other week who either stayed for a few meetings or stopped coming after their first time. Audrey learned a lot from those critiques and the different styles of writers.

Over time, the flavor of the group metamorphosed. Gone were the two hours of serious reading and discussion, positive critique, and gentle support. Social chit-chat ate into the time. Fewer people even bothered to keep up with their writing and presentations to the group, but always offered, if not a disapproving critique, less than substantive comments.

Audrey, soon bored and unfulfilled, decided to take action. She discussed with a few dedicated writers the idea of forming a more focused group, one where the members concentrated on the goal to be published one day—the goal of every serious writer—and offered beneficial suggestions toward that goal.

Hence, Shades of Ink.

The group started with five charter members and, by invitation, had increased to a comfortable eight. By accident, but appropriate for the group's name, each writer worked on manuscripts from a different genre. Mystery, romance, western, science fiction, biography, horror, young adult, and historical. Also by accident, gender make up ran seven to one with Jason Strately—science fiction—referred to with affection as the "token male."

Audrey, with the help of the others, developed simple rules for the group. A majority read aloud one week, with the others reading the following week. The system helped those who struggled with writer's block or were developing an outline, character creation, or repairing plot holes. Everyone offered a concise, impersonal critique of the selections, either as it related to the novel or to the current chapter.

The group discussed attending several writers' conferences around the Midwest, and Fran Gerard—romance—working on her second book, already had an agent reply favorably to her first submitted manuscript.

After the last person commented on Cheryl's story, Audrey ended the meeting. The Urbandale Public Library closed at eight, but Deanna Brooks, who wrote Young Adult and worked circulation at the library, had made a deal with the director to allow Shades to meet until "No later than 8:45." However, if they ran longer, such as tonight, no one quibbled.

While everyone gathered notebooks, powered off laptops, and checked cell phone messages, Audrey excused herself to go to the restroom, accompanied by Miki Garcia—biography. They laughed as they walked to the back corner of the main room, joking how only two of them needed to visit the restroom tonight. Some weeks, Jason, poor man, sat alone.

The writers met in the central open space. To save energy, they extinguished all but a few of the library's lights. Tiers of bookshelves disappeared to either side in grayish-yellow gloom. Silence hummed in the air, save for the shuffling of footsteps and the muffled activity of members preparing to leave.

Miki checked her make-up in the mirror by the sinks. When Audrey exited a stall to wash her hands, Miki commented, "I'm so into your mystery, Audrey. You've got the chauvinistic bastard of a bad guy down pretty solid."

"Profiling the character wasn't difficult," she replied. "I just modeled him after my last boyfriend."

"It was cute the way Jason squirmed when we all started trashing men."

Audrey laughed. "He's a dear, though." She smiled at Miki by way of her reflection in the mirror. "You should ask him out. I notice how he keeps sneaking glances at you."

"Well...yes, but if you want to know the truth..." Miki's voice dropped to a conspiratorial whisper. "I've been talking with Kristen—"

A scream echoed against the bathroom tiles, cutting off the rest of her sentence.

Audrey was one step ahead of Miki out of the women's restroom door. By the time she'd run half an aisle, more shrieks and curses filled the library.

"What's happened?" Audrey cried.

A short-lived yelp sounded behind her. She whipped around to see Miki's legs disappear around the end of a set of shelves. Audrey ran to rescue Miki but halted when a gray amorphous form rose in front of her.

She screamed herself and bolted back up the aisle toward the exit. In her frantic headlong flight, she tripped over a bloody form.

Jason's corpse lay mutilated, strips of flesh peeled away from his abdomen, and chunks missing from his legs. Blood flowed from countless wounds.

The other writers of Shades of Ink and the lone library attendant waiting to lock up fought a Punch and Judy battle gone ballistic. Gray silhouettes, somehow solid enough to attack, fought over bodies like dogs with chunks of steak. Red-eyed shadows rendered their victims to bloody scraps of clothing and skin. Blood arced in spatters, as amorphous gray claws gouged soft parts. To on Audrey's left, Cheryl jerked as if from an electric stimulus, her scream gurgling to silence as the shadows gashed her throat to bloody destruction.

Audrey stumbled, fell again, and crawled toward the front of the library, hands and legs slick with carnage. She shrieked as one of the creatures hissed close behind her. At the glass double doors, her blood-soaked hands fumbled with the release bar. The raspy crunching sounds grew nearer every second.

She clanked the bar, pushed open the door, and dashed outside...where more shadows engulfed her before she reached the bright glare of the lit parking lot.

•   •   •

Joe Konopski was tired.

His usual eight hours became an all-day shift with an occasional temporary relief for bathroom breaks, greasy, fat-saturated meals, and he still had a half-hour's drive home from Altoona to Waukee. He kept reminding himself, however, of the overtime compensation.

Most days, he didn't mind the monotony of the job. He enjoyed the noise and bustle of the crowd and the clatter and mock screams on other rides at Adventureland Amusement Park. He always shared a smile and laughter with the customers, keeping them entertained with jokes and stories so they wouldn't get bored waiting in line. After all, the people paid his salary and if they didn't enjoy their visit, they wouldn't return.

Several people returned to Joe's ride throughout the day. He remembered a few faces of those who made second or third-round trips. His amusement ride didn't pack the thrills of the roller coasters, but he tried to make the experience the best.

Joe operated Pirate's Glory, a gigantic contraption designed to resemble a sea-going pirate vessel. Individual seats fitted with pull-down locking harnesses filled the inner chamber, one half facing the other. After he pushed the start button, the ship swung back and forth until the bow or stern—the best seats—rose above the top of the swing bar. The downward motion caused riders' stomachs to flutter with the increased G-force.

Today, his relief operator had called in sick, so Joe agreed to man the mainsail the entire day.

Closing time drew near. The glare of the midway lights held total darkness at bay. When a voice over the park's public address system announced "Closing in ten minutes," Joe could begin shutting down.

After one more ride. Up the stairs trooped another group of eager and still energetic teenagers hoping for one last thrill. Waiting at the bottom, a couple of weary adult chaperons shifted stances, just as anxious as Joe to go home. He recognized a few of the kids from earlier. The disparate groups had coalesced into one large party, maybe on a prearranged schedule.

Joe winked at the adults, forced a smile, and greeted their laughing wards gaining the waiting platform. "One last ride, folks?"

They cheered and joked as he gestured with one arm. Teens in shorts and T-shirts scrambled for the ends of the boat. He turned to the waiting pair of adults at the bottom of the stairs and offered a silent "last chance" welcome motion. They waved exhausted "Thanks, but no thanks," so Joe hit a button, hydraulically lowering the harnesses. Another button fired up the gears to start the gigantic ship swinging.

The kids disappeared into the evening gray as they swung above the lights, delighted squeals from the girls and celebratory shouts from the boys erupting as the momentum played havoc with their internal balance. Stomachs swooped and blood rushed through arteries and veins in vain attempts to compensate for the unnatural sensation.

More screams in the night. Joe frowned at the concerned looks on the escorts' faces as they watched their charges arcing back and forth. A second later something splattered on Joe's face.

Some idiot spitting. Always one jack-off in every group.

He raised a hand to wipe away the offensive fluid and his fingers came away red.

His brain noted the changed nature of the screams. He whirled around as more red spattered all around him.

Gray shadows roiled over the pirate ship. Red-eyed devils ripped and pummeled the hapless, helpless teens pinned in their seats. Back and forth went the ship. Blood sprinkled like intermittent rain with each upswing. Sheer horror froze Joe from shutting off the ride.

The feasting of the shadows continued, and Joe didn't notice the one emerging from below his platform until it clamped onto his ankle and dragged him to the depths below Pirate's Glory.

•   •   •

The suburb of Windsor Heights covered approximately a mile and a half square. The boundaries comprised 63rd to 80th east to west while the freeway and Hickman respectively formed the northern and southern borders.

Officer Janet Quist's patrol took her out of her territory, but the neighboring departments didn't mind. She and other officers often assisted with accidents and any requested backup.

With the spate of recent murders, every officer in every metro department pulled extra hours, double shifts, sometimes not even bothering to go home, snatching a few restless hours' sleep at desks or on break-room tables.

Her radio squawked. "Polk County Dispatch to 218."

She clicked her handset. "218."

"Two car vehicular accident on Douglas and 86th. Can you respond?"

The location placed the incident in Urbandale, not too far away, but Quist couldn't believe she was the closest unit. The Urbandale patrols must be tied up somewhere.

"Affirmative," she answered.

At the next intersection, she took a left on 73rd Street, went all the way to Hickman, and up a long hill until she reached Northwest 86th. The metro's reasoning behind the naming of streets required the Rosetta Stone to be understood. Sometimes the numbering stayed consistent in the suburbs, but most times, not. For example, the long stretch of Northwest 86th in Urbandale changed to 22nd Street at the West Des Moines line.

The Perkins restaurant on the far corner sparked a memory. New Year's Eve, three years ago. Her boyfriend at the time had been away on a business trip over the Christmas holiday and returned to town three days shy of year's end. He had already decided on her presents, and they waited for her in the stores. By lottery, she chose the order in which he purchased them. They made an adventure out of the last day of December. However, when evening rolled around, he'd forgotten the number of people patronizing area restaurants. With no reservations, they had to settle for the Hickman Road Perkins. Later, he made up for the slight by taking her dancing at the Val-Air Ballroom. Afterward, at her place, they celebrated the start of the New Year with a bang. Well, two bangs, with lots of pre-game fun.

As Quist eased into the left lane, she wondered where Mitch had ended up. Not two weeks later, his company transferred him to the Pacific Northwest to be regional manager or some such title.

Oh, well, she soon met Randy, and boy—did he ever live up to his name...

What the hell?

She stomped on her brakes, ignoring the horn from a tail-gating car. Its driver swerved around her and roared on.

The parking lot of the Urbandale library was a vast sea of lit concrete. At this time of night, the library should have been closed.

A half dozen cars filled parking slots, and someone sprawled near the front door captured her attention. Even from fifty yards away, she recognized blood pooling on the pavement. She cranked the wheel hard into the entry drive. Her eyes cast about looking for any movement from a furtive suspect's departure or a beckoning witness. Nothing. She braked twenty yards from the body and exited her car.

She had heard descriptions of the recent murder victims. The scene in front of her was far worse than she'd imagined.

She edged back toward her unit, one hand clicking her shoulder-clipped radio, the other releasing the strap holding her weapon. As she opened the door, she caught a shifting of the darkness inside. Two red eyes peered with fiery malevolence from the passenger's foot well.

She slid the Springfield XD .45 caliber from her holster and backed away. The shadow advanced but retreated when it touched the glare of the parking lot lights. From the grayness of her car, it glared hungry hatred at her.

Quist's eyes darted to the corners of the lot, the doorway of the library, checking for any other signs of attack. No other movement or sound except cars passing on 86th, her sudden ragged breathing, and the shadow's soft raspy rustle, like faded static from her car radio.

When she looked back into her vehicle, the eyes had vanished. Where did it go? What was it?

She moved toward a brighter area of the parking lot, weapon still aimed at her open car door. The other hand, shaking from fear, clicked her shoulder radio.

"218 to Polk County Dispatch. Officer in need of assistance." She gave her location, situation, and requested an ambulance. "They damn well better hurry!"

•   •   •

From the outside, the Polekat Klub didn't look very impressive. A single-story building, white clapboard, no windows, with a cracked, uneven blacktop parking lot. A red neon pole on the roof and its accompanying neon cat dancer provided sleazy glitz to the place.

David drove his battered Vega into the lot, jounced through a pothole, and parked on the far end where the pavement devolved into gravel. Shutting off the car, he grinned at his friend, Mark, riding shotgun. "You ready for this?"

Mark grinned like a fool. "You know it."

They exited the car and walked toward the main entrance. Nervous, and unable to figure out what to do with their hands—in pants pockets or out?—they kept straightening their shirts, finger-combing their hair, both trying to look cool, as if they belonged.

A short, enclosed section, like a partial concessions stand, jutted from the building. A bored woman wearing too much make-up sat behind a cut-out window.

"Ten bucks," she droned. She sniffed once and gave them a disinterested frown. "Each."

David jammed a hand into one pocket and tried to withdraw his money, but ended up spilling single bills, several coins, and nail clippers on the ground. After retrieving the items, he withdrew the correct denomination in the wad of money and handed it to the woman. She rolled her eyes and pushed across a ticket. Mark followed suit, and they entered through the doors.

Inside, they met a man the size of one of those stuffed bears collectors have mounted standing upright on pedestals. He stuck out a skillet of a hand, narrowing his eyes at the two newcomers. "Tickets," he grunted.

They produced the tickets. The bouncer jerked a thumb over his shoulder at the main room. "Enjoy."

David and Mark rounded a corner and stopped in their tracks, flabbergasted and speechless. They stood at the end of a darkened room lit by neon and stage lights. To their right a black-haired man in short sleeves and another cosmetically enhanced woman with brassy hair and sparkly eye shadow tended the bar. To the left stood several curtained partitions. Painted cats dressed in various kinds of attire and wearing human expressions decorated the walls. Men of varying races, dressed in anything from slacks and polo shirts to jeans and T-shirts sat at tables or in single chairs. A row of chairs lined each wall.

What caught David's and Mark's attention, however, were two of the most beautiful bodies on the planet dancing under spotlights on the stage. Already naked, the women gyrated and twirled, stretched, and spread to the music from hidden speakers. Who cared if their movements didn't quite match the beat? They oozed pure, raw sex.

The two buddies stared and smiled at each other. This paled whatever their imaginations had dreamed up. Sure, as young men of the world, they'd been around—gawked at the magazines, and seen the videos. They'd even spied on girls in their dorm rooms and the campus gymnasium showers. For a week they'd planned, scraped together the money, and counted the days. They'd imagined what they'd see, but to witness it live, to watch the women stripping...and maybe more...

Real live naked women, and they danced for David and Mark.

Well, not just for them. Twenty other guys sat at the tables or in the prime spots at the stage's edge. The summer blonde dancer slid over to the edge, accepted a dollar, and treated the guy to—

"Did you see?" David elbowed his friend. "I mean, did you see what she did?"

Mark's head bobbed up and down. "Y–yeah."

"She put his face between her—"

"Yeah."

"We gotta get her to do that to us."

"Oh, my!"

For the next hour, they never moved from next to the stage, offering bills to the dancers as soon as one popped out from behind the curtains. The last woman, after her dance, announced she and the previous ladies would be available for dollar lap dances, or for a special price, private performances in one of several cubicles scattered around the joint.

"What do you think, Mark?" David asked. "Each of us buys a session?"

Mark nodded, too busy fantasizing to speak.

Soon, the half dozen dancers hit the main floor and started making the rounds, trying to entice the customers into dollar lap dances.

David elbowed his buddy. "Which one do you want?"

Mark pointed a quivering finger at a busty blonde wearing something blue, tight, and very revealing. Before her routine, an announcer had introduced her as Serena, pronouncing the name with a series of rolling R's.

"Yeah," David said. "Great choice."

"And you?"

David had chosen the moment he walked into the strip club. She'd been the other woman on stage when they'd entered. A leggy brunette with glistening tanned skin and wavy brown hair. And what a body! Whew! Never mind if some parts were artificial. Hell, whose weren't in this place?

"I'm gonna get Lexie," David said.

"Aw, man," Mark mocked. "You can't handle her."

"Watch me."

They approached the bar and spoke to the middleman. He towered over them, linebacker huge and smiling like a serpent. He stroked his goatee as he listened to their desires, took their money, and after ushering them to individual cubicles, went to collect the specified women.

A single shaded lamp illuminated David's cubicle. He waited with hammering heart, erection already pressing against his pants. Two minutes later, Lexie slunk through the curtain. He stared as she explained the rules in a sultry, sex-dripping voice.

The erection turned painful against the pants crotch as Lexie removed a cup of her bikini top, exposing one round, smooth shiny breast. She eased her crotch down on one of his knees and twisted and ground into his leg. He became enthralled by the way her upper body seemed to move independently from the lower. She took his hands and placed them on her thighs. While he caressed her, she shoved her chest forwards, millimeters from his bug-eyed face.

His hand inched up upward—would she allow him to squeeze her ass—but she moved away, teasing him further.

David, so entranced by the stripper, paid scant attention to a movement behind her, a shifting of blurry gray in the far corner. Someone silhouetted behind the cubicle, maybe the next performer moving in front of a stage light.

No, wait. The cubicle, though curtained, was solid black, and he wasn't seeing anything over the top. In the corner, something rose.

David forgot sexy Lexie and her bountiful assets as red eyes opened. Before his shrieks erupted from the cubicle, Mark screamed from somewhere nearby.

Lexie jerked away from him to be enveloped in dark shade. Her strangled cry cut off almost as soon as it started. David scrambled out of the cubicle and into hell.

The entire strip joint had transformed into a live-action gore magazine, splashed in red. Bodies twisted and gyrated, but instead of dancers pouring out sex for the customers, shadows mauled and mutilated their helpless bodies. The men with dollar bills stuffed in their pockets writhed on the floor or sprawled across tables while crazed gray shapes shredded their clothes and skin. Broken, slashed bodies lay strewn about the floor.

David managed two steps toward the door before the huge bouncer rose before him. A swirling shadow shook his massive body back and forth. He fell away and David faced another living, flowing, growing entity. It blocked his path to the door. Two red eyes shone deep and evil.

He was denied a quick death.

CHAPTER 16

Harry raised his head to gaze at Misty's serene, relaxed face and caught a movement in his peripheral vision.

A shadow.

His hand reached for his gun as he assumed a defensive posture. An ache of butterflies whirled in his stomach when the shadow matched his own shifting body, created by the light next to the bed. A few moments passed before he relaxed his hand. He hadn't removed the weapon from its holster, but his fingers twitched in anticipation. Eyes darted everywhere, seeking other, unnatural movements.

Nothing.

Quiet steps took him to the room's doorway. No one in either direction along the hall or at the ICU desk. Harry didn't like it. A nurse exited a room down the hall with a soft squeak of sneakers on the tile and entered another. Numerous times over his career he'd visited hospitals at night. Without exception, they all were similar. Eerie quiet. Dimmed lights. Distant echoes. There was a hint of emptiness, of abandonment despite passing headlights flashing through the windows of darkened rooms, the hum of central air, the soft buzz of fluorescent lights, and the intermittent blips of patient monitors.

Hospitals at night were creepy. He imagined himself as the only person walking around, the only person alive.

Ironic in a place where medicine reigned supreme. Scary, too, considering the terrifying events he'd witnessed today.

Shadows.

Back at Misty's room, he stood in the doorway. His eyes took in the entire open space.

Too dark. Too many...shadows.

In the bathroom. Under the supply cart. Under Misty's bed.

He grimaced and flipped on the light switch. Then he did the same with the bathroom lights and the one over the bed. Ever-changing scenes from a muted television helped. A few dusky patches in the corners and beneath the bed still existed, but Harry was satisfied no shadows could attack.

Not as if the increased illumination was going to bother Misty. He wished the brightness could irritate her into waking.

He re-seated himself in the chair and pulled it closer to the bed. Folding his arms on the firm mattress, resting his chin on his hands, he viewed his wife's soft, beautiful face and bed-flattened hair in three-quarter profile. The bright light made her cheeks and forehead shine. Her chest under the thin blanket rose an inch, then lowered with each monotonous breath.

Harry had read somewhere that if one thought one didn't deserve the love and companionship of another, then one probably didn't. The article tried to dissuade people from seeing themselves as inferior, placing others so far above the norm some shift in the natural had to have occurred to gain the desired person's attention.

From the beginning of their relationship, Misty had never treated Harry as an inferior. She supported, encouraged, and rewarded his efforts. She instilled confidence in him, brought out his masculinity and his romanticism. As equals, they gave and received as needed but neither was selfish.

However, the truth was he yearned for her smile, got high on her laughter, melted at her touch, and sizzled with each kiss. She said he gave her the same feelings.

Not even close.

The chinks in the armor of their life came from her parents. His mom and dad enfolded Misty into their lives from the start. Even before they were married, his parents invited Misty to Christmas, Thanksgiving, and many weekends with his sister and her family. Never did she have a problem, or experience an uncomfortable moment.

His in-laws were complete opposites. The Stokes never believed Harry good enough for their daughter. They desired a businessman in a large respected company who wanted to rise to the top of his profession. Or they envisioned her a hard-working farmer's wife, continuing the sheep business, and raising a passel of children.

Not married to a cop. Not to a guy who went around looking at dead bodies and associated with lowlifes.

Despite the ill will between him and her parents, their marriage had prospered. Both were satisfied with their jobs, hung out with several mutual friends, and cherished each other's company.

Her agency dinners, his police events, their date nights.

Cooking dinners together or one treating the other to "special" evenings. His romantic gestures out of the blue. Her seductive techniques.

During the last several months, they'd discussed having a baby. He imagined the time he'd spend with his child.

Changing diapers. Bottle feeding. Baby asleep on his shoulder. The kid grasping his finger.

The first laugh, the first words, and the first wobbly steps.

Teaching his son baseball or seeing his daughter excel at martial arts.

Watching his son mature and move from toy blocks to model rockets to books to girls to...enjoying success in whatever employment he chose.

Marveling at his daughter's growth. Dolls to crafts, girl to young lady, savvy enough to kick the ass of any horny boy, if her father didn't get to him first. Rising in the business world to be a leader.

A child. Grandchildren. All lost.

A savage attack had ripped those dreams and plans to shreds. An attack by what? Shadows? How? Why?

His mind could not wrap itself around the concept of killer shadows. What had he seen earlier behind the blues club? What had slaughtered the couple in the hospital chapel? Why had he set every light in the room to its brightest setting?

He jerked upright as a monitor's beeping changed pattern. Misty's breathing staggered and her body shuddered beneath the blanket. She relaxed, but a minute later her breathing again faltered. This time she didn't settle.

Harry thumbed the call switch. When no one appeared, he dashed into the hall only and almost collided with the nurse.

"She's having problems breathing." He pointed at Misty as if the nurse couldn't see her patient on the bed. She bustled over and inspected the monitors and the IV unit.

On the verge of demanding to know the problem, his cell phone rang. He fumbled it from a pocket and stabbed a button.

"What?"

A voice he recognized as Belsom's said, "Harry, where are you?"

"I'm at the damn hospital," he snapped still looking at Misty. "Where the hell else would I be?"

The medical examiner moaned. "You, uh, you need to get over to the Polekat Klub. Right now."

"Why?"

"Harry..." Belsom choked up. "There's been a—"

"Oh, shit. Isn't there anyone else you can call?" He didn't want to leave Misty.

"Everyone's out," Belsom stammered. "Multiple calls. Harry, just get over here. I need to..." The medical examiner's words trailed off into incoherent mutterings.

Harry paused, appealed to the nurse. "Well?"

"Your wife is fine," the woman answered "Her breathing is back to normal. I'll keep watch and call in the doctor if there are any further problems."

She's not fine, you dimwit. That's why we're standing in the blasted hospital.

Belsom's voice interrupted again. "Harry?"

"All right. I'll pick up the Feeb and be right over." He ended the call, and with another look at the nurse, who nodded assurance, plus a last look at Misty, he headed for his car. "Leave the lights on," he ordered as he left the room.

"What?"

"Police order. Under no circumstance turn out the lights. Just...trust me."

•   •   •

Images spun as blown by a whirlwind in Lori's dream. No longer did she watch herself from above. She watched in confusion, trapped in a hurricane of pictures, words, and voices. The wall blocking her memory shimmered, on the verge of collapse.

Thousands of petroglyphs surrounded her. Crude depictions of animals, birds, a bat, a stick figure representing a pregnant woman. Other weird shapes and symbols, some faded through time and indecipherable.

Desert stretched beyond the rocks. Mountains dominated the horizon. Looming clouds portended rain. Wind blew cold.

Someone stood beside her in the scene. She couldn't focus on his face but caught snatches of words she didn't understand. Then, the excruciating pain in the dark and the creation of the wall.

Instead, from the depths of the wavering inky black, appearing as if rising out of the devil's tar pit, an object, a half size larger than an encyclopedia. She'd never seen it before but recognized what her imagination had conjured.

The Sarmangous.

Evil resonated from the cover, emanated from the unnatural symbols and figures.

Why did they strike a note of familiarity?

The book disappeared as ominously as it had arisen, descending back into the pool of black sludge. She reached out imploring arms and cried, "Wait, don't go away! Come back! What are you?"

The images returned. The dirty streets and drawn and tired Mexican faces of downtown El Paso. Then the dream faded to gray.

Lori opened her eyes to her bright hotel room, any shadows the afterimages of her dream. There might be a connection between the pictures on the rocks, the Sarmangous, and whom she became after she awoke with the amnesia.

Had she fallen? Struck her head on a boulder? What role did the person standing beside her in the dream play in everything?

She was so close to discovery. If she could keep it together.

Some instinct told her the connection she sought had already arrived, in this city. If she stepped outside the hotel's front door, she might see it, be able to grasp it...

...but you don't hold on to shadows.

Campisi blinked as her cell phone chirped a second time. She'd fallen back into a light doze and groped for the phone. Her fingers clutched at the phone and, without checking the caller's identification, answered the call.

"Campisi!" Harry's weary yet sharp tone spiked Campisi's adrenaline. She shook off sleep in a few seconds.

"Campisi," he repeated before she could answer. "Get your shit together. I'll be by to pick you up in ten minutes."

"Why? What happened?"

He paused and she could hear him inhale. "As I understand the situation, Des Moines has become one giant slaughterhouse."

CHAPTER 17

Saturday morning

Chaos reigned. Hell had come to Des Moines.

Harry Reznik operated on minimal sleep, stolen gulps of cold coffee, and not much else. Campisi didn't look much better. The once stolid Vulcan exterior had transformed into a collage of emotions: concern, confusion, and exhaustion.

Over a dozen attacks reported around the metropolis overnight. Task force members, unable to stay on top of everything, called in other suburban departments' detectives while stretching forensics teams to the breaking point. Not knowing where else to turn, Lieutenant Gravatte requested assistance from the local FBI to have more investigating bodies out on the streets.

Harry still could not grasp the idea Campisi did more than a "regular" agent. He hadn't had time to process all of Friday's events. The task force meeting, the revelation from Campisi about shadow creatures, the attack on Misty, and dealing with Reverend Samuels all jumbled into one long, continuous event.

The previous night he'd wrapped up the killing of the drug dealers and gone back to the hospital to suffer fewer than two hours of fitful sleep at Misty's bedside before he received the phone call from Belsom. He'd picked up Campisi, and rushed to the Polekat Klub, a strip joint just south of the interstate on Northwest Second.

Frank Belsom met them at the door. The dedicated and inexorable medical examiner had reached his limit.

"You don't want to go in there, Harry." Belsom leaned against the side of the building, sweating, his coloring tinged a pale green from exposure to too much death. "It's a GD F-ing bloodbath. I've seen cleaner kills from hyenas."

Blue, white, and red lights swirled from police and emergency vehicles. Combined with the slinky neon cat on the roof, the lights added a surreal, psychedelic atmosphere to the night.

"I've had it, Harry," Belsom muttered, head hung low. "I thought I was tough. Could handle anything."

"Frank—"

"Gotta be tough." Belsom spoke from his own world as if Harry hadn't spoken. "I snickered when others passed out in medical school at their first hands-on Y incision. H, Harry, a fifth of my class dropped out by the third year. You have to be tough. Can't shrivel up at the sight of a little blood. Get your hands in there. Grab hold of some guts and spleens and livers and brains. You do it 'cause it's your job."

He thumbed toward the double door, "What's in there, they don't teach you about. Why?" His voice rose and he lurched forward and grabbed Harry's lapels. "Because it's not supposed to happen. Damn it, Harry! It's not supposed to happen!" Belsom, beside himself, forgot his swearing by initials.

He released Harry and staggered back against the wall. Any words would be ineffectual, so Harry left the medical examiner to his muttering and inner turmoil and entered the strip club followed by Campisi.

The description of an abattoir was incorrect. Blood frenzy was more apt. He and Campisi stood just inside the entrance to the main room.

Crime scene techs wandered as if lost amid a battlefield of bodies in various stages of mutilation. Corpses lay on the floor, draped over chairs, twisted, gouged, mangled. Blood spatters covered every surface, staining the walls, the suave decorative cartoon tom cats in tuxes and suits, and the curvy female felines in bikinis and negligees. The stage resembled something out of a crazy old-style magician's theater act where the master illusionist simulated the sawing in half of his beautiful assistant with an overhead circular blade, the blood flying, the audience terrified.

Harry couldn't take it all in, didn't know where to look next. Not ten feet to his right a burly muscular man, a bouncer maybe, lay with his torso facing one way, his lower half the other. His abdomen was ripped open as if someone had used a hand-held garden tiller. A dancer sprawled near the bar, most of one blood-soaked breast missing. The color of the streaks of blood matched her hair, tangled as if from the worst case of bedhead.

Others lay in even more gruesome conditions.

Harry rubbed his face, screwed his fists into his tired eyes. Words caught in his throat. Beside him, Campisi stood also nonplussed and speechless.

He opened his eyes to see one of the crime technicians nearby. "Any survivors?"

"A few," the man said, his expression lost and wretched. "If you want to call them survivors. Me, I'd rather be dead than suffer what they're going through." He gave Harry a grim smile. "Sorry, Detective. I didn't mean it like..."

Harry lwaved the man's words away.

"This isn't even the worst," the tech stated. "Back in the privacy booths, we can't tell where one body ends and another begins. What part belongs to—"

"All right," Harry interrupted. "I get the picture."

He and Campisi gathered what evidence was available, then went to Mercy Hospital to speak to some of the injured. Most, like Misty, lay in states of deep unconsciousness, but a few sat in muted shock. Others babbled nonsense.

One man, around twenty years old, refused to acknowledge any questions put to him. He kept screaming, "Red eyes all around me! They came from everywhere, all around. The shadows!"

They were soon brushed aside by scurrying nurses and doctors working with fervor and desperation until reinforcements could arrive. As dawn broke, they stood outside the hospital gripping Styrofoam cups filled with cold coffee. The cool morning air refreshed after the sterile hospital and a slight breeze nipped around the corner of the building. A cloudless sky promised lots of sunshine.

"You called it, Campisi," Harry said. "You told me more people would die." He read the expression in her eyes. "No, I'm not jumping all over you. Just admitting you were right. What happened last night? Why the increase in kills? There are corpses all over the city. We're going to have a full-scale panic, and maybe a mass exodus."

"I don't know," Campisi answered in a dull tone.

"Listen, Campisi, I may not be coming down hard on you, but you say you've handled cases like this. You're supposed to be the expert. Tell me what we have to do. How do we stop them?"

She started to speak, then stopped and he could tell she just couldn't find the words. She appeared as stymied and dumbfounded as everyone else involved.

"Let me tell you what's going to happen," Harry added. "Your FBI is just the beginning. I guarantee, if this doesn't stop and shit like this happens again today or tonight, we'll have more alphabet agencies walking around this town than we can handle. Some of them may be called in today. Then we'll have the National Guard trooping in, and this entire damn city will be quarantined. Don't think it won't happen. In the span of a few hours, this situation has become bigger than any task force can take on.

"Campisi, I'm desperate. I've got bodies piling up. Victims are insane and the M. E. already is half-crazed. Meanwhile, the media are having orgasms with these deaths. They love this stuff. I'm open to any ideas, as wacko or stupid or far-fetched as they may sound. Give me something. Anything!"

Harry pleaded with his eyes. He had once scoffed at her shadow creatures theory, but matters had escalated. Now he'd accept shadows, bogeymen, even Martians.

Campisi returned his look. "I received some information last night that might be relevant. It concerns a particular book."

Harry's cell phone rang. "What?"

"Detective Reznik, this is Officer De Santos," said a female voice. "I'm sorry to bother you. I know you're busy—"

"No kidding. What do you want?"

De Santos drove patrol, at least until her paperwork for a recent promotion to the Narcotics division passed through the appropriate channels. A good cop, professional and hard-working, who enjoyed boxing. She threw a hell of a left hook.

"I'm here at 1914 Crocker, a block east of M. L. K. Parkway. With everything in disarray this morning, dispatch gave me your number to call you direct. I hope you don't mind."

"What's up, De Santos?"

"Well, sir, there's been another attack."

"What a surprise. I didn't think you'd be calling to report a stolen car." He broke off his sarcasm. "Sorry. What happened."

"This is something different. I don't think it's a normal murder."

"De Santos, none of these have been normal."

"Sir, this looks like—the scene, I mean—it looks like...a sacrifice."

"What?"

"Dispatch said you were busy with the strip club, but I think you need to see this."

Harry growled deep in his throat. "De Santos, if you're trying to get out of writing up a report, I'll kick your ass."

"No, sir!" Her vocal salute offered respect, then her tone lowered to a half-desperate request. "Please, Detective. Just come, if you're able."

"Aw, hell," he groused as ended the call. "Let's go, Campisi. Looks like we're in the shit again."

•   •   •

Harry disliked change. He wanted things to stay the same. Sure, if a store or building became an eyesore, then tear it down. However, he wanted to leave the lot clear, not have something else built there. He resisted all new work policies, be they stupid or efficient. This made the latter twice as difficult because he strove for efficiency.

The recent road construction and reconstruction around the metro proved a nuisance. New wide multi-lane streets hadn't lessened the amount of traffic as projected, and he didn't want to discuss the chaos of the freeway through town. Plus, the new streets did nothing to change the state of the neighborhoods through which they ran.

The Crocker Street neighborhood on the northwest part of the Sherman Hill district, for example, still retained its middle to lower-middle-class atmosphere despite the previous year's widening Martin Luther King Parkway. Plain homes, some showing peeling paint or broken gutters. Small lawns with token bushes and tiny porches. De Santos, once she was in Narcotics, might find herself visiting a few of the neighborhood buyers and sellers of various illegal products here.

The house at 1914 Crocker sat back from the street, almost hidden by its neighbors. Even in the bright morning sunlight, the nondescript box appeared withdrawn from the world, hiding in the shadows.

Harry shuddered. The house presented such an uninviting sight. If there hadn't been a police car parked in front, he might have driven past the small extension of Crocker and continued south on Nineteenth Street with hardly a glance. Plain, gray-white, old shingles, rusty gutters. Small bushes hunkered, forlorn and neglected, at the end of a gravel driveway. Basic front door with a two-step concrete walk-up, no railing.

Officer De Santos stood on the top step as Harry and Campisi approached. Harry shot her a look, indicating she'd better explain why she thought this scene more important than two score corpses at a strip club.

De Santos, the color of a bleached sheet—maybe remembering what she'd seen inside—still showed her professionalism. "A Schwan's salesman making morning rounds trying to drum up new customers stopped and knocked. After no response, he peeked through the front window, saw a bloody hand, and called us."

"Whose residence is this?"

De Santos hesitated. "Well, sir, I don't know."

"What do you mean you don't know? Come on, De Santos, don't screw around. I'm not in the mood."

"This is what I didn't tell you, sir. I wanted to wait until you had arrived."

"What are you talking about?"

"I don't know how to put this...but there is no one living here. In fact, there is no house at this location."

Harry, tired and not hiding the fact, fought to keep his exhaustion from turning to anger. "I'm looking at a house, De Santos," he said, keeping his voice calm. "Or are you saying I'm hallucinating?"

"No, sir. I'm sorry, sir. I'm just as confused as you are. I've checked and rechecked. There are no records of a house at this location." She pointed to the door. "No numbers either on the house or on the mailbox. I assume it's 1914 because it's between 1912 and 1916." She pointed to the houses on either side. "I can't come up with a record of ownership."

The first stab of a headache pierced his brain. "Listen, De Santos. Someone owns this property. Taxes have to be paid. Insurance premiums, utilities. There's a name somewhere. What do the neighbors say?"

"Nothing, sir." De Santos's tone remained in control, although Harry caught a hint of impatience creeping in. Did she think he was insulting her, questioning her ability to perform her duties? Who the hell knew anything anymore?

De Santos continued. "No one claims to have seen, much less have an acquaintance with, the owner. No car, no pet. Some say they don't recall ever seeing lights. Until we asked them, I don't think any of the neighbors paid any attention to this place or would claim it even existed."

Another shudder passed through Harry and he glanced at Campisi who stood a few paces away, quiet, observant. Here sat a house, unnoticed by neighbors, not attracting attention, maybe not wanting to be seen in the first place.

He shook his head to clear the encroaching grogginess. "What's inside?"

"Two bodies. One male on the first floor, one female in the basement. No ID yet on the woman, though the male might be a Peter Monaco. There was a journal of sorts in the kitchen with that name on the first page. We started a cursory search, then I called for the crime lab."

"Take a number and get in line." Harry stepped to the door. "We'll have a look. Oh, yeah, this is Federal Agent Campisi. She's with me. You, uh, find something on this house and Monaco."

"Yes, sir."

As De Santos walked away, a strange expression clouded Campisi's face. Instead of the bland Vulcan, she had a far-away pained look. Was he seeing a new side to her? Did something about this case, maybe this house, bother her?

"Something wrong?" Harry asked.

For a moment, she acted as if she hadn't heard him. Then she shook her head like a dog irritated by fleas. "Nothing. Everything is fine."

He studied her for a couple of seconds. "All right, come on."

They stopped just inside the front room.

"Maid's year off, I guess," Harry commented.

The carpeting was so dirty, dingy, and dusty, no trace of the original color or pattern remained. The few pieces of furniture fit right in. A two-cushioned couch, the cushions flat and dead and the armrests broken and faded reminded Harry of the couch in the old camp office he'd bunked in one summer up in South Dakota.

He'd taken a summer job in Keystone, a tourist trap town at the foot of Mt. Rushmore. Earlier hires had claimed the beds, so the late-arriving resident had to sleep on the couch, a dead piece of furniture, like this one, home to spiders and other critters. He had drawn the short straw.

Harry shuddered at the memory and studied the room. A rusty recliner with cracked and torn vinyl. A television tucked into one corner—unplugged, but who cared? A black hole gaped in the screen as if someone had swung for center field. No pictures or paintings anywhere. Harry deduced candles from various clots of dirty wax ground into the carpet.

The body lay at the far end of the room near a short hallway. One arm outstretched, perhaps the man's vain attempt to crawl. Pieces of flesh were missing from his neck, arms, legs, and buttocks. Pieces of a ripped and shredded purple robe, its fabric sewn with strange symbols, clung from his decimated body. The man's head lay sideways, the expression on his face frozen in permanent horror.

The detective and the agent moved through the house. A living room, a kitchen, and one bedroom with bath. An open door in the hall led to the basement. The flight of steps curved to the right halfway down.

"Let's save that for last," Harry suggested. "I'll check the bedroom. You take the kitchen."

He continued along the short hall to the bedroom. This back room, with black plastic duct-taped over the single window, resembled the front room. A cheap wooden dresser, scratched and dusty, tilted off-center in a corner, two of the four drawers askew. A ragged and thin blanket lay crumpled on a thin mattress. More candle drippings coated the dresser and floor. The room, also like the other, smelled musty, but other odors included urine, sweat, and dead mice. He decided he didn't need to investigate the attached bathroom.

"Abandoned," opined Harry to Campisi when they met back at the basement door. "Or complete apathy for cleanliness."

"I've seen worse, but it's been a while," Campisi replied.

"What do you think about De Santos's saying this place isn't listed anywhere?"

"Uncertain at the moment. I know you can hide a personal identity, but a property?" She shook her head.

Harry paused and said, "Well, Agent Campisi, shall we descend into the bowels of this fine abode?"

"After you, Detective."

"Do I hear reluctance in your voice?"

She cocked an eyebrow and said nothing.

•   •   •

Lori Campisi stared at the dark stairwell. She stood alone at the top of the stairs while Harry went in search of flashlights since Officer De Santos had forgotten to inform them the basement wasn't wired for electricity.

Her chest and stomach ached with a hollowness borne of anxiety and fear, not of shadow creatures attacking, although the possibility still existed. She just assumed they would have already attacked Harry, her, or the officers before them.

No, this fearful anxiety she'd experienced on other occasions, during other cases. The empty ache always preceded discovering a revelation, a major key to the case—if not the factor in reaching a resolution to the situation.

Did a discovery or resolution to this mystery lie at the bottom of the stairs? Or in the few passages of the journal she'd scanned in the kitchen?

She looked at the body of Peter Monaco lying nearby. Who are you? Is Monaco your real name?

Her vision blurred, and her head swam from a mental collision of several powerful forces. This, like the heightened anticipation, was familiar, but not so intense. This one always hit her at night when, on the verge of sleep, just as she poised on the edge of unconsciousness a shot, a slam, a bang, something mentally heard and felt exploded in her head. She'd sit straight up until dizziness forced her to collapse.

Just like now. Her equilibrium gone, she stumbled and made a desperate grab for the banister.

She jolted back into the nightmare, before the wall. This time the blockage quivered with even more transparency. Instead of pure black, it swirled between shades of dirty milk gray. She wanted to reach out and touch her hand to the wall, push through it, maybe grab hold and tear it to rubble. She yearned to reveal the truth on the other side—of her identity as a child, of who or what had caused all of this.

Peter Monaco. The name produced a hazy image. Not of the ravaged body on the floor, but someone, somewhere, else. But the image faded, and she slumped against the wall. She couldn't focus, couldn't concentrate. The visions swirled in her mind, too overwhelming for her to piece them together into recognizable patterns. Her body toppled forward.

Two hands grabbed her under her armpits and lifted her upright.

"Hey, Campisi, you all right?" Harry's voice cut through the rush of images, drove them back. She blinked several times to focus.

"Yes," she mumbled. "Yes. I, uh—"

"Shit!" Harry ejected the word in disbelief. "I just came round the corner and you were falling like someone conked you on the head. Look at me. Are you okay?"

"Yes," she replied. "Just a sudden dizzy spell."

"Did you get any sleep last night or breakfast this morning? You haven't overtaxed your federal reserves, have you?"

His laughter at the play-on-words brought her senses back to normal. He should know she hadn't eaten, as she'd been with him all morning. However, she even offered a small smile at his attempt at humor. It disappeared when she tried to evaluate the past few moments.

What had happened during those other times? During the night spells, she'd have a flash of memory—slam against the wall but expose nothing further. Could this be a further breakdown of the mental barrier, one in an ever-increasing series since she'd come to Iowa? Another quick glimpse of insight through the shimmering haze, almost penetrating the shield of amnesia?

What did it mean at this moment? Regarding Peter—

Harry's voice again interrupted the confusion within her. "If you need a break, I can take the basement alone." He glanced around and repeated her conclusion. "This looks like another shadow attack, but from the condition of Mr. Monaco, well, I think these beings or creatures are long gone, else we'd have been dessert by now."

"Yes," she said. "I agree, and I'm all right. The dizziness has passed. I'm fine now. Let's continue."

She reached for a flashlight and took the lead on the first of the basement stairs.

The basement held the remains of a body, and those two words—remains and body—understated what the attack had left. Hell, *attack* even understated the scene. Mutilation? Slaughter, perhaps. Wild, violent, psychotic.

Harry, who stood behind her, gasped, and his light wavered as his hand started trembling.

Descending the stairs, they had avoided stepping in the ragged trail of blood left by Monaco on his ill-fated crawl toward freedom. How had he had the strength or the ability to make it as far as he had? At the bottom, their flashlights revealed the origin of the bloodlust.

Copious amounts of blood covered the floor and made grotesque splatter patterns on the walls. Scraps of flesh dotted the gruesome tableau. A partial, and partially skinned, body lay ravaged, torn asunder, near the far wall. Appendages torn from their sockets, and other body parts—blood- and gore-covered—were strewn in a revolting jumble, like disposable leftovers from a slaughterhouse all thrown together in a vat.

Something had torn away the victim's face. Half an eye rested on the floor next to a mangled ear. Her hair resembled paintbrush bristles stuck under the gory liquid splashed on a nightmare canvas.

"How the hell did De Santos know this...this was a woman?" Harry's whisper was raspy and raw.

Campisi's light touched upon the answer in the red-streaked mound of one breast, in a corner.

"Holy shit!"

"Wait! Move your light back," she ordered. "No, to the left. Stop."

Her eyes widened at the object Harry's flashlight illuminated. Although she'd never seen it, not quite believing in its existence, she knew what rested on the blood-soaked dais.

The Book of Sarmangous.

She aimed her light and started to step into the room. Harry grabbed her arm and pulled her back.

"What the hell do you think you're doing? You can't go waltzing across a crime scene."

"Detective Reznik." She stared into his shadowed eyes. "We need that book."

"Listen, there are procedures—"

"No!" Her voice resounded clear, strong, in control, in command. Harry started at the authority in her tone. She took hold of his shoulder for emphasis. "No, Harry. You listen to me." She lowered her volume, but her voice lost none of its urgency. "I don't care about procedure. Procedure doesn't mean shit at this moment. I'm telling you this is the most important thing we can do regarding this case. You asked for an answer. There it is. We do not allow your forensics team to lay one finger on it. We do not allow anyone to look at it. I don't even want to touch it. In fact, why don't you go back upstairs and find a plastic garbage bag and we'll wrap it up."

He opened his mouth to protest.

"Don't say anything, just trust me. I cannot stress the importance of this. The book has a direct relation to the shadow creatures. Don't ask me for any details right now, but it does."

"You can't remove evidence," Harry said, gritting his teeth.

Campisi controlled her breathing. "Damn it, Harry. Haven't you been listening to me? I know you don't want to believe in these living shadows, but you cannot deny what you've seen. De Santos said this looked like a sacrifice." She spread her arms. "The candles, the dais, the symbols on the walls, the book. There's the victim. What else would you call this?"

"And Monaco was the high priest?"

"It is possible."

"What happened to him? Why did the shadows attack him?"

"I don't know. Maybe something went wrong. We're running out of time. Now, I'm getting the book. It's the key to everything. Up to this point, I haven't forced the issue, but if you try to stop me, I'll remind you who I am. I can override you, and I will." Her grip on his shoulder loosened and her voice lost its hard edge. "But I need you. I don't want to do this without you. Come on, Harry, take a leap of faith with me."

In the diluted flashlight beam, Harry's eyes narrowed, and she imagined the tug of war between police procedures and their situation ran through his mind.

Duty. Procedure. Trust.

Shadow killers.

His wife in a coma.

A low rumble sounded deep in his throat. "Damn it! I swear..." He kept his rage contained, not uttering the subsequent threat. Instead, his eyes never leaving hers, he took a step back up the stairs, then another, until he faded into the gloom.

Had she been mistaken about the Sarmangous? No, she couldn't be wrong. Everything fit. If the book lived up to even half of what it was purported to be—if it contained as much power as rumors and vague references said it did—then she needed to be very careful handling it. Would the plastic bag Harry was searching for be enough protection?

Protection for the Sarmangous...or for them? Her stomach returned to the familiar empty aching depths, this time to deliver an extrasensory warning. The situation called for extreme caution.

She didn't hear Harry's return, just the plastic crackle of the trash bag being thrust at her. He said nothing as she accepted it and offered no support when she stepped lightly, on tiptoe, around the splatters and pools of blood and flesh, trying to avoid contaminating the scene and soaking her shoes as little as necessary.

When she reached the stand, she shone her light on the open pages, memorizing some passages and drawings so she could access the same spot later. Using the plastic to cover her hands, she placed one hand on the left page, moved the other under the cover, and eased the book closed. Then she enfolded the ancient tome within the plastic like a badly wrapped Christmas present.

All the while, Harry's light shone the way. She retraced her steps through the carnage and rejoined the detective at the bottom of the basement stairs.

"Now what?" he asked. "You just stroll outside with it tucked under your arm?"

"Yes," she stated.

"What about all this?" He gestured to the bloody scene.

"Your forensics department will arrive in due course and process the scene." She then added as an afterthought, "According to procedure."

As she reached for her cell phone to call Hound, Harry said, "What are we going to be doing?"

Ignoring his question, Campisi walked past him and left the basement.

CHAPTER 18

Ten minutes later, Campisi directed Harry east, then north on the freeway toward the interstate. She hadn't explained the first phone call or the second one, just gave him orders once they returned to the car. Harry acquiesced but once out on the freeway, he decided not to follow her lead without a further explanation. "Where are we going?"

"Iowa City."

"Where in Iowa City?"

"The University."

"Half of Iowa City is the University," Harry said. "Could you be any more specific?"

"Rudolph Whitehead, Professor of World Literature. Ph.D. in Ancient Literature, Ph.D. in History."

"So he's intelligent, eh?"

Campisi ignored his remark, too busy quelling her mental turmoil. She hoped Professor Whitehead would be able to show them the procedure to stop the shadow creatures by using the Book of Sarmangous that lay in the back seat, still encased in the trash bag.

Hound had given her the path to follow, and she trusted him. Besides, no other option presented itself.

However, a niggling *something* scratched at the rear of her mind, a connection she couldn't put together at the moment. If put in the correct position, it would interlock with the rest, forming the link between all the puzzles in this case.

Why did the Book of Sarmangous strike such an ominous familiarity? She had to fight to keep her vision from blurring and her mind from drifting back into the struggle against the amnesia. The temptation and the promise of relief seduced her. The old witch's words might be coming true. She suffered more and more the closer she came to the answer. The Sarmangous was the biggest step yet.

Harry brought her back to the present. "How'd you find this professor?"

She took a deep breath and refocused. "I have a contact in my department back in Washington, D.C., as I told you, who sends me research material. Last night I asked him to send me any information relating to this book and the name of a person whom we might ask for further assistance. I called the University and—although the campus operator couldn't reach him—she mentioned he spends many Saturday mornings in his office."

Harry sighed. "You asked for a leap of faith. Well, this is a big one. We're leaving a city full of dead bodies to hunt up some professor? You realize I'm risking my job by going with you without first checking in with the lieutenant."

"You may call her if you wish. However, what explanation would you provide?"

He pursed his lips, contriving logical reasons for leaving town during the biggest and worst case in metro history. "I suppose, I could say was following a hot lead."

"Weak, Detective Reznik."

"Yeah, it sounded lame even to me."

"She would order you back to Des Moines, and then what would you do?"

He shook his head and shrugged.

"In my experience, it is sometimes easier to ask forgiveness than permission," Campisi said.

"Ah. I wait until she calls me."

"Yes. However, you have already powered off your phone. By the way, how fast are you going?"

"Seventy," he replied. "Why?"

"I needn't remind you time is of the essence."

"Are you going to explain should we get stopped by the State patrol?"

"I am a federal agent," she reminded him.

"Okay, then."

They left the city limits and raced east on Interstate 80. His handling of the vehicle impressed her—how he anticipated the traffic ahead and shifted lanes as needed.

The sun had resembled a pale orange when they left Monaco's house. Now, sunlight beat down warm and glaring. In one way, the bright light benefited them: fewer, not-so-dark shadows.

"Don't you think you owe me an explanation about why we did what we did and what that thing is?" He jabbed a thumb at the back seat.

"Yes, Detective."

"First off, let's cut the formality. You've called me Harry a couple of times. I think we're past local versus Fed." He paused for her to respond and, when she didn't, he added, "I promise not to get in your face about your authority status, and I agree to have an open mind. Hell, I'm probably out of a job, anyway. I can start believing in anything."

"If there is a problem, I'll square it with your lieutenant, even your chief, if the need arises," Campisi said.

"Another cover-up?"

She looked askance at him.

He barked a short laugh. "Shit, Campisi, cover my ass all you want, I won't object."

"Will do," she said and added, "Harry."

"Great." He took one hand off the steering wheel and offered it to her. A gesture of a new beginning. Damn, even with his new attitude, he continued to be a pain in the ass.

She took his hand, however, and they shook once.

"Now, what the hell did we steal?" he asked.

Campisi paused before speaking. "Do you know what a grimoire is?"

"A what? Sounds French."

"It is a magic book or a book of spells. They gained popularity in Europe between the 1500s and the 1700s, although some were written earlier, with most of the material derived from sources even further in the past. There is evidence a few notable persons mentioned in the Bible and even a Pope wrote grimoires."

"Sounds like something an Old West snake oil salesman would carry in his wagon."

"Yes. The so-called 'magicians' of the time claimed their wares' veracity just as vociferously as those selling potions and salves in the nineteenth century."

"What were these spells supposed to do?"

"Various things, including incantations to control spirits or demons."

"Why?"

"To do the magician's bidding."

Harry nodded, so she added, "However, none of the grimoires' spells worked. Like the balms and pills, the seller gained fortune by scamming gullible people."

"So what's in the back seat and why did you get all fired up about us taking the book from Monaco's house?"

They passed the western exit for Newton. After a moment, she said, "Because, this could be the real thing."

"What? You're thinking this Peter Monaco lit a few candles, read a few words, and voila, abracadabra, we have killer shadows on the loose?"

"Maybe. I don't know, but it does, with some shaky logic, fit with what's happening." She paused, then said, "The supernatural has fascinated me since high school. I have researched numerous materials. Knowing what I've seen and read about those grimoires, I remained skeptical when I ran into a few references to a secret, all-powerful book. I assumed it was just another sham, a legend passed down through the centuries. Another story to tell the naïve. A macabre mystery designed to sell the fake spell books, to con some money out of people."

"It's a reasonable assumption."

"Partial journal entries, old and faded parchments, eroded inscriptions on walls and tombs. They all sounded like hype. I likened them to Lovecraft's stories about the Necronomicon."

"The Necro-what?" he asked.

"The Necronomicon."

"Sounds like an illegal sex act."

"Stay on track, Harry," Campisi scolded. "H. P. Lovecraft lived in the early 1900s. He wrote numerous short stories featuring an infamous book—or grimoire, if you will—called the Necronomicon, written by a crazy Arab and said to contain secrets of past civilizations. One could call upon old gods or control monsters and bring them to our world. It's interesting reading, and there are similarities to this book."

"What's this one called? The book we have."

"The Book of Sarmangous."

"Sure, it would have to be something scary and foreign-sounding."

Campisi described some of the references she and Hound had discussed, including the journal entry from the Turkish scribe.

"Some of the citations claim a 'great power' to be obtained from the book. Others mention a 'guardian' who protects the Sarmangous from those who are unworthy. As I said, it all sounded sensationalized."

"But now…"

She shook her head. "I hate to keep saying this, but I don't know. I'm not sure. I'm hoping Professor Whitehead will be able to—"

Crash!

She and Harry jolted back into their seats, and for a second, Harry lost hold of the steering wheel. The LeSabre swerved to the right.

"What the hell?" Harry managed to regain a hold of the wheel before—

Crash!

Campisi looked out the rear window. A silver Land Rover edged forward to rear-end them again. Just visible through the off-road vehicle's windshield, were three figures, one driving, the second riding shotgun, the third leaning forward from the back seat. She couldn't make out their faces hidden beneath...hoods?

"Harry!"

"I see them," he cried. "What the hell do they think they're doing?"

"I don't believe they're State Patrol."

"Now she throws the one-liners. Good guess, Miss Sherlock."

Harry glanced once in the rear-view mirror, then ahead. "Shit."

Traffic congested up ahead. Several cars, a couple of pickups, and three semis all jockeyed for position to pass a slow-moving car towing a camper trailer.

"Harry."

"I know, I know. Shut up for a second."

She gripped the door's armrest, fear-stricken, as Harry attempted to avoid another collision with the Land Rover by changing lanes, then swerving back again. The trio of hooded figures lost no ground.

One car, a bruise-purple AMC Pacer, now trailed the camper trailer. It had to wait while two semis already in the left lane passed. The third semi had already returned to the right lane in front of the tow vehicle. Other cars and trucks moved on ahead of the pack.

"Hang on!" Harry made a feint of switching lanes again, then reversed back with a hard right and onto the shoulder. He slammed the accelerator to the floor. The car raced over short sections of grooved blacktop spaced near the shoulder of the hard road. Rapid fire rubberized burps warned drivers against drifting too much further off the interstate.

They passed the purple bubble car and the trailer. Harry stayed on the shoulder to overtake the first semi before going back on the interstate. The Land Rover sped toward them. The driver had fallen for the fake, but recovered in a second and gained ground.

"Here they come," she said, her voice ripe with quivery terror.

Harry's jaw tightened as he urged the Buick faster. He pulled ahead of the semi, a flatbed hauling agricultural machinery. A long peal of the truck's horn blared. He executed a quick jerk on the steering wheel and lurched in front of the Peterbilt cab.

The second rig moved alongside and a few feet ahead of the flatbed. The Land Rover appeared on Campisi's right. She swore as she recognized the hooded driver's intention.

He eased the vehicle closer trying to box the Buick between it and the semi to the left. The Land Rover swerved, trying to force their car into the big rig, a solid, extra-long-cab Kenworth pulling an England-brand trailer.

Harry pushed back, mere inches separating them from crunching the side of the truck's cab. Campisi tried to read Harry's strategy. He couldn't slow, even though the Peterbilt had, allowing some distance for what he must think we're a pair of maniacs playing dangerous highway games.

He couldn't speed up because he had to fight with the Land Rover's constant sideswipes. The impacts left her side mirror hanging by a thin wire, and the fender and door caved in.

A few seconds of space opened up before the Land Rover attempted another maneuver. Harry slowed just enough to draw the off-road vehicle into his plan. The Peterbilt loomed. Harry edged over to the left and the Land Rover followed. He positioned the Buick midway along the length of the England trailer.

"What are you doing?"

"Getting rid of this asshole," he growled.

He stomped the gas pedal and jerked the wheel right. The Buick's rear passenger door caught the front fender of the Land Rover. Although the four-wheel-drive vehicle had the advantage of solid mass, the surprise worked. Harry pushed and forced the Rover's driver to concentrate on not careening out of control. Both vehicles slowed.

"Just a second." Harry ground the words out between clenched teeth. Again, he slammed the pedal to the floor and shot past the Rover as it ran over a half crescent of old rubber discarded by some big rig's giant tire exploding.

Campisi viewed the scene out the back window. The Land Rover jounced over the chunk of tire and the driver must have tapped the brakes to prevent losing control. The Peterbilt, unable to avoid the collision, clipped the back corner of the Rover, spinning it off the road. The vehicle hit the ditch and rolled several times into a grove of trees fifty feet down the embankment.

Harry and Campisi sped off, knowing they couldn't stop and explain matters to the authorities and lucky no one else had been injured or killed.

All the way to Iowa City, she urged the Des Moines detective to increase his speed, wanting more distance between them and the trio in the Land Rover.

CHAPTER 19

Harry drove to Schaeffer Hall, the southeast point in the Old Capitol Pentacrest, just off the heart of downtown Iowa City. Frustrated by the one-way streets seeming to lead him away from their destination, he managed to get onto Clinton Avenue fronting the broad lawn and the monolithic chunk of the lecture hall. However, parking was prohibited on the near side, and the vehicles crammed the metered spaces on the other side.

A car up ahead eased away from the curb. Risking losing the space if he took the time to drive up a block and make a proper U-turn he grabbed the steering wheel with both hands, gave the side mirror a cursory glance, and yanked the wheel hard left. Signals at the next intersection dammed the flow of traffic. He maneuvered the damaged Buick into the parking slot in front of a restaurant called The Summit.

Harry switched off the ignition.

"Subtle," Campisi commented.

He smirked. "Didn't want to walk halfway across the damned campus."

As they exited the LeSabre, Campisi carrying the wrapped book, Harry reflected the previous two statements were the longest bit of conversation they'd had since the incident with the Land Rover. Neither had any answers other than Campisi's certainty it was all connected with the Sarmangous.

The Summit was out of place in this neighborhood, the establishment going for the haughty upper-class look amid a row of typical college stores. A bookstore on the corner, a couple of bars, a computer supply store, and a joint called The Airliner. The latter place was busy, with a variety of university types hanging out front. A tall muscular jock wearing a gold and black jersey imprinted with the distinctive Hawkeye logo had his arm around a curly-haired brunette in jean shorts and loose T-shirt who carried a couple of textbooks. Nearby, a bearded youth denied the warmth of springtime with an oversized army-green denim jacket. He spoke with a pair of women dressed for a performance art exhibit complete with black plastic glasses, short-cropped hair, and brown berets. Striped shirts clashed with faded bleach-stained jeans.

Harry waited for traffic to ebb and then he and Campisi crossed Clinton Street. Prevalent food and exhaust odors wafted in the warm morning air. Harry narrowed his eyes at half a dozen grunge-dressed youths who rode by single file on skateboards. He suspected the damn punks had joints or baggies of coke tucked into their backpacks. The students rolled up the sidewalk to the Old Capitol, the building enclosed by a construction fence.

Four lecture halls, one doubling as the Natural History Museum, surrounded the central building topped by a golden cupola. Harry studied the placard of a map guide on the grassy lawn just off the sidewalk but couldn't understand the layout. The numbers on the drawn map weren't in any decipherable accord with the listing on the left.

Schaeffer Hall loomed three stories high, a solid mass of gray stones, one of them etched with the building's construction date, 1898. A formal grandeur resonated from the monolithic structure. Inside, four marble columns greeted them on the main level. Wide halls, marble floors, pale yellow walls, high ceilings. Just inside the front entrance, they studied a map showing large lecture rooms in the middle of each floor and at the ends of each hall. Smaller classrooms along each corridor with tiny professors' offices tucked in the corners and a library on the third floor.

A few classes were in session. Harry and Campisi wandered the floors until they reached a lower level. A lone student sat on a wooden bench reading a thick textbook. Harry caught the title. *General Applications for Statistics and Actuary Science.*

Whatever the hell that was. When he'd attended Iowa State, he never would have considered taking a course with such a ridiculous name.

When Campisi inquired about Whitehead's office, the student gave a knowing smile. "Weirdo Whitehead, huh?" The kid nodded. "Yeah, you're lucky. He doesn't have a class this hour. I see him in the campus library lurking in the dark corners, but I think he's in his office today."

"Could you please direct us to it?"

The student pointed toward the far end of the hall. "Take a left. You'll see a door marked 'stairs.' His office is in the sub-basement. You can't miss it. He's the only one crazy enough to be down there."

"Thank you," Campisi said.

As they walked away, the student snickered. "Good luck. There are rumors that some people who visit Weirdo are never seen again."

Proceeding down the hall, Harry stopped to study one of the many cork bulletin boards hung on the walls. As with the others, papers, fliers, and notices covered the entire board. Apartments wanted or for rent, cars for sale, alumni news, graduate studies updates, upcoming events with listed speakers and times. All the papers overlapped, some buried two and three sheets deep. Harry stared, amazed by the chaos. He shook his head and moved on.

The door to the stairs was opposite the elevator. The ascending stairs wee illuminated by natural sunlight through narrow, mullioned windows. The descending flight disappeared into an unknown realm...full of shadows.

Professor Rudolph Whitehead's office, the last in the line of otherwise empty offices along the snaky sub-basement corridor, looked like the result when a disorganized second-hand book store meets a forgotten dungeon. Books and more books lay everywhere, overcrowding shelves and stacked in piles on the floor. A small portion of an old wooden desk showed through the piles of folders, pamphlets, and lecture papers. The dungeon ambiance came from no direct source. Maybe the urine-yellow lighting or the black, moldy, gooey substance striping the dove-gray walls. The dust and cobwebs choking the rafters and the corners added to the eerie atmosphere.

The man himself gave a startled jump as he exited a smaller room in the rear corner. He wore a sleeveless, pilled brown sweater vest straight out of the 1940s over a half un-tucked white shirt, pale yellow sweat stains under the armpits. Brown slacks and an old belt with stretched holes, scuffed shoes.

"Oh, my, I'm sorry," Whitehead apologized, with a slight jitter in his voice. "I didn't hear you knock. I was...well, I..." He gestured behind him.

"Professor Rudolph Whitehead?" Campisi followed the man's quick nod by introducing herself and Harry.

"Yes. Oh, my," Whitehead said, impressed and nervous at the same time. "How may I help you?"

Campisi showed him the wrapped item. "We'd like to learn what you know of this."

"What is it?"

The federal agent hesitated, and then in a flat voice stated, "The Book of Sarmangous."

Whitehead's eyes widened to the extreme, and he stumbled back a step, catching hold of the edge of a shelf. He pointed a shaky index finger at Campisi.

"Are you trying to play a joke, madam?" His finger waggled in a scolding motion. "If so, I'll ask you to leave."

"I'm afraid it's no joke, sir," Campisi replied, her tone flat and serious. "The book was in the basement of a house in Des Moines. You may have read about the recent murders."

Whitehead gasped. "The shadows!"

"Yes, sir."

"You…I mean, are you telling me this is the Sarmangous?"

"Yes," Campisi said. "We need to know more about it and if it can help put a stop to the creatures. My contact informed me you had the most extensive knowledge of the book."

"Yes, yes, yes." The professor's eyes never left the package. Then he leaped forward and with one arm swept two piles of books and folders off his desk. They crashed to the floor.

"Put it here," he said. "Carefully."

While Campisi placed the book on the desk, Whitehead rummaged in the bottom right hand drawer and came out with a pair of leather gloves, cracked and peeling with age. He slipped them on, approached the trash bag, and—with meticulous precision—removed the item within. Soon it lay on the desk in all its ugliness.

Whitehead covered his mouth with one hand and stared. "It's true," he whispered. "It does exist."

"What can you tell us about it?" Harry asked.

"The Book of Sarmangous was written in a time long before the ancient Sumerians first became a culture," Whitehead said.

Professor Whitehead had cleared two chairs, offered them to Harry and Campisi, and sat in his at the desk, not taking his eyes from the closed grimoire. Campisi sat near the desk, but Harry chose to lean against a bookshelf in the corner. He blew a dust cloud and stifled a sneeze.

"No one is certain of the author," the professor continued. He was much calmer, less fidgety, though no less awestruck, after his initial reaction upon first seeing the Sarmangous. "He might have been the local version of a mystic, shaman, magician, what have you. I have to correct myself because 'written' is a misnomer. The contents, all the words, symbols, etcetera, are more likened to tattooing." He brushed a gloved finger over the cover. "As you can see, the cover and the pages within are a combination of animal hides and skin stretched, processed, then inked."

Harry curled his upper lip. "Human skin?"

"Yes, Detective. The cover has been blackened and inscribed or otherwise imprinted with many shapes and symbols."

"How 'otherwise'?"

"Supernaturally, of course," Campisi answered.

"Yes, my dear," Whitehead cooed. "The Sarmangous is many, many centuries old. How else could it have survived to today except by magical and supernatural influences?"

"Figures," Harry muttered. "Listen, Professor, I don't want to rush you, but time is of the essence here. What do you know about the shadow beings? Did some kook call up those things?"

"Oh, yes, yes. But before we discuss the shadows, let me continue speaking of the unnatural influences. Ms. Campisi, you showed wisdom when you wrapped the Sarmangous rather than holding it with your bare hands. I'm afraid we wouldn't be speaking if you hadn't done so."

"I suspected as much. Please, fill in the details."

"The Sarmangous has power," Whitehead said. "It offers power. The author understood it contained knowledge the world wasn't meant to have. Oh, to think of the life experiences he must have endured, the wherewithal, the courage to put it all in writing."

"The insanity, you mean," Harry piped up.

"Yes, Detective. No sane person would dream of doing this. Why he undertook the effort, and why he didn't destroy it afterward, is all due to the supernatural influence. Insanity, yes. This includes the seekers of the Sarmangous. All must have been quite insane."

"The seekers?"

"Only the most desperate, the strongest-willed, and yes, the person most driven out of his mind, would be worthy of claiming the power of the Sarmangous. Alas, it is all a lie."

"Why?"

Whitehead gave him a sad smile. "Because the Book of Sarmangous has always had a Guardian. See, when someone, after agonized years of searching, finds the Sarmangous, disposes of the current Guardian, and touches the tome, he is given two choices. Here, let me show you something."

He scurried to a far shelf and removed several books hiding a small safe set into the wall. After several revolutions of the combination dial, he opened the hinged door and withdrew several folders with scraps of paper spilling out the sides and pockets from the safe's depths.

The professor swept more of the desk clear and slapped down the folders. He riffled through a stack of papers, each labeled in faded ink Finding the one he sought, he offered it to Campisi. Harry stepped away from his corner and peered over the agent's shoulder.

"The original text is on top with the translation underneath," Whitehead explained. "It's a passage from a series of papers written by a Chinese general's aide who chronicled his master's adventures. Most of the papers are lost or destroyed. Someone discovered and smuggled out this parchment and a few others from the basement of a Beijing library if you can believe it."

Harry squinted at the narrow, unintelligible Oriental figures, and then read the English translation written below the original Chinese characters.

My lord has departed and I fear I have seen the last of him. Maybe it is for the best. I pray he finds deliverance from his madness.

I may be beheaded for revealing this, and I may bring dishonor to his family name, but most I have no doubt my lord is insane and has been for some while.

I sympathize with those monks to the west who would not reveal their secrets until my lord general put into practice his knowledge of the most excruciating forms of torture. I pray for the souls of those who died, may they forgive us. After countless years of questing for this forbidden book, we entered a forgotten and alien part of the underworld.

The darkness of those caverns might have been endless. I estimate we traveled hours, but I cannot be certain. Time and distance might have been altered, so deep we progressed. Although he didn't detail what was forthcoming, he affirmed he understood what challenges awaited him at the end. My lord fought valiantly, his stamina and resilience strong despite his madness. I would even say the derangement buffered him, intensified his skills to heightened ferocity. The vanquishing of his opponent was almost anticlimactic, but with the last plunge of the sword, my lord had won his sought-after prize.

He gazed at it for long minutes but would not touch it, saying that he had prepared his chambers at home for the time when he would lay hands upon the ancient tome. With meticulous care, he wrapped the object in a protective cloth and we made our return trek back to his home.

My lord did not grant any servant, even I, his trusted aide, access to his inner chamber the night he first touched the Book of Sarmangous.

Oh, I still cringe at his screams and the rampages my lord had perpetrated upon the sacrosanct room. What maelstrom of horror he must have experienced because of that infernal, evil book!

This morning, before dawn, my lord came to me in my bed chamber. He still bore evidence of his battle with the warrior in the caverns. Cuts and streaks of blood he had refused to wash away crisscrossed his face, making him look like a crazed tiger. Fresh wounds gaped and oozed, and I choked back anguished cries. In his delirium, he had blinded himself in his left eye. A line of black viscous fluid trailed down his cheek, dripping a repulsive path in his wake.

He clawed at me with one scarred, scabbed hand. The other had a talon grip on the evil book. I could not decide whether to stare at the accursed tome or my lord's death-mask visage.

He uttered words raspy and strained, his breath cold, stale, lifeless. "After all my...boasts, my tales of glories to be mine...ours...I cannot...I am weak." Tears mixed with blood, and sobs choked his words. "So weak. The Sarmangous brings pure madness! No, don't touch it! I have and it found me wanting. My choice is made."

I implored him to explain, even as he shivered in fear and terror, eyes darting in every direction. I shudder to think he might have killed me if he'd tarried. He managed one final warning. "I will protect the Sarmangous so no one else may suffer. It is a lie, my friend, a falsehood. Be not deceived."

Then he departed, stealing into the gray dawn, cloaked and shrouded by the morning fog. He staggered north until I lost sight of his once handsome, strong, and muscular figure, now a mere fraction of a man, the damned Book of Sarmangous wrapped in his arms against his chest.

Professor Whitehead replaced the paper in the folder.

"That is a fine story for Halloween, Professor, but tell us about the shadows," Harry said, frustrated.

"Ah, the shadows, yes." Whitehead opened the Sarmangous. "The shadows are but one of many spells and bits of sorcery this book contains."

Campisi peered at the spells as the professor studied the pages with reverence, "What are some others?"

"Later, Campisi," Harry interrupted. "Let's stick with one disaster at a time."

"I agree," Whitehead agreed. He flipped through pages until Campisi said she recognized the characters she'd seen when the book lay open in Monaco's basement. Whitehead studied the first couple of passages. "Here, take a look."

Harry approached the desk and also peered at the thin sheets of...what? Paper? Skin? He shivered. They contained a hodgepodge of symbols, figures, and characters of some ancient system of letters, a language dead and all but forgotten. The writing, as Whitehead had stated, was tattooed and faded, but nowhere near obliterated.

The professor studied the text and uttered curious *hmm* noises.

"Don't tell me you can read this garbage," Harry said.

"Oh, not in its entirety," Whitehead answered. "I have seen some of the language mixed in with others I have studied and in some of the documents I've picked up in my travels."

"Hey, wait a minute—" Harry started, and stepped back, ready for action. "Are you saying you've been looking for the Sarmangous, too?"

"Are you questioning my sanity, Detective?" Whitehead smiled.

"Frankly, yes."

"Ha! Don't concern yourself, my dear officer. In truth, any scholar of ancient history looks for the Sarmangous at some point, though a fair number discount its existence. I have a successful career here at the University and although my interest may exceed that of some others, I promise you I shall not go crazy. I'm quite content to remain 'Wacko Whitehead' in the eyes of my students and colleagues."

"I think the kid said 'Weirdo,'" Harry corrected. "Yes, perhaps."

With a wary eye on the eccentric professor, Harry returned his attention to the alien text as Whitehead pointed to the left-hand page.

"This is the spell to bring the shadows to life. Or rather to open the portal allowing them access to our dimension."

"So, they do come from some other universe," Campisi said. "Yes."

Harry pointed at the Sarmangous. "Why would someone do this?"

"For power, of course. It's what the entire book is about. Power. See, this other page explains it. The follow-up spell, so to speak." He ran an index finger down the page indicating certain drawings and star-pointed symbols. "Here and here. These are the important aspects of this ritual."

Campisi followed Whitehead's progress through the ritual. "What is the intended result?"

"To have the shadow beings under the control of the person who brought them into the world—who gave them free rein. To accomplish this goal, the shadows require a sacrifice. I, uh, assume the Sarmangous was among the dead?"

"Yes," Harry answered. "A woman in some guy's basement. He didn't make it through the living room."

Whitehead nodded.

"The officer at the scene mentioned the scene mentioned a ritual sacrifice," Harry added.

"Yes," the professor said. "As I said before, the power deceives—lies. The one offering the sacrifice is blinded to the truth. He is the ultimate sacrifice. He won't control anyone or anything, and the shadows can now run amok, killing at will."

"Which they have," Harry stated. "Listen, Professor, I'm just a city detective. I don't know a lot about magic, rituals, and all the rest of this shit, but there's always a counter-spell. Something to put things right, get rid of these shadows. You mentioned the opening of a portal. Isn't there some spell in this godforsaken thing to close it again?"

"Of course. Evil must be tempered by good and vice versa." He turned a page. "Ah, here. Logical it should be on the next page." He read a few lines. "Very interesting."

"What?"

"The spell will be difficult, but it can be done. There is evidence of at least one previous success. This Persian scribe who—"

"I read the same journal," Campisi said.

Whitehead laughed. "It's amazing, everyone associated with the supernatural writes journals."

"Let's get on with it," Harry said. "How do we find this portal? It wouldn't be as easy as returning to this guy's house."

"I regret to say no." Whitehead frowned. "However, the Sarmangous should direct us."

"Like a homing device?"

"Yes."

Campisi said, "Professor, I have a question. The house we visited...it's as if it's an anomaly. The officers could find no record of ownership, no paperwork pertaining to the property."

Another professorial nod. "Ah, the eternal mysteries of the Book of Sarmangous. I could show you another writing of an entire castle disappearing."

"Before we go any further, Professor," Harry said. "We ran into a bit of trouble driving over. How much danger are we in other than the shadows?" He described the incident with the Land Rover.

Even before Harry had completed his story of the cloaked figures, Professor Whitehead had again backed up against a bookshelf, terror in his dilated eyes.

"I–I—" he stuttered.

Campisi stepped closer, alarmed at the man's reaction. "What's the matter, Professor?"

Whitehead managed three labored breaths before he answered.

"I apologize. It's...just...I forgot. It's another condition associated with the Sarmangous. Forgetting the dangers."

Harry spoke up, now on edge. "What are you talking about?"

"The Triune," Whitehead said. "No one knows who they are."

"The Triune?"

"Sorry." Whitehead again apologized. "Like so much of this, it's vague. The Triune. A trio of...what? Humans? Demons? Who knows? They pursue all who seek the Sarmangous. It's unclear whether they protect the Sarmangous, like the Guardian does, or whether they want the object themselves. They're ruthless and swift in their executions. You may consider yourselves lucky to have survived."

"How did they know we had the Sarmangous?"

"Another mystery of the supernatural."

"Well, they'll be hard-pressed to follow us," Harry said. "Their vehicle had a problem with a tree."

"You underestimate them, Detective." Whitehead scurried to and fro gathering papers and re-wrapping the Sarmangous in the trash bag. "We may have tarried too long as it is. We must go."

Campisi picked up the book. "What materials are we going to need for this portal-closing ritual?"

"Ah," the professor said and reached a hand under the desk near the center drawer. A portion of the rear set of bookshelves snicked open. With a slight flourish, Whitehead pulled on the camouflaged entrance. Behind the shelves lay a cubbyhole the size of a small walk-in closet.

"What the hell is this?" Harry squinted at the motley collection of mystical paraphernalia. Various sizes and colors of candles lined the walls. Fronting them, labeled bottles of oils, herbs, and powders. Necklaces and rings engraved with unrecognizable patterns, jeweled knives, and other assorted weaponry hung from hooks. More piled books on ancient languages and demonology threatened to topple onto the professor's head.

Campisi noted several objects of interest with an inquisitive and appreciative eye.

Whitehead demurred. "Just, um, my little private collection of items gathered throughout the years."

"Impressive," Campisi said. "You have a few books not in my own library."

Harry shook his head and muttered, "Great, my city is going to be saved by the founding members of the Loony Admiration Society. Come on, people, let's move it. I'm going to be in enough trouble as it is."

Professor Whitehead gave Harry a withered grin. "Indeed." He perused his eclectic collection and began his selection.

CHAPTER 20

Lieutenant Glynis Gravatte slammed the phone receiver hard into its cradle the base dinged in protest. The growl in her throat came out low and gravelly. She hated playing liaison between her detectives and her superiors. It was one of the less-enjoyable responsibilities of her rank. She tolerated politics and reports with grace, even aplomb.

Not today.

Not after this week of hell.

She stuck her head out the office door. "Where the hell's Harry?"

"Not answering his cell phone," the nearest detective replied and answered his own buzzing phone.

"I'll kill him," Gravatte muttered through gritted teeth. "I'll carve him up."

"Lieutenant?" a detective interrupted.

"What is it, McNeil?"

"Another attack reported. This one at the Econolodge on Merle Hay."

"Well, get someone on it."

McNeil threw up his hands. "Who?"

"I don't care!"

"Come on, Loo, I've got three cases going here myself."

"Pull in Vice," Gravatte suggested.

"But they're—"

"McNeil! I don't care. If they're busy, get the damn Rat Squad if you have to." Gravatte slammed her door shut when her nerves jangled a split second after her phone did. "Harry, for the love of heaven, you'd better be doing some good wherever you are."

•   •   •

No one knew. No one could see.

She could do nothing anyway. The injuries, the damage, and the ever-strengthening power of the shadows dominated her mind.

Why, she didn't know, she experienced the terror of other survivors, also unconscious, also sinking into the abyss. With every attack, each decimated individual brought ever more madness.

Misty no longer cared whether anyone or anything could put an end to it.

•   •   •

Fate, Harry reasoned, could be one nasty bitch.

Since leaving Schaeffer Hall, he'd taken to glancing at his watch every few minutes, à la Frank Belsom. He was in a hurry for a solution, but he wasn't comforted by kooky Professor Whitehead and his collection of ritual accouterments, even if he and Campisi had to rely on the guy to solve the shadow problem. Also, with every passing mile, he considered and rejected various explanations to Gravatte upon their return to Des Moines.

If they ever did return.

Back at the car, Harry sneered at the expired parking meter and that some diligent authority figure hadn't recognized official license plates and placed a ticket under the driver-side wiper blade. Harry crumpled the official notice and, with a growl, tossed it into the middle of the street where it disappeared in the rushing wake of a passing pickup. The ticket paled to insignificance to the flat left rear tire.

Campisi and the professor stood at a discreet distance while Harry wrestled with the annoying mechanics of changing the tire. Back on the interstate, they reached the U.S. 218 exit before being stalled by traffic due to a three-car accident. Officers on the scene monitored the one open lane.

"Shit!" Harry was trapped in the right lane, the other drivers refusing to offer an open slot. "Campisi, you are going to owe me big when this day is over."

He wrenched the steering wheel left, forcing an open space, and eliciting a few honks. He drove off the shoulder into the expansive grassy median. Praying for the Buick's suspension, he hit the gas. He ignored the confused and angry stares of the officers as he raced past, but Campisi helped matters by pressing her credentials against the window.

He jounced back onto the pavement well ahead of the accident, stayed in the left lane, and inched the speedometer ever higher.

"Well, aren't we having fun?" Whitehead chirped from the back seat.

Harry's stomach reminded him he hadn't eaten in more hours than he cared to count, and lack of sleep gnawed at his eyelids as the miles passed. His two passengers ignored his gastric complaints and served as distractions as they conversed further about the Sarmangous.

Campisi had retaken possession of the ancient tome. It lay on the floor at her feet. Harry kept shifting his eyes to the damn thing, then to the dashboard clock, then to the traffic. He listened to their conversation while creating one he might later have with Gravatte.

"Professor, you mentioned the Sarmangous would act as a homing device to locate the portal the shadows are using," the federal agent said. "How?"

"Do you remember the text from the Turkish scribe? I believe you said you had read it."

"Yes."

"Well, I have in my files another entry from the same journal. When the scribe's master died, presumably killed in the same fashion as your Peter Monaco, the scribe had to take steps to stop the shadows."

"Just as we're doing," Harry put in.

"Yes. He found someone akin to me, someone who understood the Sarmangous's text, and they started looking for the portal."

Whitehead had brought with him a gray, hard plastic briefcase. He placed the case on his lap, maneuvered the latches, and popped the top. Again, he fingered through the stack of papers he'd taken from his desk and handed Campisi the specific document.

Harry glanced at it. Like the other, the paper contained the fragment of a journal entry in its original form with a translation beneath.

Campisi skimmed the page. "The beginning of the entry is obscured, but the person may have been the local Muslim Shaman or holy man."

"Yes, I believe so," Whitehead agreed.

She read from the text. "'The Osama said he was uncertain how we should locate the doorway. He was sure since the Sarmangous had been used to open the passage between worlds, it could find and close it. In all honesty, I cannot say I believe in this other world, but I am but a poor scribe and not worthy of such knowledge. Still, I have seen the shadows and the remains of my brethren, so maybe the idea of another place beyond the scope of my earthly vision is possible.'"

"Amen to Allah, brother," Harry muttered.

"'We walked for many hours in places seeking the gateway,'" she continued. "'As we neared a low rise of foothills dotted with many caves, the Sarmangous began to respond. The contours and ridges of the infernal tome's black cover began to glow, aye, even to pulse. First in rich silver, then as we neared a certain cave, a blazing gold so bright I had to avert my eyes. I understand the cover is made of skin and the pattern of gold lines reminded me of veins as on the inside of my wrist. As we approached the cavern, my guide cried out. I dared look and there the gateway swirled in a purple hell-storm. I fell to my knees and prayed—'"

Campisi stopped speaking and Harry, annoyed, said, "What? What happened?"

"That's the complete entry."

"Cripes, Campisi, you sound like my scout leader who cut off the end of a good ghost story around the campfire and sent us all to our sleeping bags scared witless because we didn't know what came next."

"Sorry."

"Yes," Whitehead commiserated. "The journal exists in various fragments. It's a wonder even partial entries survived."

"Great," Harry said. "How did you happen to have this piece?"

The professor hesitated. "Well, let's just say it came to me by...unconventional means."

"You stole it," Harry stated.

"Uh, yes."

"I'm beginning to wonder about your 'minimal' level of interest in this Sarmangous." Harry glared at Whitehead in the rear-view mirror. "Listen, Professor, let's get back to this Triune you discussed earlier. What are the chances of running into those creeps again?"

"It's a definite possibility, Detective," answered the professor. "As long as we have the Sarmangous, we will be a target."

"Do you have any idea what they want?"

"It is assumed they're a secret group surviving throughout the centuries, somehow in tune with the Sarmangous and those wishing to find it. Who knows, maybe it is the same original trio. Most people who've seen them are dead. There are even fewer references to the Triune than for the Sarmangous itself."

"I guess we'll have to keep our eyes open and be ready for anything." Harry pushed the accelerator closer to the floor.

Lori Campisi shifted in her seat to speak to Professor Whitehead. "Describe this ritual to rid our world of the shadows. What other items besides what you've brought will we need? What are our roles?"

"Yes, well..." Whitehead hesitated. "I must admit, Agent Campisi, beneath my lighthearted exterior, I'm quite concerned, even a trifle fearful."

"What can we expect to happen?"

"Since there is no recorded version of the full ritual, I have to say we'll be, um...well, to put it bluntly...winging it."

Campisi caught Harry's narrowed look. Just remember, his glance expressed, you picked this geek.

"It's not the pronunciation of the words I'm worried about," Whitehead continued. "It's more of what will happen. From what I can decipher, if we can find the portal and close it, then the shadows, in effect, die. They are connected to their dimension through the doorway."

"You mean the creatures derive their power from this other dimension, and as long as the portal is open, they continue to survive?" Campisi asked.

"Correct."

"Close off the power source, they die," Harry added.

"That's the hope," Whitehead answered and consulted a small notebook taken from a back pocket. "We have candles, a ceremonial dagger, and special powders. It's funny, but tradition had to start somewhere. Nothing much has changed in the magical, supernatural world for many centuries."

"Yeah, yeah," Harry urged. "Get on with it."

"We'll need light, several spotlights and flashlights."

Campisi said, "What's the procedure?"

"Well, the idea is to draw the shadows back to the portal."

Harry flipped a hand up. "Back? Why would we want them back?"

Campisi wished he'd just concentrate on driving. She tried not to watch the traffic congestion.

Whitehead fidgeted as he spoke, betraying his anxiety. "We'll create an area for the shadows to gather and trap them there. Then we can close the portal."

"Why do we need them back, and how do we bring them back to the portal?" Campisi tried to think of any weakness in the plan. "How are we certain they'll all return?"

"Answering the third question first, I'm sure once they sense the portal being tampered with, they'll come back to defend it. I don't know why we need them all in one place. The ritual just demands it. Maybe to make it easier to close the portal. Plus, once we offer them some extra...enticement, they'll show."

"What enticement?" Harry asked, but Campisi suspected they both understood what the good professor meant.

"Blood," Whitehead confirmed. "It's, uh, traditional."

"I assume we can't ask the Red Cross for a spare bag of A-Negative."

"Uh, no."

"Of course not."

"After the shadows are trapped, a few handfuls of the powder and the correct sequence of words, then..."

"What?"

"I don't know."

"Gee, Campisi," Harry groused. "He's been hanging around you too much. He's picked up your habit of not answering the important questions."

Whitehead shrugged. "The ritual doesn't say how it happens, if it happens, or if the portal closes or blows up."

"Or if we all die," Harry added.

The professor shrugged again.

"I think the first things we need are the lights. Any idea how we can get those?" Campisi asked Harry.

In a moment, he snapped his fingers. "Misty told me about a project she once did for the agency. She needed extra lights for a particular exhibit at a show. Now, what did she say was the name of the place...Roderick's? That's it. Roderick's Audio/Visual. Said she spoke with a woman named, uh, Bobbi. Hold on." He reached for his cell phone. "I'll call Misty for directions..."

His voice trailed off as the circumstances dawned on him. Even Whitehead suspected calling Misty would be impossible, even if he didn't know the details.

"Anyway, it's in the phone book," Harry said, his voice low. He returned his concentration to the interstate.

"Professor Whitehead and I will get the lights," Campisi said. "I'm sure my badge will work more efficiently than yours. Besides, Harry, you'd better check in with your lieutenant. I'm thinking we're going to need some help."

Harry stared out the windshield. "What time do we do this ritual? We couldn't just grab the items and go?"

"Again, no," the professor stated. "Tradition, you know. After nightfall."

"Not midnight?"

"In this case, we're lucky. Just a dark sky. Besides, we still need to find the portal. That could take time."

"Why don't you keep that thing in the open once we reach Des Moines?" Harry said. "While you're getting the lights, maybe you'll get a...I don't know...a blip on its radar. I'd hate to have to drive all over the metro trying to get something. I'll work on coming up with a strategy if we do." He gave a short laugh. "Tradition should put the damn portal in a cemetery. Believe me, there are a few scary ones in town. Hell, the cemetery on the other side of MLK Parkway from Monaco's house is eerie even in bright sunlight. Besides, Professor, I don't think we're going to have to wait for nightfall."

"Why?"

For an answer, Harry pointed toward the horizon, where cast-iron-black clouds gathered, low and ominous.

"Our ghoulish hunt wouldn't be complete without the traditional thunderstorm, would it?"

CHAPTER 21

Harry let the engine idle when they arrived back at the DMPD. "Time to face the music. GG is probably hitting the ceiling by now. I'm not sure what explanation to give her."

"Detective Reznik, considering all we've seen, I would opt for as much of the truth as you think she can handle." A grimace rearranged his face. "Do you have any other choice?"

"I know, I know," he groused. "I'm trying to imagine how it will sound. 'Hey, GG, killer shadows have invaded our town. A professor, the Feeb, and I are going to say a few magic words, toss around some powders, and make them disappear. Feel like helping out?' I can imagine her reaction."

"I imagine it would resemble the one you exhibited yesterday at lunch when I brought up the subject."

The grimace deepened.

Whitehead's voice piped up from the back seat. "I think it would be prudent—"

"You stay out of it," Harry snapped. "Your job is to keep focused on the hocus-pocus to get rid of these creatures."

He withdrew a small notebook from a shirt pocket, snatched a stray pen from the well between the seats, and scribbled on one page.

"Here," he said as he tore off the page and offered it to her. "I just remembered directions to the audio/visual place. It's below the Eighth Street Bridge. You get what you need and meet me back here. If you hurry, you'll be able to save me from GG ripping me a new one." He spoke to the man in the back seat. "Prof, you have everything else required?"

"Yes, Detective."

Harry and Campisi exited the car. They met at the left headlight.

"Listen, Campisi," he said and lowered his voice. "Keep your eyes on the good professor. He has a weird glint in his eye. I don't think he's playing with a full deck."

"He's here to help us," she said. "We can't do this without him."

"I understand, but you couldn't miss his expression when he saw the Saran Wrap book."

"Sarmangous," she corrected.

"Whatever. What I'm saying is, I can recognize obsession when I see it, and Whitmore—"

"Whitehead."

"I don't care if he's named William Morris," Harry snarled through gritted teeth. "He's trying his damnedest to keep his orgasm in check over this thing."

"Crudeness does not become you, Detective."

"Just watch him, okay? Get back here as soon as you can."

A few moments later Campisi and the professor headed for downtown. Campisi glanced at the reflection in the rearview mirror. She'd given him the Sarmangous, and he held it to his chest as if to prevent the grimoire from floating out the window. Recalling Harry's opinion, she tried to formulate a conversation starter.

"Judging by your collection back at the university, Professor, you must have done a lot of traveling."

"Oh, yes," Whitehead said. "I also have a collection at home, although not as extensive. I spend most of my time lecturing or traveling, and when in Iowa City, I'm in the office."

"How did you amass such a variety of Sarmangous material?" She rechecked her directions. Eighth Street was a one-way going north. She drove a block further, took Ninth south, and circled back to the bridge at Eighth.

"During research or field trips, along with the normal itinerary, I'd look into Sarmangous rumors, gather tidbits of information. I've visited four continents and several island chains," the professor said with pride.

"When did you become interested in the occult, the paranormal?" Campisi made a left down a sloping street leading to parking lots for several businesses tucked under the overpass.

"I branched out when my field of study ventured outside the normal areas."

The insipid façade of Roderick's Audio/Visual Supply was tan stone, thin roof-line, tiny deep-set black-bordered windows, and the business name printed in uninspiring letters above the dark tinted glass door.

"And the Sarmangous?"

Whitehead waited until they both stood outside the car before he said, "I've been interested for a number of years." He clutched the book to his chest as if he didn't want to take the chance of leaving it in the car.

Lori raised an eyebrow.

He cocked his head like a parakeet. "Worried about me, Special Agent?"

She paused a moment. "You've read the same information regarding the Sarmangous as I have. You know the history and how much evil the book contains."

"You don't think I can resist the temptation?"

"I've seen what magic and the lure of power can do to people." She walked to the door of the sound and light business.

They entered a small lobby, the obligatory potted plant accompanying a pair of light tan foam-filled plastic-covered chairs. Beyond a double-paned sliding window was a receptionist's office, just as bland as the lobby. The woman behind the desk was no older than thirty, with average features, straight seventies parted hair the color of the lobby chairs, and eyes the same shade as the plant.

Synchronicity.

The woman rose to meet the visitors, sliding half of the window to one side. Campisi flashed her identification. They didn't have time for nonsense. She could be direct and to the point when needed.

"Special Agent Campisi," she stated. "May I speak with Bobbi? I require lighting."

A minutes later, she repeated her request to the owner, Andrew McGuire, a mustached, middle-aged man with a receding hairline, thin wire-rims, a loosened stretch-fabric tie, white shirt with the sleeves rolled to his elbows, and dusty, faded black pants.

"Bobbi is out sick," McGuire said. "But I believe Billy can fulfill your needs."

He introduced her to a young man, reed-thin, whose tousled black hair hung over his ears to his shoulders.

McGuire acted as if he expected a horde of agents to storm through the front door Waco-style. Billy, on the other hand, gawked in awe of an actual federal representative present in his storeroom. He was eager to show Campisi every single light in the place including, if given the opportunity, the ceiling fixtures.

Campisi deferred to Professor Whitehead regarding the available choices. He held the trash bag-wrapped book close while studying various wattages and light stands. When he viewed a spotlight with a two-foot diameter, his face lit up like the bulb on the box in front of him.

Over the years, Campisi had practiced patience so often it had become a key aspect of her makeup. However, after a discussion with plenty of technical terminology passed back and forth between Billy and Whitehead, with McGuire adding his two cents' worth, she was close to interjecting a Reznik-like, "Get on with it!"

Several hands loaded trunks of lights and cords and stands into the Buick. Through it all, Campisi wondered about Whitehead. Was something going on beneath the scientific exterior? Was it her imagination, or did she see a peculiar sparkle of something...abnormal...in the man's eyes? Did the supernatural aura of the Sarmangous affect him?

She had to admit an uncomfortable sensation in it presence.

Throughout the drive to and from Iowa City, and during the visit with Whitehead, she fought an internal battle to stay focused, to keep in check the dizziness and nausea. Endless images flashed in her mind's eye. If she succumbed to them, the barrier might fall, but how much time would she lose...and what about the condition of her mental state afterward?

Harry, already leery of the professor, did not need to suspect anything unusual happening to her as well. She couldn't take the chance of harming the plan to destroy the shadows.

She'd have to hang on a little longer.

*   *   *

Harry was in deep shit long before he reached Homicide—even before he reached the lobby elevators.

He wondered if Gravatte's attitude had filtered throughout the building. Officers from various departments bustled about like lackeys on one of Misty's favorite television shows, The West Wing. Everyone he passed gave him the same worried look.

The third-floor department contained harried-looking detectives typing, on the phone, or both. Upon noticing Harry's entrance, a couple made excuses to be elsewhere.

Calm and collected most of the time, Gravatte's demeanor would have cowered the she-devil goddess Kali. As Harry stepped through the doorway to her office, she slammed shut a binder and threw it against the far wall. Rounding on him, she launched into a diatribe that raised the bar on ass-chewing. Not known for foul language, Gravatte used more multi-syllable words than Harry knew existed. His peripheral vision caught another detective making a beeline for the exit, frantic to escape any spillover in GG's tirade.

"Then, some eagle-eye Altoona cop sees you driving like a bat out of hell east on the interstate." Gravatte upped her already loud voice level. "Just what I need, a panic-stricken city, my task force in complete disarray, and my best detective goes gallivanting out to the country with the freaky Feeb. Now, you come strolling back in here as if you and she enjoyed a pleasant picnic. I'll ask just one time, Harry, and if you don't give me a damn good story, I'll throw your ass in front of the next semi-truck. Just where the hell did you go?"

Harry repressed the urge to mention the Peterbilt that almost had fulfilled the lieutenant's desire. Instead, he said, "Finding answers."

Before his superior could explode once again, he held up a hand, worked his face into a serious, pleading expression, and stated in a flat but commanding tone. "Let me talk. We don't have much time."

He explained everything: The shadow creatures. Peter Monaco's house and the discovery of the Book of Sarmangous. The rushed trip to Iowa City, the conversation with Professor Whitehead, and the planned ritual to close the mysterious portal. He related the incident with the cloaked figures driving the Land Rover and the further danger the Triune presented. By the time Agent Campisi and Whitehead returned to the station, Harry thought he had Gravatte all but convinced.

She paced her small office, muttering all the while. "You people are out of your ever-loving minds. Lord, why did I ever become a cop? Dad said, 'Please, baby girl, don't be a cop, you can't imagine what shit you'll face every single day.'"

Harry, glad she no longer threw things, said, "Lieutenant, believe me, I know how nuts this sounds," he said. "I've been dealing with it ever since Campisi first told me yesterday about these creatures. I haven't had a chance to share the information because afterward, everything started going to shit. The attack on Misty, Reverend Samuels, the junkies behind the nightclub, and everything this morning. I've been riding the wave and I don't understand it all myself. Hell, no one does." He shook his head. "I don't know why, but in some inexplicable way, it makes sense. If there's a chance this ritual or spell will work, I'm willing to give a begrudging trust to Campisi and this professor. He is a little flaky, and I have my suspicions about him, but Campisi, for all the crazy stuff she's told me, seems to be the most level headed-person in this whole mess."

"I've all but lost control around here," Gravatte said. "We've got the Feds sniffing around. The governor placed the National Guard in key locations to quell any violence, and said governor, the mayor, and every other official are jamming the phone lines. Not to mention there are more media pissants hounding our asses than we've got bullets in the armory."

"Listen, Loo," Harry offered. "Campisi says she's got some pull with the Feds, her being in this special department, which will, in effect, make this all go away when it's over."

"God couldn't make this go away," Gravatte countered.

Harry gave her a sarcastic grin. "I tend to agree. I'd like to see what miracle Campisi can cook up.."

His lame comment brought a reluctant smile to his superior's lips before it disappeared as she raised her eyes to look behind Harry.

Campisi entered the department followed by an excited Whitehead. The latter carried the Sarmangous.

"Let's talk in the meeting room," Harry suggested.

* * *

Lori Campisi had learned to read subtle facial expressions better than any sham mind reader. When she, Harry, Whitehead, and Gravatte walked to the room where the task force had first convened, it too little effort to tell the lieutenant held in check some major fire just below the surface.

Harry's eyes darted a message she interpreted as, "Don't push it, just go with it."

Gravatte chased a couple of detectives out of the meeting room with a pit bull snarl. To Campisi's relief, Harry spoke first. "How did you two make out with the lights?"

"They are disassembled, but we have several cases in the trunk," Campisi answered.

"Good. I was explaining to the lieutenant here about—"

"Then you may explain it to us as well," interrupted Brandon Talbott as he entered the room, Sally Walcott trailing close behind. "We're supposed to be a task force, a team, but you obviously decided to duck out of the line of fire. What's the matter, Reznik, couldn't take the heat?"

Campisi understood Talbott's sniping, but she also recognized the weariness behind it. Sally Walcott said nothing, just leaned against the wall, lit cigarette between her lips.

With all the chaos of the past few hours, Campisi doubted anyone dared give a grievance to the Clive detective regarding the No Smoking policy. The individual who tried might wind up with Walcott's foot up his backside.

Gravatte held up a hand to stifle what might become a useless exchange of retorts and heated words. "Harry, tell them what you told me."

Campisi stepped forward. "Excuse me, but it might be easier and more credible if Professor Whitehead explained what he told us earlier."

All eyes redirected to the sandy-haired man in the natty sweater.

"Oh, well yes, I suppose I could. It's just, well, you see..."

"Get on with it," Harry commanded. "I want to stop fooling around and end this thing."

The history professor launched into a hasty explanation about the shadow creatures, the Book of Sarmangous, and the spell to eliminate the shadows. As he spoke, Campisi kept her eyes on the other three team members being dragged into the loop. There hadn't been time to ease them into the notion of ancient books and shadow beings from another dimension.

She and Harry had spent too much time at the university, and with the storm on top of them, minutes were crucial. These people needed to be convinced, otherwise, she might have to play her federal trump card and take control whether the local authorities liked it.

During most of her cases, the difficulty lay in convincing people the supernatural existed. Even with the proof before their eyes, the die-hard skeptics stood their ground. She never exhibited aggressiveness in her dealings with local authorities but hoped her calm demeanor kept everyone focused and on track.

She studied the faces in the room. Some nods of reluctant acceptance, but no outright disagreement. Even the arrogant Talbott backed up a step, though his twitching and fidgeting continued. "Hell," he said as he finger brushed his hair and scratched his left biceps. "This isn't any crazier than what I've been hearing all day. Sally?"

Walcott, who'd hadn't moved from her wilted position against the wall, raised her bloodshot eyes and mumbled around her cigarette. "You're all nuts, you know." Then she shrugged. "Shit, what else is there? I'm in."

Now all eyes looked to Lieutenant Gravatte who, except for Campisi, had the final say.

"I still don't understand how we locate this portal," the lieutenant said.

"Oh, I've been waiting to tell you." Whitehead hopped from foot to foot like he was dancing barefoot on hot coals. "The Sarmangous—it's detected the portal!"

"Where?"

"I don't know but close. We received a strong reading coming back after getting the lights."

"It intensified as we headed into downtown, then weakened when we headed south," Campisi continued. "I'd say the portal is somewhere north of Locust."

"Hold on a second," Gravatte cut in. "What are you talking about? What is intensifying?"

"Watch," Whitehead chirped. He again donned his leather gloves before he unwrapped the Sarmangous. "I kept it protected when we entered the station so no one accidentally came in contact with it."

The object of attention lay in all its ugliness on the table. What kind of power did this book offer people, what force did it hold over them? The others were unable to look away.

Huddled at the table, she and the detectives watched the change in the otherwise black cover. A portion near the lower right corner of the book started glowing, the minute black folds of skin lightening and growing more intense as if someone was manipulating a dimmer switch.

The glow ebbed from nickel-plated silver to rich honey gold. Then it started to pulse. As the Turkish scribe had described, the lines of pulsing light resembled the slight thrumming of blood coursing through vessels felt when touching a person's wrist. In other words, a heartbeat.

Talbott stepped back a pace. "What's it mean?"

"Based on how it reacted in the car, I'd say the portal is somewhere to the northwest," Whitehead answered. "Not too far from here."

"The area glowing is smaller than before," Campisi added. "Earlier, the light consumed almost half the cover."

"Yes," the professor agreed.

"Across the river, somewhere downtown," Harry said.

Talbott piped up. "Well, what are we waiting for? Let's go close this thing, blow it up, or whatever needs to be done."

Campisi deferred to Gravatte. She in turn gave a sharp look in the agent's direction, gave a quick nod, and said in a no-nonsense tone, "Do it."

CHAPTER 22

Three cars drove east on Court Avenue from the station, crossing the Des Moines River in parade fashion. The occupants stayed in contact with each other over a special radio channel Lieutenant Gravatte had reserved for only the people involved in what Brandon Talbott had dubbed "Operation Shadowbusters."

Harry suppressed the urge the asshole when he started humming Ray Parker Jr.'s theme from the movie *Ghostbusters*. Although Talbott used humor to cover anxiety and fear, Harry was in no mood for the guy's levity. Not with Misty still in a coma because of these devil creatures.

Agent Campisi sat in the passenger seat, attention focused on Professor Whitehead who held the Sarmangous, ready to give direction changes to Harry based on the ever-glowing cover.

Talbott and Walcott rode in the second car. Harry speculated Talbott still whined to his partner about all the things wrong with the plan and Walcott ignoring him. In the task force room, after listening to Whitehead's discourse on the ancient grimoire, the shadows, the ritual, and the dangers involved, she accepted the situation almost at face value, asking no questions, anxious to proceed.

Two members of the tactical squad occupied the third car, both experienced in weaponry—though Harry didn't see how guns were going to be useful in this case—courage, and intestinal fortitude in critical situations. Filled in on the operation, they accepted their orders without questions.

Harry gave a wry grin, amused at what people believed, or at least acknowledged as possible when their world was going to hell around them. Maybe they needed a stereotypical ritual with potions, a dagger, and some sacrificial blood to stop the madness.

Street lights flickered, their sensors registering the lack of sunlight. Storm clouds roiled, dark and ominous. Lightning sizzled in the air and thunder rattled the windows. Harry recalled the previous evening— only last night?—when he worried about shadow creatures in his car.

Tonight, closing the portal took precedence. Could they find it in time? He didn't want to imagine the carnage created if they didn't.

Fat drops of rain spotted the windshield as he went north on Second Avenue. With each drop, his heart rate increased.

Whitehead spoke from the back seat. "Can we go west again?"

"We'll be on Grand in a second," Harry answered.

Sparse traffic allowed the trio of official vehicles, bubble lights flashing, all the space they wanted. Slow but steady won the day. They didn't want to pass by a necessary turn and have to backtrack.

At Eighth Street, Whitehead yipped like he'd been bitten and Harry planted a foot on the brake.

"What the hell's wrong with you?"

"We're close," the professor said. "North again. Need to go north."

As he passed the east side of the Principal Building, Harry was relieved the book hadn't led them to the state's tallest building. Over forty floors with countless offices, utility, and maintenance rooms. He'd hate to be stuck in the elevators.

However, something niggled at the rear of his brain. He had the slightest inkling of the portal's location. He so wanted to be wrong, hoped it would be elsewhere, but...

His fear was confirmed as they reached the intersection of Eighth and Pleasant and Whitehead cried, "Stop!"

The interior of the car pulsed with yellow light. Campisi shaded her eyes as she tried to look at Whitehead.

"Well?"

The professor stayed silent for a moment.

"Come on, Whitehead," Harry commanded. "Where to now?"

"There!" The professor's gloved left hand shot past Harry's nose, pointing to the building on their left. "The portal is in there. It has to be."

The radio squawked and Talbott's voice said, "What's the matter? Are we there?"

Harry grabbed the microphone and clicked the button. "Hold up, everyone. We may have something." He glanced over his shoulder. The Sarmangous' pulsing light cast eerie shadows on the professor's features. "Are you certain?"

Whitehead nodded.

"Shit!" Harry slumped back in his seat. When he spoke, he had to increase his volume over the pounding rain. "I think I know where the portal is located. Inside, I mean."

"Where?" Both voices spoke in unison.

A couple of years ago, he explained, Misty had gone through an arts and culture phase and dragged Harry along into a world that he neither comprehended nor cared about. While he respected the talents of classical artists such as Michelangelo and da Vinci, and even in some warped sense, Dali, he thought ninety-nine percent of the rest of what people ostensibly called "art" was incomprehensible crap—stupid, and silly. The stuff wasn't worth the time and energy it took to create, and not worth the time to look at, let alone study for some hidden meaning of life.

Misty immersed herself and Harry in the art scene, so he ended up wasting too much money and too many hours going to art museums, fairs, and special exhibits. They visited galleries and listened to discussions about painting, sculpture, clay modeling, and charcoal sketching. He stopped short of attending art classes at Drake University but shelled out a ridiculous amount of cash at the state fair for a piece of garbage some nitwit had put together using pieces of old bronze from the capital, discarded after its seemingly endless renovation. Colored a pale algae-green, Misty liked it. "Wouldn't it look nice in the side yard?"

After two months, Misty conceded the godawful thing didn't fit in with anything in or around the house. Harry sold the damn thing on eBay for $500, making a nice profit.

On one of their later excursions into the world of art, they took a free tour given by the Principal Company, an insurance/financial investment firm, in its complex of office buildings on the northern edge of downtown. From traditional to modern, the half-dozen buildings featured various forms of art.

Harry gestured to the building. "If it's the one I'm thinking about, the damn exhibit is scary all by itself."

Campisi peered through the rain at the front doors. "What is it?"

"It's called *The Final Gasp* and...well, describing it is...difficult. You can't get a feeling for it until you see it."

"You believe this is where the portal is?"

"I think it is the portal," he said. "When you see it, you'll understand."

Campisi nodded. "Then let's go."

The storm raged on. Wind drove the sheeting rain. Lightning and thunder created a wild light and sound backdrop.

After instructions shouted over the radio, seven pairs of hands grabbed light cases and duffel bags. Seven pairs of legs raced up several long, broad tile brick steps, past a covered designated smoking area to the company entrance, a revolving door. By the time everyone maneuvered their baggage into the lobby, they—and the items they carried—were soaked.

Harry directed the tactical unit men to deal with security personnel at the public entrance to the rear of the building off Ninth. Harry remembered guests and other visitors registered at the welcome desk.

The front lobby measured at least fifty feet by thirty with a high ceiling and elegant carpeting. Hulking square planters with tall, brown-spotted green fronds shooting into the air stood like sentinels along the walls. A central waiting area with couches and chairs separated a pair of escalators connecting the first floor with the skywalk level. Tall windows offered an expansive view of the pounding rain.

This area, as Harry recalled, was an early stop on the art tour. To his right stood a piece of schlock the guide had fawned over for several interminably long minutes. A trio of headless skeletal figures made of blued bronze stood in front of an acrylic-painted background of the same figures. Harry remembered the guide droning on about the artist's concept of life, continuity, and the incompleteness of living. Misty had loved it. From him, it elicited a pained wince of confusion.

One of the backup officers returned. "I think we're too late, sir. Two bodies behind the desk."

"Make a quick run-through for any other employees," Harry ordered. "There are eleven floors in this building alone."

"Yes, sir." The man rushed back to help his partner.

"Where are we going?" Talbott still shook off water like a wet poodle.

Whitehead had dropped his duffel bag of ritual goodies and withdrawn the Sarmangous. The tome blazed like a golden sun. The professor aimed the book in various directions.

"We're very close," he whispered.

"Put that thing away until it's needed," Harry said. "We're going through the doorway over there." He pointed to a darkened opening to their left. A framed notice hung on the wall listing the name of the exhibit—*The Final* Gasp—the artist, and a brief paragraph explaining both.

Harry said, "Prepare yourself. You ain't ever seen anything like this."

The artist had designed the exhibit to affect the senses of sight, smell, and hearing. Before the group trouped through the entrance and down a short black hall into the main room, Campisi skimmed the notice. The artist wanted the viewing public to stay inside for up to an hour, or more if possible, allow the mind to drift, experience the changes within, and when back outside, to see the outside world in a new light.

Harry mentioned Principal employees called it the Red Room. The room measured fifteen feet by twenty-five feet. A pair of benches sat on either side of the door. Two sets of small double diffused spotlights in each of the front corners near the ceiling provided illumination along with the main attraction: a "window" of sorts, an open square in the back wall ten feet high and sixteen wide. Soft maroon light filled the window, giving the room its nickname.

Hidden speakers emitted what sounded like a television tuned to an off-air station with the volume low. The air smelled clean, like lightning-created ozone.

Everyone set their cases on the carpeted floor and stared.

In the few minutes she stood and stared, the "window" appeared to be a strange movie theater screen at one point, then filled with red-tinted fog the next. The noise evolved from television white noise to water running through a toilet with a loose gasket.

Campisi had investigated haunted houses, recorded ghostly voices in old prisons and sanatoriums, tracked a woodland devil through the Virginia Appalachia, and—although the famed Winchester mansion in San Jose remained an open case—she'd once braved the house and all its mysteries for an entire night.

She wasn't prepared for *The Final Gasp*. The pervading sense of malignancy and malevolence struck an all too familiar and enervating chord.

The cave. A monster.

Something rising to touch her, seize her.

No, it had grabbed her leg!

Her mind drifted, unable to concentrate. The portal captivated her. "It's so alien," she whispered, then exclaimed, "Oh, shit!"

Her outburst broke the mood.

"What the hell is this?" Brandon Talbott's voice had a nervous edge.

Harry just shook his head.

Sally Walcott said, "I think my college roommate described something like this when she took some bad drugs."

"Amazing," Whitehead said, breathless.

"Listen up, everyone," Campisi spoke in a commanding voice. "We can't allow all of this to sidetrack us. We have a job to do. The longer we're here, the more danger we're in."

"She's right," Harry agreed. "I'm surprised we haven't encountered any shadow creatures. We've invaded their territory just by being here. Let's get moving. Professor, how do we set up the lights?"

Under Whitehead's guidance, they unpacked and assembled the spotlights, fourteen five-hundred-watt Lowell DP lights, packed in five cases. Each case weighed forty pounds and contained extendable tripod stands and extension cords. One case held three six-outlet surge protectors.

Campisi had asked Billy if the outlets would be able to handle the amount of electricity needed. He hadn't recommended using all the plugs, and she now related this information to Harry.

"We don't have a choice," he said. "I see only two wall outlets. We'll have to hope for the best. Just pray lightning doesn't blow the fuses in this building—or we don't trip them ourselves."

They arranged the spotlights to form create solid pools of illumination bisected by a column of shadowy gloom.

"To allow the creatures access," Whitehead explained. He pointed to an area left unlit in front of the portal, save for the misting red. "This will be where the creatures gather. We need to keep them here."

Talbott grasped one of the light's maneuvering handles. "Why can't we just shine these spots on them?"

"Basic physics, Detective," lectured the professor. "You move one light and you create a dark area in the space where it used to be. Besides, they may escape back into the portal. Not a bad thing, mind you, but we need to contain them."

Campisi surveyed the room, shading her eyes against the bright white from the lights near the walls, all raised to a specific height. "Professor, we couldn't illuminate some areas between and behind the lights. Won't the shadows slip in there?"

"Use the flashlights to keep them at bay. Everyone must stay in full light. Keep away from the walls and the middle. There will be shadows all around us, here in front, in the corners, and above us, but we've set the lights high enough we should be protected."

Harry clicked on his light. "Are we supposed to do anything during the ritual?"

"Monitor the shadows, keep them contained. I need one assistant. I believe Agent Campisi would best fill the role."

Campisi nodded. "What do I do?"

"You hand me the correct bottles and light the candles in the order I tell you."

The professor made his "altar" adjacent to near the left pool of light near the portal. Since he didn't have a dais, he would have to hold the Sarmangous with one gloved hand, open to the correct page. Campisi would wield the dagger and, at the appropriate time, slice into Whitehead's bare palm.

"You're demented," Talbott cried. "This is all bullshit. Candles, daggers, blood—"

"Shut up!" Walcott grasped the West Des Moines detective's shirtfront. Her words came out clear and cold. "Close your mouth and pay attention. I'm sick of your griping. Do as the man says. I swear I'll bust your teeth if you screw around."

Harry smiled in a newfound respect for the woman.

She said, "We've been here for a while now. This is supposed to be the portal to the other dimension."

"Yes, my dear."

Walcott pursed her lips. "Why haven't we seen any shadows yet?"

"Damn it, Sally!" Harry pointed to the entrance. "You spoke too soon. Look!"

All eyes stared at the entrance to the room. The red room became redder as dark, shifting forms with glowing blood-colored eyes flowed through the doorway. A slithering sibilance overpowered anything from the exhibit's speakers.

The shadows had arrived!

CHAPTER 23

Everyone yelled and moved at once. Walcott screamed. Expletives cut off as people knocked into others, trying to back away from the creatures.

The shadows slid up and around, flowing over and through one another, the number of red orbs increasing every moment.

"Stay in the light," Whitehead shouted. "Agent Campisi, we should begin."

"No shit, Professor!" Harry jockeyed into a stable position. He flicked on his flashlight and aim it at the mass of shadows.

"Wait," Whitehead ordered. "Let them come. They'll follow the path. Agent Campisi, here next to me."

She moved to stand next to him. He already had the Sarmangous open to the page containing the ritual.

The wraiths swirled around the small pool of light. With each arriving shadow, the incessant, nerve-wracking crackling hiss rose in volume, an electric squelch in Campisi's ear. From somewhere, gusts of warm wind blew through her wet hair. The phenomenon exacerbated the others' panic and confusion. She hated moments like these, but in every special case she'd investigated, the climactic moment always arrived when people least expected.

More memory flashes, terror-inducing images one after the other flickered in rapid succession through her mind. She focused all her concentration on the moment, to fulfill her responsibilities.

The wind and the static white noise forced Campisi to move closer to Whitehead and shout. "What do we do?"

"When I call for a certain object, hand it to me," he shouted back.

She nodded, then screamed a warning. "Harry, behind you! Behind the tripods!"

Through the cacophony, the detective heard her and aimed his powerful flashlight at a dark shape rushing between two of the light stands. A rising patch of red-eyed gloom skittered away.

Whitehead touched her arm. "Are you ready?"

She nodded again and prepared to grab whichever bottle or powder or even the dagger should the Professor call for it.

Back in the basement office in Schaeffer Hall on the university campus, History and Language Professor Whitehead spoke in a nasal, higher-pitched voice, on the cusp between wispy tenor and effeminate. He paused and hesitated, stuttering often, but his energy and vitality were unmistakable. Those qualities now changed his voice during the ritual to clear, commanding, powerful tones as he enunciated each ancient word, snapped out important phrasing.

One gloved hand balanced the open grimoire, the other, bared, traced strange patterns in the air. Indecipherable shapes with impossible angled borders overlapped and replaced each other with every motion of Whitehead's palm.

Campisi stayed near, ready, watching. She kept one eye on the professor, the other on the group of detectives and special unit officers who tried to keep the shadows in check, not allowing the creatures to sneak into the small patches of darkness. Quick darts of the bright flashlights forced the shadows to disperse and stay on the move. The officers assisted and directed one another and even doubled up when needed.

The column between the pools of floodlights became a mass of swirling black shapes and red eyes, with more shadows entering the room every minute.

A hand on her shoulder startled her.

"The dagger! I need the dagger." Whitehead pointed at the foot-long shining weapon, gold hilt with embedded jewels, engraved with alien figures and symbols. The blade glimmered the brightest silver, its edge honed to a sharpness to draw blood at the merest touch.

She offered the dagger, but he refused and motioned for her to hold it hilt up, like a priest presenting a cross. She did as instructed and he created more shapes around the dagger while speaking more words.

Then he offered his palm. "What?"

"Cut me," he ordered. "We need the blood to draw the rest of the shadows and to complete the ritual."

It was a rare occasion when she exhibited resistance to finishing an operation to cease supernatural activity. At that crucial moment, she hesitated and couldn't say why. Maybe because of the overwhelming presence and power of the Sarmangous, or the chaos and mind-numbing noise all around her.

She couldn't deny, however, the flashes of imagery infiltrating her mind like a film projector gone berserk. Pictures of events experienced and places visited. Horrible places and numbing terror. Her nightmare returned in full force.

Petroglyphs.

The cave again.

Someone screaming.

A blurred vision of someone nearby. A man reaching for her, desperate to save her from whatever burning force prevented her from escaping.

"Agent Campisi!" Whitehead's shout brought her back to the present. "Hurry. You must slice my palm!"

She held the blade over his hand. With meticulous care, she made a single, swift motion, a diagonal four-inch cut across his palm. Blood oozed. Whitehead winced, but he raised his arm high over his head. Red streamed down his arm, staining his shirt and sweater before fat droplets splattered to the carpet.

The red window-portal changed. Zigzagged lightning sizzled as the center darkened to a deep, cloudy purple.

"Professor! What's happening?"

The roiling fog cycled through deep purple, to black, then gray, and back to purple.

"It's the portal," he said, his voice reduced to a raspy croak. "The other dimension is opening again, allowing more shadows to come through. We must finish the ritual or we'll be overwhelmed."

Whitehead pointed at a clear glass bottle and a bronze tin the size one might use for storing wooden kitchen matches. "I need those two items."

She handed the professor the bottle, noticing the blood still flowing from his hand. She'd cut him deeper than intended. Deftly uncapping the bottle, he flung the liquid in various directions like a priest with holy water.

"My hands are a bit full, my dear," he yelled and gestured to the tin. She removed the lid. Control and strength returned to his voice. "Would you mind? Take a small handful. Just enough. Now, pretend you're scattering breadcrumbs to ducks and fling the powder toward the portal."

She did as instructed. The fine grains fizzled like mini sparklers as they made contact with the portal. The hurricane forces within the portal darkened, expanded out and away from the wall, advancing closer. Whitehead continued his litany, but his voice grew more hoarse and strained with each passing moment. The wind, the white noise of the shadows, the shouted orders of the troupe of officers almost drowned out his words.

Someone screamed. Shadows enveloped Brandon Talbott's torso. He'd stepped into an area where the spotlights' glare faded and the shadow creatures had attacked serpent-quick. The flashlight flew from his hand.

He shrieked again, his face deformed by terror and the shadows' embrace. Once one had a hold, others massed. Soon the detective writhed in the air, covered in red-eyed gloom. In seconds, the monsters had dragged him back into a corner. Several flashlight beams arced to ward off the attack, but they arrived too late. Talbott, or what remained of his destroyed body, collapsed into a blood-soaked pulp. His screams ceased as the shadows ripped open his throat. The rest of his soft parts gushed, a ragged bloody nightmare.

Harry rushed toward Whitehead. "How much longer? We won't be able to contain them at this rate."

Fulfilling his prophecy, the last spotlight on the left flared for a microsecond and, with an explosive squeaky cough, blinked out. Shadows swarmed to fill the darkened section. Walcott's quick reflexes saved her from being the next casualty. She stumbled and Harry caught her before they fell.

Something boomed throughout the room. Campisi couldn't tell if the storm outside had worsened or if the deep rumble originated from the whirling dervish of the dimensional portal.

The wind howled.

Whitehead's voice ululated with what Campisi hoped was the final part of the ritual.

The shadows, like frenzied ghosts, rushed willy-nilly. Crackling white noise deafened.

Another 500-watt bulb literally exploded. Thin shards of glass sprayed outward. One of the tactical men, lurched away, avoiding blindness.

From the portal, a massive shadow creature began to emerge from the swirling purple and black, its red eyes—wider than the others—blazing with evil fury. Tendrils of its essence reached for her, came within mere inches.

Someone else screamed. Campisi realized the sound came from her own throat.

A flash, another ripping explosion. And then…

CHAPTER 24

Silence.

Nothing.

A familiar, endless darkness.

Eyes squeezed shut so tightly they hurt.

The woman who became Lori Campisi would not, dared not, open her eyes. For she would see...what?

Nothing. But the other woman, or rather the preteen girl who had experienced so many wild adventures, encountered too much evil, yes, her, she would see —

No! Don't look! Too late.

A deep dark cave.

What's in there with her? Where is it?

The girl remembered the burning pain, someone grabbing her, pulling, and the jolt of impact on hard ground. A sense of motion...riding in a car? Then whispered words and the formation of a rising black wall shutting off her past.

"Daddy?" Her voice a peep in the forever night.

"Campisi." A faint calling from the far reaches of the dark confused her. The voice sounded familiar, but it had to be...

"No, Daddy," she cried. "Don't go away. Don't send me away!"

"Campisi!" The voice grew stronger, drew closer, but her terror rose inside her, filling her. Her weak cries dissolved to wails.

"Daddy!"

Something grabbed her, pulled. She slammed against the solid floor, fought against her captor. She wouldn't succumb again, having a hollow sensation of being forever lost every minute of each day, never quite finding herself. Legs kicked and arms flailed, but the dark's strength overwhelmed her. The shadows ruled. The monster in the cave had returned.

Several hands held her, preparing her for the creature's excruciating touch. Then she'd hear the words, the alien syllables to shut down her mind. This time there would be no escape. She refused to open her eyes, would not watch as the horror engulfed her, ate her up, chewed her up, tortured her.

"Hold her, damn it. She going into a seizure."

Why did the voice seem familiar? This wasn't the voice from all those years ago.

"Shit. She's as strong as a tiger." Another voice, this one not recognizable at all.

"Campisi!"

She was trapped, secured, despite her thrashings, but if death had come to claim her, she'd die fighting. Another voice, calm, intellectual.

"Detective, I don't think it's physical. She's seeing something in her mind."

"What, are you a damn shrink now, Professor?"

Who spoke? She ought to know.

"She needs to open her eyes, Detective, to come back from wherever she imagines she is."

"Shut up! Aw, damn it to hell. Hold her arms."

A weight bore down upon her. Maybe this time she'd have no pain, hear no words, but suffer crushing agony before death.

Smack!

Pain speared her cheek.

"Campisi!"

Two hands grasped her lapels and lifted her head and shoulders. Instead of hard rocky ground beneath her, she lay on a hard carpeted floor. Her arms dangled, released from others' grips.

Smack!

Her other cheek burned.

"Agent Campisi, come back to me. Open your damn eyes and look at me."

Hot breath wafted over her face.

By minute degrees, the blackness faded into a harsh dawn. With each second, the terror evaporated, leaving coldness inside her. She gasped and the fresh air hurt her lungs. Fluttering against the sudden brightness, she forced her eyes open. A sweat-streaked, yet strong-jawed face and wild, windblown hair loomed above her.

"H-Harry?" she said with sandpaper-dry throat.

He nodded. "Are you all right? What the hell happened?"

After a few more blinks, she regained some clarity of vision.

Harry's hands still fisted in her shirt. Her legs protested the two hundred pounds sitting on top of them.

She gasped. "Harry…get…off me."

"Not until you tell me you're not going to continue to act like a bucking bronco on speed."

Her senses returned, and she glared at him. "You're crushing my legs."

He moved to stand, easing her up at the same time. Other hands lent support until she stood upright and stable.

"Thank you, I'm all right, but—" She reached up and touched her inflamed cheeks. "Who slapped me?"

"I did," Harry admitted. "I didn't know what else to do. What happened to you?"

She shook her head. "I don't know. I think it was…the past." Then she remembered where she was and why these people surrounded her. "The shadows!"

"All gone," Harry confirmed. "The portal closed, the shadows disappeared, and this place is back to being a silly, if creepy, art exhibit. Its creator will have to do some repair work, though."

"Why?"

He gestured to the large open space, once red and foggy. The bruised gateway to another dimension had disappeared leaving a pale, white wall.

"Neon tubes inset into the window created the hazy red effect. All of them exploded."

"And the portal is closed? Just before I blacked out, there was a flash."

"Lightning from nowhere destroyed another spotlight, burst the tubes, and fizzled the portal. Looks like the ritual worked. I know Whitehead was relieved. Then you were on the floor thrashing around."

The other members of the group hovered nearby, a couple of them glaring at the bloody remains of Detective Talbott, but she didn't see the professor. "Professor Whitehead? Where did he go?"

"What? He was here a minute ago. He kept trying to diagnose your seizure."

"The Sarmangous," she cried. "He took the book!"

Harry's eyes widened. He bolted for the door, Campisi on his heels.

"The rat bastard," Harry growled as they reached the lobby. "I knew he'd been scamming us. Which way?"

"Outside," Campisi said and hurried through the revolving door out onto the patio.

They both blinked at the change in weather. The black clouds had moved off to the eastern horizon and the blue sky shone bright with sunlight.

Campisi squinted as she searched for the professor.

"Wait, listen," Campisi said. Rapid footfalls slapped a wet rhythm on pavement. "Over there."

They ran to the corner of the brick-paved patio. Across Eighth Street, fifty yards away, lay a courtyard, centrally located within the company's complex of office buildings. The courtyard, also brick-tiled, stretched from the street to the far building.

Professor Whitehead sprinted across the courtyard, heading for a small round platform upon which stood a square arch made of frosted glass cubes. Under his arm, he carried the ancient grimoire like a running back sprinting for the end zone.

Harry cupped his palms around his mouth. "Whitehead!"

The man looked back and missed seeing the danger materializing before him.

"Oh, no." Campisi pointed. "Look!"

A trio of cloaked and hooded figures emerged onto the courtyard and from three points of a triangle each zeroed in on the frantic professor. A terror-filled shriek erupted from Whitehead's throat as he collided with the nearest two, who grabbed his arms before he could react..

The third produced from the folds of his garment a wicked-looking knife. Its twelve-inch silver blade glinted with pure evil in the sunlight.

Campisi and Harry stood motionless, unable to prevent the inevitable.

Just as the knife-wielding figure prepared to impale the professor, a sudden hiss echoed in the spacious courtyard. Upon the platform, the cubes belched white fog, like a special effects machine at a concert. Either they'd tripped a sensor or it reacted to the afternoon sun.

The fog billowed up and out, obliterating the arch.

The elaborate mechanism's initial hiss must have distracted the Triune from their goal of murdering the professor. Each stopped, frozen as if to determine if another threat had popped up. Whitehead must have felt a loosening of his captors' grip. With a desperate lunge, he ripped free, pieces of his shirt tearing away. He stumbled once then made a mad dash straight for the foggy arch. Before his would-be killers could take a single step in pursuit, Whitehead vanished into the enshrouding fog.

"What the hell?"

Campisi shared Harry's confusion. For Professor Whitehead had entered the billows of fog in the arch...and hadn't emerged out the other side.

"What's he doing, just standing there in the middle?" Campisi shook her head. "I don't think so."

With another hiss, a timer noting the end of the cycle, the fog dissipated, leaving a mist-covered arch. Condensation beaded on the frosted cubes and the brick tiles. The professor had disappeared.

"Don't tell me..." Harry started.

Campisi shrugged once. "I surmise Professor Whitehead suspected or sensed another doorway leading out of his predicament. I don't believe, however, we'll have to destroy it. I think he just used it to transport elsewhere." Her voice had regained its flat, calm, resonant nature.

"At least we can round up the wild bunch. Come on."

"Don't bother, Harry."

The cloaked triplets, the Triune, understanding their quarry had escaped drifted toward the corner of the glass and metal office building. As one, they gave one last glance at the Harry and Campisi and disappeared around the corner.

Campisi stopped Harry with a hand on his arm. "They're gone, Harry. We wouldn't be able to catch them."

Harry sighed. "Good riddance. To them and that squirrelly shit of a professor. He and his damned book can be the best of buds for all I care. Just so he doesn't conjure up anything more around here."

Campisi gave the arch a last glance. "I believe, he's far, far away." Then she added, "I would venture to say he regrets his actions."

"Come on, Campisi." Harry took her arm. "We've got a case to clean up. Shit! Sorry, wrong thing to say."

Campisi also remembered Talbott's corpse still inside the art exhibit.

"I know what you mean," she said. "You take care of Talbott and the rest of your team, and let me show you how well my federal powers can make all this go away."

•　　•　　•

Special Agent Lori Campisi of the Federal Bureau of Investigation stayed true to her word. A few persuasive phone calls to the right people and within days the media provided the public with a story accepted by the masses, however improbable the scant details. Officially, those responsible for the murders had been captured and transferred to some unknown federal venue for questioning and indictment. People wanted to put all the killings and the chaos behind them and find ways to move on, one way or another.

He and Campisi stood in the airport lounge waiting for the announcement of the latter's flight to Washington, D.C. Given his hard-nosed nature, he had struggled to find words of gratitude. He struggled to understand the events of the past week, but was grateful for the agent's assistance.

"You're unique, Harry," she said. "I know despite what you've been through, you'll survive. You have the strength."

"Yeah, sure." He sighed. "How about you? Going to be okay?"

She nodded. "Yes. I've experienced worse...but I can't remember just when."

"Right." Harry barked a sharp laugh. "So, where do you go from here?"

"Back to Washington."

"No more ghosts, goblins, or demons?"

"Not for a while. Just the usual drug stings and bank robberies."

"So your 'special' work isn't the daily routine?"

"It's ongoing, but not constant. Listen, I have to go, Harry."

Her tone relaxed for a slight moment. "You take care of yourself. Maybe I'll see you around sometime."

She stepped onto the escalator. When she reached the halfway point to the terminal level, Harry called out, "I hope not. You stay outta my city, Campisi, you hear?"

She gave him a wry smile. "I'll try."

The few who understood the truth about the shadow murders remained silent even among themselves. Those involved in the final hours of the ordeal took paid vacations to settle their inner demons. Harry dealt with a psychological battle scar for a long time, startled—if only for a second—at shadows. He'd hesitate for a terrified second before entering a darkened room. Dusk would become a period of heightened anxiety.

Shell shock, or the sterilized *post-traumatic stress syndrome* always would lurk in the hearts and minds of those who had seen evil up close.

Brandon Talbott, the arrogant twerp of a detective, received a hero's funeral.

Sally Walcott quit the Clive force and moved out west, wanting distance. Harry sympathized, but she could never run far enough from her nightmares.

County Medical Examiner Frank Belsom also left the metro. Several months later, he sent Harry a postcard stamped Acapulco, Mexico. To everyone's surprise, including Belsom himself, he'd accepted a job as a pathologist. On the back, he wrote, *"And the worst I'll see is some F-ing tourist who drowned after slipping on a wet patch poolside and smacking his head."*

Lieutenant Gravatte solidified her job security by proving her leadership in a crisis. A few federal words in the right ear and she emerged with several commendations.

She told Harry she took all the medals and certificates home and stuck them in a drawer rather than hanging them in her office as a reminder of a few horrific days of blood and bodies. She did, however, accept a promotion to Captain with an appropriate wage increase.

Misty Reznik remained comatose. Harry visited her every day, sometimes staying overnight, threatening to shoot any silly-ass security person who requested he leave. He often cried himself to sleep. His suffering doubled with the never-ceasing animosity from his in-laws.

In one sense, Misty and the other comatose victims who either remained unconscious or later died were lucky. They didn't have to remember and try to live each day knowing the horrors existing behind the curtain of everyday life.

Horrors in the shadows.

CHAPTER 25

No more pain...at least not the physical kind. No more overwhelming force from the shadows. No more suffering the celebration of death.

No more shadows...

...but the Night, the special place and time, remained.

...and she, its sole entity. Alone. Lost.

She didn't drift through the void searching for the light—for a path back to the bright, warm world. Instead, she huddled like a small frightened child. Abandoned.

She'd read once how some comatose patients heard voices of loved ones, trying to coax them awake, pouring out love and endearments to comfort the unconscious.

There was no sound now, although Harry must be near and her parents must have flown in from Wyoming. She sensed nothing.

Alone. Lost.

Logic seeped in. She recognized what had happened. The shadows' presence had filled her with pain and torture. They had presented each death as another victory over humanity. With their departure, they had left her mentally stripped. Naked, with no protection, no strength. No will and no resilience.

Forever in the empty darkness.

She curled in upon herself and wondered which condition was worse.

• • •

Minnesota, near the Canadian border
Cold.

Most of the country enjoyed the warm spring, the south suffering temperature extremes reaching the upper nineties as they experienced every year. In the thick preternatural forest of upper Minnesota, spring was just beginning to awaken, opening one eye during the day and burrowing under the covers at night, letting the last bits of winter hold reign.

Dark.

Sunset in the woods caught people unaware. Shadows grew long, the gloomy spaces between the tall trees thick enough he thought he might be able to touch them. Touch the shadows. Research regarding the Sarmangous—and oh, what a wonderful majestic book it was—had provided him the spells to open doorways that would lead him to other places. Not other dimensions, just elsewhere in the known world.

He could not say how he knew this was the very northern part of Minnesota, near the undefined border with Canada. The proximity of the book and its power conveyed the information, as it helped to locate another doorway very near the dimensional portal he helped close. The one under the fog-enshrouded arch.

He hadn't told the detective and the federal agent all he'd researched, had held back vital pieces. Because if he ever had the chance of having the book…

Now, here he was. The known world, but in an unknown, isolated part of it. No nearby roads, no towns, not even a lake for the avid fishermen.

Trees stretched to the sky, tall and looming. Silence.

No animals stepping through the leaves, not even the irritating noises of insects. It was as if his sudden presence, his emergence from the doorway, a gaping hole in the trunk of a dying tree, had caused all other animal life to depart the area or at least to cease making identifiable sounds.

He sat on the cold ground and placed the Sarmangous in front of him. His skin registered the chilled air, but not his mind. It focused on the object of his desire.

With long slow breaths, he relaxed after his hasty flight from the Des Moines office building. After waiting to see if the federal agent would recover from her sudden seizure, he waited until everyone focused their attention elsewhere. Then, with great care, he donned both gloves, closed the Sarmangous, and stole out of the room. Within seconds, he departed the office building and raced across the street, reciting the proper incantation to cause the fog machine to operate, opening the door. One terror-filled moment encountering the Triune, and he made his escape.

He laughed to himself and reveled in his success. Oh, the detective and the agent both had their suspicions, sensed the true fascination and awe he'd expressed for the Sarmangous.

True. How true.

His emotions lurked just below the surface, waiting. Given more time and further exposure, the woman agent, with her connection to the supernatural, also would have succumbed to the book's charm.

He removed the gloves protecting his skin from direct contact with the ancient tome. Now was the time. His time.

He contemplated the upcoming choices. In the past, the power of the Sarmangous deceived those whose warped conceit told them they were strong enough not to run and hide, to become a Guardian.

However, he was also certain, if certain words were spoken, the proper spells cast, the amount of mystical protection sufficient, the power could be harnessed, controlled, and he'd have true Power. He imagined the possibilities, the ability to fulfill all desires, to grant each wish, to bring to fruition the dreams of a lifetime—of several lifetimes. Millennia of supernatural energy would be his and his alone. The world would lie at his feet. It was his time and he would not be deceived.

With reverence, he lowered his hands and touched the Book of Sarmangous, wrapped fingers and thumbs under the length of the front and back covers.

Death.

Professor Whitehead, the man, History Professor at the University of Iowa, died. His soul, his spirit, the very essence of him disappeared into the void, the sudden emptiness replaced by something more, something bigger. It surged out every orifice, effervesced from every pore.

A sudden tornado, disturbing not a single leaf or bush, rushed over and through him.

Trapped in a mental theater of horror, he suffered hell-spawned screams, ungodly wails, and inhuman shrieks blasted from hundreds of unseen speakers. Horrible grotesque doom-infested evil images exploded upon the projection screen. Blood and entrails gushed down the aisle. Rivers of red flowed under and splashed over his feet. Flames rose all around to consume a nearby patron, extinguishing for a moment, then flared again to claim another victim.

A throat-wrenching sound grew from deep inside him. "Noo-aahh!"

He fell to one side, still gripping the Sarmangous. No longer did he glorify the book. Now he cursed and damned the author of this infernal tome.

Agony. Torture. Despair. The obsession, the insanity.

Mere feelings, emotions, and states of mind written in many journals and papers and manuscripts. No way any mere sane mortal could comprehend the full meaning behind the words. The awful, detestable reality.

He recognized his obsession, and insanity always lurking below the surface, ever watching, always waiting, anticipating the possibility of finding the Sarmangous. By mere chance—or destiny?—someone else brought the grimoire within reach, and those mental states blazed to the forefront, tempered by the need for reason, a small sliver of conscience to aid and assist in the problems of man. Once the little shadowy menace had been dealt with, the need, the overwhelming desire, coursed through his bloodstream faster than he had run across the courtyard.

Now, after touching the book, he hadn't even the strength to stand, let alone run. His body lay amid the grass and dirt, and his voice shrieked against the inner hell he experienced. His heart beat out of control, the convulsions and jerky motions of his body so much more intense than he'd seen the woman agent suffer.

How long he endured the torment, relived again the agony of pain and suffering, he couldn't say. Internal chaos reigned, then...nothing.

No sounds, no images of grisly inhuman deaths, no blood, no wailing. All vanished without warning, leaving the resounding echoes drifting into the void and his erratic breaths. The battle was over and he had lost. His selfish desires for god-like power faded like the last rays of sunlight against the inevitable darkness. He was not strong enough to accept the challenge. The Sarmangous's offers, its enticements, were lies, but he thought he could overcome the possession. Obsession, and yes, insanity, as with all the others, had blinded him.

His inner weakness of spirit and character made the choice. He would not take the extra step, could not withstand the agony to yield to the temptation of ultimate power.

With the other option selected, the future held one path. He must now hide, go far away, farther than even his present location, to a place maybe no one would discover for years, centuries...maybe never. If, however, some mad individual indeed sought him out and located the Sarmangous, then he would battle with all resources and reserves available to protect the individual from the horrors inside the book. He would fight until the day when one who felt worthy, or rather to whom the Power of the damned book deemed worthy, defeated him.

He picked himself off the ground, collected the Sarmangous, and ran deeper into the woods. Without pause, without exhaustion, weaving around the trees, through the shadows, leaping small streams, guided by an unknown force, mile upon mile, into the mysterious wilds of Canada, farther and farther until...

...Midway up the side of a brush-choked hill, he entered an opening all but hidden from discernment. Beyond, a tunnel fashioned for his purpose, designed for his new lifetime role as Guardian.

Into the tunnel, along the interminable length to a chamber far, far down in the earth. Here he would remain, provided for by...what? The supernatural? The book itself? He didn't know or care.

He placed the Sarmangous in a niche dug out of the earthen wall, then sat on the dirt floor. A fire blazed to life, fueled by nothing, yet existing. Nearby food—meat and fruits—waited.

The fire offered warmth and the food sustenance throughout the long, lonely vigil.

But...maybe not so long.

Around the world, supernatural signs and guideposts transformed. They now pointed in another direction, to a new location. Sigils and symbols rearranged to direct future seekers who derived their meaning.

Deep inside his mind, in the inner depths of quantum level, he sensed...something. No, someone. A person right now, at this very moment, somewhere in the world, had crossed the un-holiest of lines and begun a quest. A search for the evil thing in the hole in the wall in the Guardian's home.

He waited...

...and he pitied this individual.

•   •   •

Lori Campisi sat on her bed in her Washington,

D.C. residence. A bedside lamp provided the illumination in the vast warehouse. She wasn't afraid of the shadows, although she glanced up at every sound until she could acknowledge the familiarity of the building's metallic warbling caused by the outside breeze, the hum of the freezer making ice cubes, or a siren wailing by on a nearby street.

The creatures were gone, the portal closed, the adventure over.

She closed the journal of Peter Monaco, stolen from his kitchen. The words on these pages would linger and haunt her for a long time.

Other memories remained patchy, but the ritual in Des Moines and the reading of the journal had broken through the wall, bringing back the incident at the petroglyph site as crystal clear pictures on her mental movie screen. She remembered the creature in a shallow cavern she and her father explored, different from the shadows, yet similar in its haunting presence. She remembered the burning touch, even through the jacket she'd worn.

Most disturbing, she understood how her biological father's quest for the Sarmangous destroyed his mind, stripped away his morals, and damned his soul. How his obsession caused him to destroy his family life, and to create the woman she grew up to be.

After years of her subdued emotions, of logical, analytical study, and step-by-step reasoning concerning the myriad of supernatural phenomena, it all fell apart. The layers peeled away, and the emotions rose to the surface.

Confusion morphed into anger then uncontrollable sobs.

She knew who she was, what she was, and hated the world for both.

Her duties and daily activities lay in the future.

For now, she railed against life and death, against light and shadows. When it passed, when the tears depleted themselves and her cries fell silent, exhaustion set in and she dropped into a blessedly dreamless sleep.

The End

ABOUT THE AUTHOR

Stephen L. Brayton is a Sixth Degree Black Belt in the American Taekwondo Association and a Marketing Associate for a software company. His first short story concerned a true incident about his reactions to discipline. He wrote for his high school and college newspaper and the script for a video project. After college, he wrote a fantasy adventure and a trilogy for a comic book. Other publications include Editor and contributing author of *The Peace Tree* Mystery; *Alpha*, the first of his *Mallory Petersen* action mystery series; numerous short stories anthologies of fiction; and poems in *Lyrical Iowa* 2018-2023.

Social media presence can be found at:
www.braytonsbookbuzz.wordpress.com
www.stephenbrayton.wordpress.com
Twitter: @SLBrayton
Facebook: https://www.facebook.com/stephenbraytonauthor

NOTE FROM STEPHEN L. BRAYTON

Word-of-mouth is crucial for any author to succeed. If you enjoyed *Night Shadows*, please leave a review online—anywhere you are able. Even if it's just a sentence or two. It would make all the difference and would be very much appreciated.

Thanks!
Stephen L. Brayton

We hope you enjoyed reading this title from:

www.blackrosewriting.com

Subscribe to our mailing list – *The Rosevine* – and receive **FREE** books, daily deals, and stay current with news about upcoming releases and our hottest authors.
Scan the QR code below to sign up.

Already a subscriber? Please accept a sincere thank you for being a fan of Black Rose Writing authors.

View other Black Rose Writing titles at www.blackrosewriting.com/books and use promo code **PRINT** to receive a **20% discount** when purchasing.

www.ingramcontent.com/pod-product-compliance
Lightning Source LLC
Chambersburg PA
CBHW060710190726
48289CB00002B/625